P9-APJ-581

ALSO BY JONATHAN MASLOW

The Owl Papers

Bird of Life, Bird of Death

Sacred Horses

TORRID ZONE

Random House ⌂ New York

JONATHAN
MASLOW

TORRID
ZONE

Seven Stories from the Gulf Coast

Copyright © 1995 by Jonathan Maslow
All rights reserved under International and Pan-American
Copyright Conventions. Published in the United States by
Random House, Inc., New York and simultaneously in
Canada by Random House of Canada Limited, Toronto.

Library of Congress Cataloging-in-Publication Data
Maslow, Jonathan Evan.
Torrid zone : seven stories from the Gulf Coast /
Jonathan Maslow.
p.   cm.
ISBN 0-679-40876-2
1. Gulf Coast (U.S.)—Social life and customs—Fiction.
I. Title.
PS3563.A7857T67   1995   813'.54—dc20   95-3000

Manufactured in the United States of America
Book design by J. K. Lambert
9 8 7 6 5 4 3 2
First Edition

HOUSTON PUBLIC LIBRARY

. R01030 78358

HUMCA

For F.R.S. and E.S.,

who took me in from the storm

Now as I have shown that the air of the torrid zone is the purest, healthiest and most temperate of all atmospheres, and the earth there is a little Paradise, always green and washed by the sweetest waters of the world: it is appropriate to show in this treatise that the Savages of these islands are the most content, the happiest, the least vicious, the most sociable, the least deformed, and the least afflicted by disease in the whole world. For they are just as nature produced them, that is to say living in great and natural simplicity: they are all equal, almost without knowledge of any sort of superiority or servitude... No one is richer or poorer than his companion, and they all limit their desires to what is useful and necessary to them, scorning all superfluities.

—Du Tertre, *History of the French-speaking Antilles*

Seven stories. Seven characters. Unlucky seven. Like seven voices rising from the graveyard, these tales rose out of the swamps and off the bayshores of the Deepest South, the Gulf Coast. They represent an area of our country that reminds me of a beautiful pearl necklace worn by an old whore. They symbolize a warmer land richer in natural plunder, treachery, and aching hearts. I didn't write them: they were told to me.

It was during travels of seven years around the Gulf Coast and the Caribbean rim that I heard, read, or collected them. I started in Tampa on the west coast of Florida, and eventually got across the Panama Canal, and even farther, through the Darien Gap, which attaches the North and South American continents like an umbilical cord. I went as far as the port of Turbo on the cocaine coast of Colombia, but turned back because Turbo was exactly the same kind of pit as the port of Biloxi on the Mississippi coast.

In Biloxi I married a woman who slept every night with a loaded .357 Magnum in the drawer next to the bed. When she started waking up hysterical in the night from nightmares, I figured it was time to pull out. I drove over to New Orleans and lived off oysters and women in the time-honored tradition. In an attic Uptown, I spent a year writing down some of these stories. Some have probably never been written before. Some are old and have probably been told hundreds of times. Undoubtedly my tellings and retellings will introduce many new lies and untruths, but this can't be helped. Time and memory turn real people into stories and legends, and our vision of the actual man or the real woman gets distorted. Only the place remains the same. It is an America of darker darkness and brighter light.

And the voices. The accents don't change. There are still Indians and conquistadors, mermaids and pirates, fundamentalist demagogues and Mardi Gras revelers living on the Gulf Coast. There's still magic in the air. Down there the dead can still speak up for themselves. They can't be silenced. If any of the characters are proven innocent, we can always change their names later.

CONTENTS

The Last Lector

"*Ay, bendito*, Carmen." Julieta Suarez was talking to herself and to the Marielita girl sitting to her right at the next work-station in the old Tampa cigar factory. "You can say whatever you like, but at least I never needed a man to lean on, like they say. For me, *tú sabes*, Carmencita, a man was strictly for children—and for love, tha'ss all. I learned a good trade when I learned to roll cigars. I could always get work in the factory. Okay, so the pay wasn't great, but I had a big family, we all lived together on Calle Diez y Ocho. What did I need big money for? Life was dirt cheap in Ybor City. There were always plenty of good-looking guys to dance with at the Club Asturiano Saturday night. Who needs a man to depend on? One thing I learned about men early—they make good lovers, but trust them? Never! *Nunca!* They see a pretty girl, well, tha'ss it! They get a case of the hard-boiled eggs, if you know what I mean. And as for their brains, there's more intelligence in a three-egg omelet.

"Believe me, I know what I'm talking about. I had seven brothers, there were only two of us girls. I was born right here in Ybor City, lived here most of my life. But I'm Cuban by blood. And just remember one thing, Carmen: a Cuban woman is never slave to a man, especially if she marries him.

"I still remember, when I was a little girl, how, when my baby brother Luis was born at home, *mi madre* looked so proudly up at me and my older sister from the bed and swore, '*Muñecas*—remember this always: he never touched me till we married!' Can you imagine that, Carmen—she was talking about *mi papa!* My sister and me, we started to laugh, but we knew what Mama meant. Make 'em wait! She meant, you have to make the man wait for the love until you say yes. She meant, even my own *padre,* he never had his way with her: he knew who was the boss. The first thing a Cuban woman does is teach her husband the most important lesson he'll never forget: that she controls the bedroom. Because the way to the man's heart may be through the stomach, but the way to keep the man is in the bedroom. I think the Holy Virgin Mother created women to save men from themselves, tha'ss right! And if it wasn't for work, men would do nothing except run after the girls, *verdad?* This is the way men repay the Virgin Mother. It's a shame, no?"

Julieta chose a moist leaf from her bench drawer and started to rub it between her fingers. She worked the leaf like soft dough. Carmen, who was only twenty-five, wore her hair coiled in metal curlers with a bright turquoise kerchief over it. She looked over at the old lady, whom she called *Tía*

("Auntie"), more out of custom than respect. When she saw Julieta wasn't paying attention to her, she slipped her right hand down into the pocket of her apron and turned up the volume on her Walkman. She was listening to Eddie Palmieri through earphones while she worked.

Julieta removed the cigar she was smoking from between her lips, blew a slow, thin stream of blue-gray smoke into the air. "You know," she replaced her cigar, "there was only one man I ever saw who never had to run after the girls, and that was Cesar Fuentes. You probably never even heard about him, you little ignoramus. You'd sell out the whole damn working class for ten free minutes in the K mart. And you call yourself a cigarmaker!

"Cesar Fuentes was a *lector*—you know what that was? In the old days, before the war—before the big depression in the 1930s—the lectors used to read to us cigarworkers while we worked in the cigar factory. They were our readers, but they were *mucho más*—our teachers and entertainers and news broadcasters all rolled into one. That was how most of us Tampa *cubanos* learned to speak English, listening to those lectors read to us while we worked. Take my family. We spoke Spanish at home. My mama, she never knew a word of *inglés*. I only started to learn English when I got old enough to hear the lectors reading in the factories. In Ybor City you could pick up three tongues listening to the lectors: English, Italian, and Union. When our people first came here from Cuba and Spain to work in the cigar factories, they demanded to have readers on the shop floors, just as they had them in Cuba. They could not speak or read *inglés*, but that was no reason why they shouldn't be able to enjoy literature, eh? My father used to say that a great writer—a Cervantes, a Shakespeare, or maybe a Tolstoy—belonged to everyone, not just to the bigshots and the bosses. Papa said the great writers were like the statues in public parks, where anyone could go to admire them, to walk and enjoy the flowers and the fresh air, no matter who they are, from the owners' class or the humble classes like us. That's what those old cigarmakers believed. The bosses didn't care if the cigarmakers had readers, they just did not want to pay for them. All they cared about was their profits. That's why they were capitalists. So the cigarmakers hired our own readers. We paid their wages out of our own. Everyone contributed twenty-five cents a week to the lectors' pay. They made more than the poor cigarmakers—sometimes a lot more, like in the case of Cesar Fuentes, like I was saying. But no one ever begrudged them. Not one red cent!

"I remember those good old days in the cigar factories." She mused over a long puff before continuing. "You could smoke as many cigars as you wanted while you worked, and get an earful of stories. Didn't anyone ever read to you when you were little, *pobrecita*, you poor little wretched thing?"

There was no answer. Carmen was zonking out on Eddie Palmieri.

"You don't know what pleasure it is to hear stories in your ears and see characters in your mind. All different kinds of characters, Carmencita, because in a story you can meet someone from all different countries and all walks of life, the good ones and the evil ones, the brave ones and the liars and hypocrites, too.

"When I was a little girl, my gang and me—my sister and a few others from the neighborhood—before we were old enough to go to work, because we didn't have schools for the children in Ybor City back then—the *patrónes* didn't think cigarmakers needed schools, we were all going to end up in the factory or on the docks, so what did we need education for? Anyway, my gang used to sneak up to the open windows of the cigar factories; we would lie down right there, just underneath the building where it was cool in the dirt, and listen to the lectors read. And the lector would be reading some story. And we would all shut our eyes tight and hold hands and pretend, you know? I remember one time it was *Wuthering Heights* they were reading, and I would pretend in my imagination I was the heroine Catherine, searching for her lover Woodcock on those foggy English moors, only that wasn't his name—what was it . . . Heathcliff! That was it: Heathcliff! Oh, he was a dark and sinister one. What a man, whose only pleasure was to inflict his own pain on everybody else. Still you couldn't help fall in love with him, he was so handsome and deep. He said the most romantic things. He said if Catherine ever forgot him that 'two words would comprehend my future—death and hell'!

"Mmm-mm." She shook her head. "Imagine how those words fell on our innocent little ears! So that's what true love felt like! And we would all twist our little tails so hard down into that cool dirt we'd dig holes under the factory! Because when you hear the story, then you start to form a picture in your mind. You feel something about the characters. How they look or how they talk. You admire them or fear them. Maybe you just feel sorry for them, who knows? And then you start to put yourself in their place, like you are trying to be them, live their lives, feel what they feel, sort of try on other people's lives, and that helps you to know who you are, because maybe you find out you want to be like some characters but not like others, but still you know it's not for real, you know what I'm saying, Carmen?... Carmen?... Carmen!"

Carmen said lazily, "Yeah, I'm listening, Tía. It's like when my neighbor Alma and me, we always go shopping to the malls together and try on lots of different clothes in front of the mirror? That way you can see good how they look on you. We didn't have nothing like that in Cuba."

Julieta ground her teeth slowly on her cigar butt and jabbed a handful of filler inside the maduro wrapper. She rolled it half a dozen times up and down on top of her workbench, then placed it into the wooden clamp to set the shape. They only kept her on at the factory to roll handmades for the company executives, but even they were quitting smoking these days. Although in her eighties, Julieta could still turn out 130 coronas a day, smoking five herself.

"Of course, the lector didn't only read stories," she continued with a sly grin. "In the morning they'd read to us from the newspapers. That's what the men wanted, to find out what was happening in the world, because we didn't have televisions or even radios at home in those days. It was the 1920s. We already had Italians in Ybor City, too, by then, so the lectors had to read a Spanish paper and an Italian one, and an English newspaper, too. They had to be real linguists, those readers, to read like that in three languages. It was just part of their job.

"Then in the afternoon they'd read us either novels or history books, but most of the time it was novels. It all depended on what the majority voted for, because not only did we choose our readers, but we voted for what we wanted them to read to us. It was always a big campaign in the cigar factory, what the lector should read next. Now, some of us girls liked to hear the romances—you know, the love stories. Then there were always some that wanted to hear Dickens or Balzac, or Conrad, or maybe Zola. Me? I really loved *Don Quixote* best. I could listen to the stories of that crazy old knight forever, but especially when Cesar Fuentes read it. I'm telling you, no one could read *Don Quixote* like that Cesar Fuentes. He really threw himself into the role of that old Spaniard with the toasted brains riding that half-starved horse, Rosinante, and Don Quixote's sidekick, Sancho Panza, who always got the kicks and blows out of all the old Don's adventures.

"I can see him now, Cesar Fuentes. He would be reading along and get to a part where Don Quixote was telling Sancho how much glory there was to be a knight in armor, doing all kinds of good and noble deeds, and Sancho was replying, 'It must be so, but I don't know. I only know that since we have been knights, anyhow since you have been one, we have never won a battle, except that with a Biscayan, and even then you came out minus half an ear and half a helmet. Since then, it has been nothing but cudgels and more cudgels, blows and more blows; then as an extra, I got tossed in a blanket, and it was done by enchanters, from whom I can't take revenge, so I'll be damned if I know what is that pleasure of triumphing over an enemy that you talk of.'

"Cesar Fuentes would read that and throw his head back and laugh out loud. He had a big, booming baritone voice, and when he laughed the whole factory started to laugh, too, and we were all laughing so hard the tears finally came to our eyes. That book was a true tonic, *mi hija,* and I say: that is the kind of book we need, books that make us laugh and forget. We would all leave the factory that day in a good mood. I always lined up all my friends and relatives to vote for *Don Quixote*. I could be very persuasive!"

Carmen nodded. She didn't have the slightest idea who Don Quixote was. She was grooving.

"You know what means *voz de oro?*" Julieta asked. " 'The voice of gold.' That's what they used to call Cesar Fuentes—El Voz de Oro. Because he was so much better than the other lectors. Oh, he really had the golden voice of an opera singer, that guy. No one could ever explain where he got it, that golden voice, but he must have been born with it. There were some who claimed it was a gift from God; that's all we knew, Carmen, because he sure didn't get it from his father. His father was a cigarmaker, a good working man, but he had a voice like a sick bullfrog. Then there were others who said it came from Cesar Fuentes's mother, Dona Anna, and here's how it happened.

You see, Cesar Fuentes's mother, Dona Anna, was a maid at the big Tampa Bay Hotel, the rich *Anglo* place Henry Plant built, where they got the college now. Dona Anna was working there when Enrico Caruso, the famous Italian opera singer, came to sing in Tampa on his way to Buenos Aires. Well, she made up Caruso's room, and she got to meet him, and of course she fell headlong in love with Caruso. After he left Tampa, Dona Anna bought a Victrola, and she used to play Caruso to Cesar Fuentes before he was even born, when he was still inside her, because she got it in her head that he should grow up to be a tenor like her idol Caruso, only I don't know—maybe that was just a story. Because there were those *sin vergüenza*, those who were without shame, who used to whisper that the great Caruso had actually taken a fancy to the hotel maid at the Tampa Bay Hotel and seduced her and gave her the baby, so that Cesar Fuentes's father was actually the great Caruso himself. Which would certainly explain a lot, though I never believed such gossip, and anyway some said Caruso was *maricon, tú sabes?*

"I don't think no one ever knows why one fellow can sing and another can't carry a tune, or why one brother is a beautiful dancer but his own twin brother trips over his feet, though he can make a lot of money instead. It's all a mystery, these things, where they come from, how they take place. I believe everyone's got *some* kind of talent. Only the thing is, most of us never recognize it, or it's something you can't make a living at, or you don't get a break, or else you just piss your talent away and become bitter, like the world owes you a living, which it does not. Oh, but that Cesar Fuentes—he had it right from the start. Such talent. There was hardly anybody in Ybor City who didn't recognize that he was going places!

"Why, when he was just a boy, eleven or twelve years old, growing up on Calle Quince—over there on the other side of the railroad tracks, you know—sometimes in the evenings he would shine his shoes, put on a clean starched shirt, comb his hair back with the Agua Floridita like the men, and come out on the front porch of his family's house to practice reciting the speeches of José Martí, the great Cuban patriot—surely you heard of José Martí, Carmencita, you little dunce, no?"

"*Sí, Tía!*" huffed Carmen, without looking up. They had made her memorize Martí's birthday at school in Cuba, along with the date of Fidel Castro's attack on the Moncado Barracks.

Julieta continued. "Cesar Fuentes knew all Martí's speeches by heart. And the people would come out into the streets from around the whole neighborhood just to listen to that boy recite José Martí's speeches about freedom for Cuba from Spain. Let me tell you, there were plenty in Ybor City back then who had actually been there themselves when the Great Martí came to Tampa to agitate among the cigarworkers for Cuban freedom. A lot of those first-generation ones had been there and seen José Martí with their own eyes, heard him with their ears, and even they used to say that when it came to reciting Martí's speeches, not even Martí himself delivered them so good as Cesar Fuentes, tha'ss right! *Ay, Dios mío,* his young voice was like an angel's, so pure and sweet, you could feel the words shoot an arrow in your heart. And he would raise up his little hand in a fist, and speak the words, 'I saw above the yellow grasses, around the black trunks of the fallen pines, the joyful bunches of new pines. That's what we are, *mís compañeros*—new pines!' And the people would be so astonished that such a small boy could make a speech sound like that, they would forget for a moment that it was little Cesar Fuentes, not the great patriot Martí himself. And they would be beside themselves with tears and shouts, forgetting that Cuba was already liberated, since the American war with Spain in ninety-eight.

" '*Ay, qué maravilla!* What a miracle!' they would say to each other. Then afterwards, they would go up to the veranda and embrace Cesar Fuentes, kiss him on both cheeks or slap him on the back, shake him by the hand, and give him coins to show their appreciation.

" 'Cesar Fuentes,' they would say to him, 'God has truly given you *el voz de oro.* And one day, if you drink warm orange juice with honey and preserve your throat, perhaps you will become the Moses of our people and lead us to the promised land—or at any rate out of this miserable Tampa, which is killing us by degrees.' Because maybe you don't know, Carmencita, but most of the *cubanos* who came to Tampa to work in the cigar trade thought they were only coming temporarily, they would go back to their homes in Cuba after the liberation from Spain, but after the war of ninety-eight, that's not the way it turned out.

"Well, having heard that kind of thing often enough—and what's more, at such an impressionable age—Cesar Fuentes had no reason to doubt it. This was not a shy boy, lacking boldness. But you know, it never went to his head, with Cesar Fuentes. He always maintained a very good, let us say, attitude. I don't mean just his posture, you know? Oh, sure, he stood up straight and tall, not all hunched over, like someone without pride. Only in him it was without a trace of arrogance. You never got the feeling from Cesar Fuentes that he was spoiled by all the adulation, or that he felt superior to anyone else. He didn't need to make you feel smaller in order to make himself feel bigger. That was what the people of Ybor City really came to love best about Cesar Fuentes— that he was something special, but he was always one of us, too. We could see the best of ourselves develop in him. It made everyone in Ybor City as proud of him as if he was everybody's own son.

"By the time he was thirteen or fourteen, he was starting to make the orations at the cigarmakers' funerals. Because in those days, Carmencita, a funeral in Ybor City—well, this was about the biggest event, next to a strike at the cigar factories. *Ay,* how I used to love a good funeral! Not in a happy way, of course, tha'ss not what I mean at all. But in the way that it was one time when everyone was together, and felt like one big family that lost a relative. Let's face it, Carmen, we were not church people in Ybor City. Our families had come from the poorest parts of Spain. The priests had been the pals of the landowners ever since the Inquisition; they were intimidating the peasants with devils and damnation and all that shit, to keep them in their place.

"But so what, you're a poor and humble person. You still got a right to a little fun sometimes in life, no? To drink some red wine, dance the merengue, or just to play some cards or dominoes. Tell me, who does that hurt?

"When it came time for a funeral in Ybor City back then, most families of cigarmakers didn't want to hear a sermon from the priests. When it came to the elegy, the people didn't want to hear about sin and salvation. No, what we wanted was someone to help us with our grief; to tell us what someone's life meant for his family and his friends, for his community—not to mention his social class. What we wanted from the funeral oration was to hear what it was that made this dead person dear to us, to remember the good things he did that might live after him, because otherwise, what would be the point of living if nothing you did good survived after you?

"Maybe it's true that we're all born in sin, and if we repent, we go to heaven: *Diablo!* I'm no expert. But I remember when my uncle on my mother's side died, Johnny Albizu, we had Cesar Fuentes to deliver the oration at the gravesite, and I'm telling you, child, that young man was an expert when it came to the elegy. He could make his words hit the emotions every time, like arrows hitting the bull's eye, one after another.

"Everyone in my family was a little bit worried, you know, because Uncle Johnny Albizu, he wasn't only a nonbeliever. Let's face it—Uncle Johnny was an anarchist. I don't mean the bomb-throwing kind; that's not the kind of people we cigarmakers were. We didn't know what violence was. Uncle Johnny Albizu, he just didn't believe in government, period! He thought the only thing governments do is to oppress the people, and the only way to solve the problem is for all private property to be owned collectively. That's what he believed.

"*Tú sabes,* it was a different time back then, there's no denying that, so we were all a little nervous about what might be said over his coffin. Not just what would be said about him, but what would be the mourners' reaction, too, because in Ybor City if someone said the wrong thing politically at a funeral—my God! They would start shouting him down or stamping their feet, and that would be a terrible disgrace for our family, the worst thing anyone could ever imagine—a political *fracaso* at a funeral! Because the most important consideration at a funeral is to maintain decorum and show the proper respect for the dead.

"Well, that Cesar Fuentes stood over the open grave. Carmen, he was built just like a willow at that time, tall and thin—he could move his body with such grace as he spoke— and those round black eyes, glowing like live coals... He was too young to shave yet, I think, but he had already developed something deeper in his voice. It wasn't pure innocence anymore, it had some, some... *sí,* some *fuego,* you know? Some fire, some flame there. Something already burning down below. He got up there to speak and I remember, it must have been a hundred and thirty degrees that day, you could hardly tell the sweat from the tears, that's how humid it was, *cariña.* And the women were all crying, and the men all looking very somber in their black suits. To me, men at a funeral, they all look like the undertakers.

"Then Cesar Fuentes started to speak. He spoke in a very straight, simple style, elegant because it seemed so natural. And he said, 'I am not going to tell you falsehoods about this man, Johnny Albizu. Because every one of you here, and everyone from Ybor City, knew him well. This man believed with the great Voltaire when he said, "I should like to see the last priest strangled with the guts of the last king." He was against the few holding power over the lives of the many. This man Johnny Albizu believed that every human has the duty to love and assist every other human, because that is all we have, each other. He has helped all of us at one time or another. That is why so many are here attending his funeral today. If Johnny Albizu had anything in his pocket, all you needed to do was ask, and he gave it to you, not as a loan but a gift. He never kept a single record of it in his entire life. He organized benefits to pay the doctors' bills if someone needed medical attention. He was one of the founders of our mutual aid society, to assist people in need. He was a member in good standing of the cigarmakers' union welfare committee. He fought injustices in the workshops every day, and when there was a strike, it was Johnny Albizu who time and again organized relief for the strikers. He was the godfather to hundreds, including myself. There isn't a single home in Ybor City where Johnny Albizu wasn't welcome.'

"Then he stopped, Cesar Fuentes, mopped his brow with his handkerchief, and took a deep breath.

" 'And this,' he went on, 'is what the Anglos call a radical, an anarchist, a communist, and worse—a Cuban nigger!'

"Ha-ha, all the jaws dropped at that." Julieta laughed. "But the truth is, that is what the Anglos called us in those times, 'Cuban niggers.' Cesar Fuentes wasn't making it up. He held his head up and said, 'But *mis compañeros*—my friends, my comrades: this man is what we should call a hero, a saint! He never tried to sell you the moon in the sky. He never tried to convince you of his ideas. No! He wanted concrete changes to come here and now on earth. Because he knew we cannot wait for eternity to happen. Because he said, "We need a piece of heaven now!" ' "

Julieta removed her cigar and savored the flavor of her memory with her tongue. She put aside the sixtieth corona she had made that day. Then she said, "I'm telling you, Carmen, there wasn't a dry eye in the cemetery. He was unbelievable that day, Cesar Fuentes, really, because instead of just praising my uncle, he went on to tell the whole story of his life, mentioning everyone in the family by name, just at the right moment, so that the crowd there could look upon the faces of the grieving family to feel their sorrow, too. And he showed how my uncle's life was our lives, how this one man's struggles represented all our people's experiences. That's just what we wanted to hear at a funeral. And Cesar Fuentes knew just how to put it. And then, when everyone there had been moved by their grief, and the moment was exactly perfect, Cesar Fuentes performed the most difficult part of the funeral oration, what we used to call *despedir el duelo*—the 'turn at the corner,' the 'farewell' to the mourning, when the orator begins to bring the crowd back from reflecting on their loss, returns them to life, so to speak, in order to finish the funeral on a high note of celebration. Tha'ss the important thing, not to leave the family feeling low and hopeless, but to pull them back up a little at the end, you know? Make them feel that this life taken from them was worthwhile."

Suddenly, Carmen looked up. Her face registered deep anxiety, as if she'd just remembered that she'd left the gas stove on at home with the baby sleeping. She blurted out, "Did you make food for the peoples, or what?"

Julieta scrutinized her workmate. "*Claro que sí!* Sure we made food—afterwards, at the house. You ever heard of a *cubano* funeral without food?"

"Oh," said Carmen. Her ears seemed to lay back flat on her head again in a position of inattention as she subsided once more into her own world.

Julieta Suarez heaved herself up from the four cushions she sat on, in order to reach her workbench, and trundled on her bandy legs over to a small bundle of wet wrappers she kept on a nearby shelf. She chose a piece, then went to work with a single-edged razor blade and a bottle of India paste, repairing a torn stem on the end of a corona and grumbling about the dryness of the wrappers they gave her to work with. When Angie the pickup girl had come by to remove the cigars she had finished, Julieta lit herself a new 45-ring corona, rotating the end till she had an even burn, then exhaled a thoughtful cumulus cloud.

"Of course he never accepted money for a funeral, Cesar Fuentes." She shook her head. "It was part of his apprenticeship, because by that time everyone knew he was going to be a lector, and in those days a lector was a lot more than just a guy that read to you in the cigar factory. He was expected to be a real leader in the community, a public figure.

"It wasn't too long after my uncle Johnny Albizu's funeral that the cigarmakers started Cesar Fuentes off as lector—the youngest to ever hold that position, if I recall. True, he was only a substitute reader at first, filling in when the veteran readers had a union meeting or maybe a rendezvous with a mistress or something like that. No one doubted Cesar Fuentes could do the job, only he needed a little seasoning, to get used to it, and then, too, you couldn't just kick out one of the other lectors and bring in a kid to replace him, even if the kid happened to be Cesar Fuentes. We had more respect for our lectors than that! Still, it wasn't long before Cesar Fuentes won everybody over with that *voz de oro*. He went lickety-split from substitute to full-time lector, first reading the newspapers in the morning, and from there to afternoon lector reading books, and from that to lector *numero uno* at La Rosa, which was always the biggest of the cigar factories.

"You can't imagine the way the shop floor was back then, Carmencita—before they installed all these machines. The workbenches were all lined up from front to back, with one center aisle the apprentices used to go get more *tripa* from the leaf tables up at the front, or to deliver the finisheds to the humidor. The rollers sat facing each other across the benches, with a low shelf between them where the master cigarmaker put his finished cigars. The benches were really packed in there, maybe a thousand people working a single shift, so in order to let them all hear the lector they built a wooden platform raised up like a pulpit above the shop floor for the reader, with a ladder for him to climb up, because he had to throw his voice so the whole factory could hear him, he didn't have a microphone or anything.

"At La Rosa, Cesar Fuentes received five times the average cigarworker's wages. Five times! But of course everyone was glad to have him. They said, 'Cesar Fuentes, buy yourself a new suit, by yourself some clothes, we want you to look as good as you sound.' So he went to the haberdashery in

Tampa, and when he came back, ooh-la-la! From that time on, all the girls fell in love with Cesar Fuentes. He could snap his fingers and they'd all come running. It wasn't that he was the most handsome guy in the world, either, Carmen, because if you want to know the truth, his eyes were a little too big for his head, and his head was a little too big for his shoulders. No, it wasn't his good looks at all, it was his face, something in his eyes, his style, and his authority. If he wanted to, I am sure he could have had a career on the stage, no doubt about it. But when he appeared at the cigar factory in that fine white linen suit, with the shining white spats and black patent leather shoes, the silk bow tie and a boater hat with a wide red and black band, freshly shaven at the barbershop with his hair slicked back with pomade—*ay-yay-yay,* when he walked in like that—the whole shop floor buzzed with excitement.

"Then he would stand in the back, Cesar Fuentes, like a star waiting to go on stage, smoking his corona and greeting everyone with a smile and a hug, a handshake, kidding someone, asking after their family, as we came back from our dinner break. I will always remember the way Cesar Fuentes smelled then—the Florida water he wore for cologne. It would float by like a sweet breeze as he walked through the factory to climb into the lector's chair. He would sit down and straighten up very tall, carefully put on his reading glasses, look up over the lenses, softly clear his throat, and nod once, like an orchestra conductor. All conversation would stop dead. You could hear a pin drop. And then he would begin to read to us. I'm telling you, Carmencita, it was like he had come down from heaven in a chariot, that guy.

"Ahh." Julieta sighed. "Long days in the cigar factory went by like a dream then. You know, a cigarmaker doesn't have much to look forward to, just work and more work, one day is like all the rest. Let's face it, it's not the most interesting job in the world, *verdad?* But somehow, with Cesar Fuentes as lector, there was at least something to keep you going every day, a new book to follow, something to keep your mind occupied. It made the work seem less boring. I remember those long humid afternoons, listening to his beautiful voice, so full of control and passion—full of intelligence, I would say, with the blades of the big fans turning slow overhead. Oooh, then when he finished reading, it would be the last hour before quitting time. The top rollers, the ones who could make two hundred double coronas in a single day, would stop their own work at maybe 150 or 175 and wander around the shop floor helping the younger rollers to finish their quotas before the time bell—usually flirting with us girls! They would come over to where we were working, you know? Because while they helped we all gabbed. And we'd have the best debates about the book Cesar Fuentes was reading. I remember thinking then how right my father was, because when we listened to the lector, and then discussed the story, it was like I could step through a door into a new world. Even then I knew in my heart it was the closest I would ever come to going to school and maybe learning something that might make me a better person, or at least let me have my own ideas about something. When you're young like I was then, and you enter the factory like everyone else, you still have some dreams and hopes. Without those lectors we *cubanos* would have remained ignorant factory workers, stuck inside Ybor City like a pit trapped inside a mango. We wouldn't ever amount to anything but a pair of hands. And nobody in this world wants to think of themselves as just a pair of hands.

"But the main thing when Cesar Fuentes was up there in the lector's pulpit—he was ours. Ours! He belonged to us. No one could take him away from us. You know, a lot of the cigarmakers' leaders in those days, the political ones, they would go on and on talking about what was rightfully ours, taking away from the rich to give more to the humble classes. That's okay, Carmen, but look at what happened in Cuba—they took away from the rich and they made everybody the same; now everybody is poor. Who wants to live there—not even you! But with Cesar Fuentes, it was different. He didn't pull anyone down, he brought us all up. His example pulled everyone up to a better level, and that's what we thought this country should be about, everyone moving up to a better standard together, not just everyone looking out for himself. Cesar Fuentes showed us a new world, civilized and beautiful. We saw that he was one of us, and we thought, *sí*, maybe we could belong in that new world someday."

She smoked in silence for a while, removing her next half-dozen cigars from the clamp and looking them over before wrapping them in maduro.

"That was long ago—back in the 1920s, when Cesar Fuentes was our lector," she resumed. "Those were good days for Ybor City, with the factories running two shifts and plenty of overtime. We had the best social dances at the clubs on Saturday nights back then. *Ay*, Carmencita, I used to dance the merengue with the boys, too, you know? Sometimes I even danced with Cesar Fuentes. I could even dream that some day we might—well, you can't ever tell what can happen in life, Carmen, eh?"

Off in the stratosphere of her salsa cassettes, Carmen sensed a variation in the old lady's rhythm that made her look up and nod.

"Everything was okay till that damn stock market crashed," Julieta continued. "You probably never heard of that, Carmencita, you dumb bunny. That was October 29, 1929. El Lunes Negro, they called it—Black Monday, when all the companies fell on Wall Street, and the businessmen were throwing themselves out of windows because they lost their money. You know, we weren't so dumb, us cigarmakers, not to know this was going to hurt us, too. After all, we were in Florida, and back in the twenties we saw the Anglos speculating in land, in that kind of frenzy they call a boom, when people get taken over by the demons to get rich quick. It came like a madness all around us, the prices driven up and up. And the land, it was all swamps and malaria, just like before. We knew, because our kids had been dying of those fevers for years, but the Anglos didn't care anything about living on the land they were buying, only about selling it the next week for a big profit. And then after the big hurricanes in twenty-five, it all came tumbling down. A lot of people were ruined, so we had already seen it happen once, and we knew that whatever went up had to come down.

"When that stock market crashed, I remember, there was one lector, we called him El Professor. He was a very studious type of man, a quiet man, who spent his time studying, a real scholar who had taught himself all about the way international finances worked. The next day, after the crash, he read to us from the newspapers the accounts of what was taking place up there in New York, about the bankers and the industrialists holding a big meeting to try to stop the collapse. And I'll never forget how one of the cigarworkers jumped up from his bench, right in the middle of the shop, and started to speak against the big bankers in the strongest language. He said, 'Damn these bourgeoisie, who have stolen everything from the working people, and I hope every one of them loses his stuffed shirt so that his big fat belly has to hang out, because as for me, I am going to laugh myself silly over this whole panic.'

"But El Professor, he looked over his spectacles, waiting patiently for the man to finish speaking. Then he very calmly continued to read from the newspaper the account of the meeting. He read to us how the panic was on the floor of the Stock Exchange, and how every few minutes the latest prices were announced, moving down and down, faster and faster. Then he read to us about the nervous feeling of those present, and how it was revealed. I can even remember the lines he read to us from the newspaper about all the Wall Street tycoons. 'They were continually lighting cigarettes, taking a puff or two, putting them out and lighting new ones. Soon the narrow room was blue with smoke and extremely stuffy.'

"Then El Professor looked up over the newspaper, and in the same calm voice said, 'Cigarettes, *compañeros*—not the cigars which we make.' "

Julieta closed her eyes for a moment and left off work. She was remembering, as if that was her real job. Finally she began again. "One era closed with those words, *hijita*, and another began. The cigarette era. After the big stock market crash in twenty-nine we were ready for a struggle. Though God knows, nobody wanted trouble. People had children and families to support, but you know, in those days there was no minimum wage, no job security, no unemployment. Florida didn't even have laws against child labor back then. The *patrónes* could do what they wanted if we let them get away with it. If the union didn't strike back, they just fired people with no notice or anything, or cut the wage in half. They could even close down the factory and tell everyone to go home. The law was all on their side.

"It wasn't six months after that Lunes Negro on Wall Street, we got word that the factory had changed hands. Before, it was always the Spanish who had run the cigar trade in Tampa. *Los españoles* had been running it for generations—first in Havana long before, then in Key West, and then Tampa. They bought the tobacco leaf in Cuba, or maybe Mexico. But what with the economy flopping, our orders died. The Tampa banks foreclosed, and the new owners who bought the company cheap were Tampa Anglos. I don't know what you have been told, Carmen, but the Anglos in Tampa never had anything to do with the cigar industry. They never had anything to do with us, either. They were always on their side of Tampa, and we were on ours, in Ybor City. They didn't know anything about running a cigar factory.

"The first thing they did was, all of a sudden they started using cheaper leaf for the cigars, tha'ss right. See, they charged the same price for it, but it wasn't the same product, and the inferior leaf wasn't so good to roll, either. The master rollers didn't like that one bit, because they had high standards in those days. We took pride in producing the best cigars in the whole world, right here in Tampa. Our union wrote a letter to the management protesting that they cheapened the product. But the new Anglo manager, Mr. Bob

Garrity, he just told us it wasn't any of our business, the grade of tobacco the company used, because we didn't own the company, we only worked there. They could use whatever tobacco they wanted.

"There was a lot of grumbling. Then only a few weeks later, they introduced a higher daily minimum quota we had to finish. That meant we had to work faster for the same pay. You couldn't be as careful then with the cigars, repairing the imperfections, till they were sending out boxes of first coronas where maybe half of the twenty-five were actually second quality. The master rollers didn't like that at all! We took pride in our work, *mi hijita*, but now if you tried to maintain the same care with the speed-up, you couldn't finish your quota, which meant a cut in pay.

"But it wasn't only a pay cut worrying the cigarmakers. We knew it only takes a little bad product out there to ruin the reputation our Tampa cigars had been building up for forty years. If they kept their policies up, they would wreck the industry we depended on for our livelihoods.

"The union sent an even stronger letter. But this time the manager Garrity was blunt. He told the union leaders we had to accept the company's policies or get out, because business was slowing down, the company's profits were getting squeezed. He said we were lucky to still have jobs, what with the big slump everywhere, and if we didn't stop complaining, he was going to start firing the troublemakers. He was a red-faced little man who only had one tooth in his head, that Garrity, a real son of a bitch—crude, you know, like he was raised in a men's room, with the language he used. He was shifty, too, never looked you straight in the eyes. I think they must have put him in there as manager just because he had a mean streak and would do whatever the new *patrónes* told him, *tú entiendes?*

"I remember we used to have a big yellow tomcat in the factory to keep the rats and mice down, we called him Omar. Well, from the very moment that Garrity took over as factory manager, he hated that cat, and the cat hated him. Whenever Garrity came on to the shop floor, that poor Omar would jump up from where he was sleeping and race away shrieking, like he'd seen the devil himself. Till one time the cat was going past Garrity's office, and the door was open. And Garrity was sitting in there with his feet up on the desk smoking a cigarette—because, by the way, he never smoked cigars himself—and then, just as cool as a cucumber, when he saw Omar walk by, he pulled the pistol he kept in his desk drawer and shot the cat in the head. Then he took it and flung the carcass out the factory doors. He was grinning that toothless grin the whole time. He acted proud, like it was some kind of game he had won. There was something wrong in his mind, I believe, to do something so cruel to a harmless animal like that.

"Well, it was just around that time that we celebrated Cesar Fuentes's fifth anniversary as lector *numero uno* at La Rosa. And guess who was in charge of the committee to choose him a gift? Me!"

Carmen smiled at the old lady, pretending to be listening, and went on with her work.

"I collected ten cents from everybody, and we presented him with a beautiful leatherbound edition of Zola's *Germinal,* which I have to admit I wanted to hear very badly, because everyone told me it was the best novel they had ever heard when read out loud, and I'd never read or heard Zola before. Of course, the easiest way to get everyone to vote for it was to give it to Cesar Fuentes for his fifth anniversary, so that's what I did. Anyway, he was very polite, and said it was his very favorite novel, too, so I just replied, 'Oh, is that so, Cesar Fuentes? In that case you must come over to my house for dinner on Saturday night, so you can read it to me when we are alone.' Because all us girls kidded Cesar Fuentes a lot about how it would be better to hear him reading to you in bed with the light on than to make love to most men in the dark.

"So then Cesar Fuentes started reading *Germinal* to us. Oh, the effect it had on me when he started reading that book! It was like an electric shock to hear that story. It's the story of the coal miners in France a hundred or more years ago—a terrible story. I won't ever forget how Zola described that coal pit as 'evil-looking, a voracious beast crouching ready to devour the world.' To this day, I still hear him describe the village where the miners lived:

'No sign of dawn; the sky was dead. Only the coke ovens and furnaces glared and reddened the shadows... And huddled in its lair like some evil beast, Le Voreux crouched ever lower and its breath came in longer and deeper gasps, as though it were struggling to digest its meal of human flesh.'

"Oooh-ooo." Julieta shivered. "The idea of that coal mine as the beast eating up the miners has stayed with me all these years. And then there was the part where the miners go down into that coal pit, not just the men but the boys and the little girls, too, half a mile down, down into black galleries where one minute it was hot as hell, the next freezing like a snowstorm, and the miners had to crawl in the dark through a shaft so narrow it scraped the skin off their backs, dragging themselves through water on their knees and elbows to get to the coal, in a place where you choked because of no air, full of dust and heavy with gases. I tell you, Carmen, I never heard anything so horrible!

"One afternoon Cesar Fuentes was reading to us from Zola, a passage of *Germinal* where the miners are talking in a bar. And one miner said to another that conditions had to change, you know? That the owners couldn't keep treating the miners like machines. That the workers were beginning to think for themselves:

> 'But now the miner was waking up under the ground, germinating in the earth like good seed... Why should the worker remain the slave of the employer who paid him?... The whole show would blow up one of these days, thanks to education. You only had to look round the village: the grandfathers could not have signed their names, the fathers could already do that much, and as for their sons, why, they could read and write like professors. Things were beginning to move little by little, and a great harvest of men was ripening in the sun!'

She moistened her lips and replaced her cigar. "Well, when Cesar Fuentes got to that passage about learning to read, his voice got darker and he looked out over the shop floor. He didn't say anything, *tú me entiendes,* because he didn't have to say anything. The meaning wasn't lost on the cigarmakers.

"It just so happened that at that very moment the manager Garrity was walking down the shop floor, though usually he stayed in the office, and he happened to hear the lector because, of course, Cesar Fuentes was reading in English. Well, that Garrity stood still, with his arms like this on his hips, and looking up at the lector's pulpit with a scowl on his face. Then he marched back to his office and slammed the door shut and didn't come out for the rest of the day, but the people who needed to ask him something came back whispering all up and down the shop floor that he was on the telephone, shouting and acting deranged. Well, when we got to the factory the next morning to begin our shift, there was a notice up on the gates. The company had changed its policy. From now on, there would be no more readers at La Rosa. Starting from that very day!

"That night the union called a big meeting at the Club Asturiano. Let me tell you, everyone showed up for that meeting. They opened the doors to every cigarmaker, no matter what nationality. Because it didn't have nothing to do with nationality, or even race. This was class warfare, pure and simple.

"The hall was packed, standing room only, with lots more people, friends and family, milling around outside on the steps and in the street."

"*Qué?*" Carmen's head suddenly snapped back. "Did you say 'Friends and Family'? I got a friend, a Russian girl, Mila, was telling me about this Friends and Family. Because, like, it's so expensive to call Havana. I got my two sisters an' my mother over there, and sometimes, you know, like you can't get a long-distance line for hours. So I was thinking of getting this Friends and Family, 'cause, like, Mila says you gonna save ten, twenty dollars on your phone bill, *verdad?*"

When she was through, Julieta Suarez calmly picked up the strands of her story. "The Club Asturiano was in pandemonium, because I think everybody was feeling the same thing. They had nickel-and-dimed us, cut back on the wages, shortened our hours, made the daily quotas higher. We knew they were going to start layoffs. But when they tried to take our lectors away from us—no, *señores*. No, no, and no! That was going too far. That was trying to take something sacred from us. And no one could do that to the Tampa cigarmakers without a fight on his hands.

"Well everyone who wanted to spoke that night. But it was mostly second-generation cigarmakers, like me and my friends. To us, making cigars was always more than just a way to earn a dollar, it was our whole way of life. It was in our blood, cigarmaking, that's all we really knew. Our fathers and uncles were cigarmakers, it was a family tradition. The people stood up there, and somebody said, 'Don't give in to these Anglo bastards, they'll ruin us if we back down now. We won't let them take our lectors away from us. They don't care about us, they just want us to be hands like in the slave plantations.' And everyone shouted, '*Huelga! A la huelga!* Let's go on strike!'

"But then somebody else spoke and said a strike was no good because the company would just close down the factory and fire everyone. What we should do was go to the factory in the morning like usual and then let Cesar Fuentes read to us, but not finish any work. And we should make a written declaration, demanding our right to hear the reader and keep the quality of the product high, and so forth and so on.

"So then, of course, after everyone had their say, it came to a vote. And we voted for the sitdown strike. Then we elected our strike committee and put Cesar Fuentes on it, even though he wasn't there that night, because he said he didn't want to influence the meeting one way or the other. He was waiting for the outcome down at his house on Calle Quince.

"The feelings were running high in Ybor City that night. After the meeting at Club Asturiano, we lit torches and marched down in front of Cesar Fuentes's home. It was just a humble worker's cottage where he lived with his mother and aunts, like the shotgun houses everyone had in Ybor City. He came out to meet with the delegation bringing news of the strike vote. He was overcome with emotion, Cesar Fuentes, that the cigarworkers were prepared to risk their jobs and even their lives to keep readers in the factory. But he was never a man at a loss for words. He stepped forward to address the crowd in front of his little veranda there. Everyone who was there that night will always remember his words. He said, '*Compañeros*, tonight I salute you and thank you from my heart. For you have done something no one else has ever done. It is one thing when the bosses take the bread from our mouths, and the working people, facing ruin and starvation, must act for our very survival. But it is quite another thing to strike for our culture, for the things that nourish the soul of humanity. Tonight the cigarmakers of Tampa have pushed history forward. And tonight we are no longer *cubanos, italianos*, whites or blacks, communists or capitalists. Tonight we are one people together. Because tonight we have defended our humanity against those who would deny us. The iron is hot. We strike tomorrow. And we will win! *Venceremos!*' "

Julieta puffed her corona, then removed it from her mouth. "I don't think anybody in Ybor City slept that night. I know I didn't, I was so nervous about what would happen. I was plenty scared, but angry too, and proud. Pride is a kind of uncle to happiness. Oh, I don't know, Carmen, with all those feelings going around inside me, no wonder I couldn't sleep!

"We used to start at the factory at seven, while it was still a little cooler, but this was in July, so it almost didn't matter, it gets so stinking hot here, it never cools off overnight. Anyway, when we got to the factory we saw they were expecting trouble, because the place was surrounded by cops. Must have been stool pigeons at the strike meeting. They were all armed with billy clubs and shotguns, while we cigarmakers didn't have anything to defend ourselves with but our own two hands. But we didn't think they would be so bold as to shoot us right there. After all, this wasn't Haiti, it was Estados Unidos, you know?

"So we all went in and took our places, like usual, and then the strike committee marched in all at once arm in arm with Cesar Fuentes in the middle. And wouldn't you know it: right there in his hands he was carrying that edition of Zola's *Germinal*. When I saw him go up the ladder to the lector's pulpit with that book, I thought I would faint; I was delirious with joy. My heart was pounding like the Eiffel Tower!

"Then Garrity came out of his office, all steamed up, just in time to hear the *voz de oro* of Cesar Fuentes, announcing, 'On behalf of the strike committee, and by the unanimous vote of our shop local, I declare La Rosa *fábrica* on strike.' He said those words. Very smooth, Cesar Fuentes, *muy profesional.* Almost matter of fact, like you would announce a meeting of the chess club. Then he started to read. And his voice was so lovely that day, Carmen, clear and crisp and deep, full of courage and determination. I swear to you, it was like every one of us was reading, only he had the voice."

Carmen again sensed something in Julieta's tone, and said without looking up, "*Oye*, Tia, one thing I don't get. This guy Fuentes—he was your boyfriend?"

Julieta ignored her. "That Garrity was so mad, he turned red as the Soviet flag! Why, you could practically see the steam coming out of his ears. He was raving like a lunatic. 'I'll show you foreign bastards what respect means!' And 'You've got exactly one hour to clear out, all of you, or I'll have you deported!' And all like that.

"Cesar Fuentes went on calmly reading Zola," she said. "We all sat there with our hands folded on our workbenches and our heads bowed. After a while, the cops came inside and stood in the hall. See, they thought they could intimidate us, but they couldn't intimidate us. We were a thousand—or maybe eight hundred—but they couldn't have been more than thirty or forty, those cops.

"It was a standoff till noontime. Then suddenly, a complete surprise. All the Ybor City kids came into the factory, bringing lunch pails to their parents and older brothers and sisters. That was something great to see, those little kids marching right past the cops on to the shop floor. I think when Garrity saw that, he must have known he couldn't use his bullying tactics on us any more, because even the children weren't scared of him and his goons. We were ready to stay there overnight if we had to, listening to Cesar Fuentes read. And I'll tell you a little secret: *Germinal* is a very long book!"

Julieta put her corona down on the edge of her workbench with the ash hanging over the floor, and sighed. "But, *ay*, Carmen, that's not what happened. What happened was this: around an hour after noon we could see through the glass in

Garrity's office a big meeting going on. He was talking to the police officers, and he was on the telephone; probably, we figured, talking to the owners. After a while, they all came out, and he was waving his arms over his head, all smiles, like a cat that has swallowed the bird, *tú sabes?* And he goes up to the front of the floor and announces that the company has said it will negotiate with us starting tomorrow. We can call off the strike and go home for the day.

"Well, for a minute, everyone just looked at each other, real quiet, not knowing what to think. Then a big cheer went up, everybody started hugging each other, and the men all threw their hats in the air. We thought, tha'ss it! The company has capitulated, and we have won.

"That night was crazy, just crazy in Ybor City. All the people in the streets talking and talking over what had happened at La Rosa, everybody so excited about tomorrow. The owners had backed down right away. It was like a fiesta, only without a saint's day to celebrate. The rhumba bands were all playing at the workers' clubs, and the people were dancing, dancing with joy. It was after midnight before everyone started drifting home to bed. It was still sweltering hot, but that didn't matter, we were all in such a good mood."

Julieta considered the worn top of her workbench for a moment, then continued. "The streets had just cleared, and some of the men were out on the verandas, chatting and having a smoke before going inside, when all of a sudden we heard a lot of loud explosions—like firecrackers going off. Then a line of cars with their bright headlights on roared down Avenida Siete, twenty-five or thirty cars, all full of men in white sheets and white hoods. You know what that means,

Carmencita? Maybe not, but everyone in Ybor City knew. It was the night riders of the KKK, Carmen—the Ku Klux Klan, the secret organization of whites who go around killing people because they are Negroes, or foreigners, Jews, Catholics, or whatever, the fascist hatemongers. They were invading Ybor City with shotguns out the car windows, shooting up the place.

"Then everyone hit the floor in terror," Julieta said. "We tried to grab for the kids and to pull them under us, to crawl under the beds before someone got shot. And they were going so fast, the dust flew out in clouds. They turned down Calle Quince, and they all pulled up in front of the house of Cesar Fuentes. The neighbors who saw it said later they were many of them shouting and staggering and laughing, a mob of drunken cowards, hiding behind their ghost sheets and their shotguns.

"But they knew exactly what house to go to. They knew exactly who they were looking for. The neighbors said later the man leading was kind of small—a lot like Garrity's build, but you couldn't prove anything with those sheets over their heads. They blew out the windows with shotgun blasts. Glass flew everywhere, and the women inside started screaming and crying. Then five or six of them, they dragged Cesar Fuentes out by the arms and the hair, beating him about the head with their clubs and kicking him. Someone said they saw Cesar Fuentes bleeding from the ears, from all the blows on the head he suffered. Then they threw him down on the ground in front of his mother's house, and they filled his mouth with dirt until he was choking.

"All over Ybor City we could hear the night riders yelling their insults, spitting on Cesar Fuentes, and one of them shouted, 'You won't be reading no more fucking books when we get done with you, you Cuban nigger shit.'

"When we heard all the noise and where it was coming from, we all ran out to save Cesar Fuentes from the mob. But before we could get there, they put him into one of the cars, doused the house with gasoline, and set fire to it, while they all drove off, leaving a burning cross in the street behind them. It was all over in five minutes. There was no time to come to his defense. We didn't have cars or trucks to go after him. The police wouldn't come to Ybor City that night."

Julieta remained motionless at her workbench, the corona in her mouth, her eyes shuttered. Only her hands were trembling. The Gulf Coast sun caught her sharp face, so tightly drawn it seemed like a mask. Softly, she said, "We found Cesar Fuentes the next morning. We sent out a search party in a car someone got God knows where. He was lying facedown in the ditch by the side of the road across town. It's hard to tell you this, Carmen, but they had mutilated that man so savagely, no one could hardly recognize that it was actually him, Cesar Fuentes. His body was missing the eyes, and they had cut out his tongue, knocked out all his teeth, slit his throat, and left him there at the roadside to bleed to death."

Julieta rolled her cigar around her mouth. Her hands had stopped shaking. She had a nearby-faraway look, as though trying to remember something from the past forgotten and beyond reach. She stayed like that for a while, staring at the ceiling. Finally, she resumed. "So that was the end of the lectors in the cigar factories. After all that, I left the cigar trade for a time. A lot of people lost their jobs then, most never went back. *Ay, bendito,* I drifted to one thing and another. You know, during the Great Depression the Tampa Bay Hotel went bankrupt and closed down. I used to sleep in the abandoned rooms. Times were hard then. I worked in a luncheonette for a while. I even picked oranges once, but they couldn't pay me enough to work out in that hot sun. I took maybe fifteen or twenty oranges at the end of the day, put them inside my shirt, and that was my pay. I just kept walking.

"But *tú sabes,* Carmen, wherever I went in those bad years, I was always thinking about Cesar Fuentes. *Nuestro lector,* Cesar Fuentes. I couldn't get him out of my mind. Every day I would see him in my imagination, striding into that factory with a book under his arm, ready to entertain us and to teach us. Maybe I was in love with him, after all. Over and over again, wherever I was, I would ask myself, '*Porqué?* Why? Why?' Why did they need to do that to him? What in God's name made them commit such a savage crime? Who was Cesar Fuentes hurting? He was hurting no one. All he ever did was read books to us, Cesar Fuentes. Was that so dangerous? Did they have to torture him and murder him? What is this evil in men, what makes them hate so much?"

If Carmen had been watching, she would have seen Julieta fighting to collect herself, her upper teeth clamped over her lower lip. But Carmen wasn't watching and she wasn't listening. Julieta said, "But I guess that's *la vida* for you, eh? Life—it's a bitch, but what else is there, you know what I'm saying, Carmen?...Carmen?...Carmen! You haven't heard a word I said!"

The afternoon had wound down, and their shift was ending. One by one the women shut down their machines. Downstairs you could hear the *ching* and *ping* of the old punch clock that still hung on the wall, as it always had, in front of the swinging doors that led out of the factory gates. Carmen clicked off her Walkman. Checking her makeup in her compact, she drew a line of crimson lipstick on her upper lip and smeared it expertly over the rest of her mouth. Then she reached over and touched the old lady on the wrist. "Tia, is time to go home now. I got to feed the kids, okay? You don't like it over here, the States, you try in Cuba son'time, you no going to like it too much over there, I guarantee. Over there they put you in the jail just for talking—and you, Tia, you don't never stop talking!

"Anyway," she said, "I see you tomorrow, babe, a'right?"

A Mermaid Pining for Her Sailor

"I was always my daddy's boy," said Stevie Rae, pressing her indisputably female bust against the bar. She signaled Salty the bartender for another beer. It was only an hour before closing time, and the place had simmered down. The hardluck choir—guys who couldn't charm, cheat, or buy their way home with some babe—were strung up and down the bar with their noses drooping in their drafts. Stevie Rae was not explaining how she got named Stevie Rae in the first place, instead of Carly Sue or Mary Alice or Faye Jean or some other Gulf Coast concoction. Rather she was explaining how she got started swimming in the show.

"I used to swim and water-ski and fish with my daddy out in the bay and the Gulf," she said. "Daddy's a *big* fisherman.

He's out there every chance he gets. Daddy thinks the worst-ever day of fishing is better than the best night of sex. He calls his fishing boat *Twin Two's* because he's got them twin 200-horsepower outboards on her? I practically lived in the water when I's a kid, so naturally when I found out they would actually pay me to go in the water, I said, 'Grrrrrreat!' That's how I got started swimming in the show!"

That's the Live Mermaid Show at Weekee Wachee in Crystal Springs, though Stevie Rae's been living on a houseboat outside New Port Richey since her divorce.

"You don't wanna know about my ex-husband, Jack," she went on. "He was a junior officer off the navy base at Pensacola? See, after the show at Weekee Wachee, they would give us girls hostess points for coming outside the auditorium and having yur picture taken with the snowbirds come down from up North to avoid the winter weather. Well, it could get real cold out there in January or February, standing around with yur butt in a wet mermaid suit for an hour after the show. I mean nasty, raw, mean, buttstinging cold. And the cold weather was, like, breaking hundred-year-old records, right? That was the winter it got so cold the manatees all swum up to Yankeetown and camped out next to the nuclear power plant there because it was putting heat out into the bay there. But, hey, those hostess points was worth three, four dollars each in your paycheck, and the snowbirds tipped if you sugartalked 'em jus' right—not too heavy, 'course, since their wives was right there.

"So this one time after the show in February, I was out there to have my picture taken with the snowbirds. And it was...we were heading toward a century freeze that night or something. I was freaked to the max that afternoon anyway, cuz this mean ole bohonker thunderstorm had come up out of the Gulf, and the lightning hit the springs where we were swimming, but they made us do the four o'clock show anyway. I was pissed, I's ready to call the federals, tell 'em they was trying to kill off an endangered species called mermaids. Hell, I mean we coulda got electrified down there!

"You know, I was always scared to death of lightning," Stevie Rae digressed. "I can't hardly plug in a hair dryer without getting a shock. When I was growing up outside Gulfport, we had these neighbors, the Beavers? Well, one day Mr. and Mrs. Beaver was in bed together doin' it when a storm struck. The lightning come right through the open window into their bedroom, hit the beer can Mr. Beaver was drinking, ricocheted off, and killed him right there and then, laid him out flat as a flounder. That's right!

"Now Mr. Beaver, he was a big guy, six foot six, weighed about three hundred pounds. But Mrs. Beaver, now she was just a little shrimp of a woman, about a buck, a buck-ten. So when Mr. Beaver bought the brewery like that, he kinda keeled over, smack on top of her. And I swear, she couldn't get him off. No matter how hard she struggled, she could not budge that fat tub of barbecued Beaver. Mrs. Beaver had to stay there three whole days, till a cat burglar came in through the open window and freed her up."

"That rigor mortis ain't as bad as it's cracked up to be," shouted someone from the choir.

Stevie Rae sipped her beer. "I wouldn't know, but anyway, the way Mr. Beaver died like that in bed with his wife, Daddy used to say Mr. Beaver came and went at the same time."

Someone down at the other end of the bar gave a throaty laugh and called, "Give that little lady a drink."

Salty poured her a shot of Southern Comfort and set her up with a fresh beer. "That lightning, it's like to kill you," continued Stevie Rae. "Anyway, after the show that one time, I was shivering out there, sitting on all these snowbirds' laps while their wives took our picture together, when suddenly this guy walks up to me and asks if I'm cold, do I want his jacket?

"I took one look at him and said, 'Darlin', could you loan me a dime? I got to go call my astrologer to see if you're in my lucky stars today.' Because, I mean, this guy was bad to the bone! Handsome? I was thinking, he's got t'be divine, I ain't never saw nothin' in nature to match him.

"So he asked me out for a beer after the show. At that particular time, we were doing the show where the mermaids trade their freedom for eternal youth and beauty? I had to hold my breath for over two minutes and twenty seconds for my part in it. I had a pair of mighty lungs back in those days—mighty everything else, too. Now Jack, he had those dark gray sailor's eyes. You could see down to the bottom of the ocean in his eyes. Trouble was, all you could see down there was that it was every shark for himself, you know what I mean? But, oh, man, that cute curly black beard! Come to think of it, he looked like the devil himself in a naval uniform. But I never had no more sense about men than a mare in heat. I just swished my little mermaid's tail and thought, Ooh, ooh, ooh, Stevie Rae, let the bontemps roulet."

"You drug him home by that beard, Stevie Rae?" said someone down the bar.

"Who, Jack?" she said, cracking her gum. "Noo. Heck, I drug Jack home by his propeller. I got one o' them $29.95 winches on my pickup truck, and I just hooked him on and hauled his ass back to my place. I figured I could show him a few things about keeping his prop lubricated he'd never heard of back home in Minne—, Minne—, Minneaposota, or wherever he came from."

"You mean Minneapolis," advised Salty.

"Aw, Minneapolis ain't even on the water, Stevie Rae," said someone else.

"I don't remember the name of the goddamn place! It was somewhere up there near Canada." Stevie Rae shrugged. "Canada's got a ocean, don't it? Wull, anyway, we had what you might call a hurricane courtship, Jack and me, because all I remember next was digging out of the wreckage.

"I remember it was Sunday morning, and I couldn't open my eyes any wider'n the three blind mice put together? I mean, talk about hung! So we decided to drive over the state line to the House of a Thousand Daiquiris on Highway 90, where you can get all these different kinds of daiquiris, like Pineapple D-lite daiquiris and Licorice daiquiris—just any ole kind you can imagine, and a lot you could never imagine, like Dr Pepper daiquiris—but on the way over we stopped at this place where a Spanish lady called Magdalena had her evangelical trailer. She had this sign out by the road that said she did readings and weddings and other, you know, psychic services, and before we knew it, we got ourselves hitched. As if that's legal or something!

"After the ceremony when we paid this lady Magdalena, she tried to sell us a big painted Indian statue. I said to Jack, 'Is that supposed to be a lawn ornament or what? Like flamingos and painted truck tires?' It was weird."

"I remember that Magdalena, she was crazier'n the Baptist pope," said a blasphemer at the bar.

"Reminds me of a joke Daddy used to tell," said Stevie Rae. "You know what a backwoods Baptist virgin is, don't you?"

Nobody said anything.

"It's a thirteen-year-old girl can run faster than her brother."

Stevie Rae signaled Salty for a light for her slim-filter cigarette, took a steep drag, and exhaled a thoughtful stream of blue-white smoke. "Everything went real good for a while," she said. "We didn't have enough money for a down payment on a house, but we were renting this real cute houseboat, docked on Cedar Key. We had everything there we wanted and decorated the boat in, you know, kind of early Navy style? We had, like, fishnet and ship's wheels on the walls, and Jack had his collection of rum bottles from all over the world—well, that was Jack's idea of collectin' antiques.

"Till Jack volunteered for missile submarine duty. That was back in sixty-eight. I remember the year real good, 'cause we took our vacation, we drove over to Six Gun City in Dallas, and we were there the day President Kennedy got shot."

"That was 1963," said some slob-for-facts down at the end of the bar. "It was the brother Bobby Kennedy got shot in sixty-eight. Bastard what hated the South."

"I knew it was someone!" said Stevie Rae. "To tell you the truth, I always did wonder why no one in Dallas made much of a fuss that day. It was like me when those astronauts got killed in space? I didn't really feel all that sorry for them. I wanted to, you know, because there was that woman astronaut got killed and all. But deep down inside I just felt they had moved on to a bigger and better show, is all I believe. Jack was the one wanted to go to Six Gun City in the first place. I wanted to go to the Grand Caymans, scuba diving on the reef with the giant sea turtles. I never could get enough of the water.

"Shoot, those submarines stay under for months at a time," said Stevie Rae. "And when they come up, it ain't necessarily where yur wife happens to live. I said to him, 'What do you want to go and do a fool thing like that for? Ain't you got what you need right here at home?'

"I told him, 'You volunteered yourself, now just unvolunteer yourself.' At first he got real mad when I brought it up. Like I wasn't supposed to say anything about it. Like it was my problem for disagreeing with him? Ain't it the way with men—now y'all 'fess up! First thing is, they do something wrong. Second thing is, stonewall and deny it, maybe it'll go away. Ninety-nine percent the guys in this world could share the same words on their graves. It'd say, 'I didn't do it. I don't know nothin' 'bout it. And if I did, I sure wouldn't tell you.' Here the son of a bitch had gone and volunteered for two years' duty on a friggin' nuclear sub and hadn't even bothered to mention it to me beforehand? The only answer I could get outa him was, 'Well, you knew I was a sailor when you married me.' As if that's an answer!

"I said to him, 'Listen, buster, if you think I married you because of yur uniform, you are out of yur cottonpickin' mind!' Anyway, I like the uniforms of those Navy Seals the best, it's just a wet suit you can get in and out of real fast. It's like the wet suit we use in the show, but without the goldsequined fishtail?

"Then Jack said it was the money, since if you go on a missile sub, you get danger pay. I told him, 'Sugar, that extra money ain't mean a thing if we never see each other anymore.' But you know how hardheaded men get. He'd made up his tiny pea brain that this is what he was going to do, and that was that. There was no arguing with him. He was already talking this foolheaded fairy tale about us having a baby with all the extra money he would get from submarine duty. Hell, I was only nineteen. Swimming in the show was my first job after high school. I told him, 'Whoa, Jack, now slow down there! Like I'm supposed to stay here and take care of the baby while you're off there twenty thousand leagues under the sea or whatever fighting World War III? I don't think that's the lifestyle I crave!'

"Then it was, well, if I didn't like what he wanted to do, he was going to get back at me for what I was doing. You know what they say: 'The best defense is a good offense.' He was on me all the time after that about swimming in the show. Wanted me to quit and get a better-paying job. So I did. I quit the show and got a day job selling real-estate lots for retirement homes by telephone, and worked nights delivering singing telegrams in Panama City, only I had to deliver them naked. Well, that was the job!

"I'm telling you, Jack wa'n't too nuts about the singing-telegram business. To tell you the truth, he went ballistic about it, pitched a goddamn fit. I told him, 'Jack, you can only work at the jobs is available. What the hell else am I trained for, brain surgeon?' Besides, I could make five hundred dollars in tips on Valentine's Day delivering those singing telegrams. I said to him, 'First you tell me we need the money, then when I start making it, you say it's wrong. I mean, really, what is it that you want to prove, anyway?'

"He didn't know. Most men don't, but I couldn't talk him out of submarine duty then. I'd made the mistake of backing him into a corner, and when he turned around, those eyes just froze me out. He goes, 'No fucking wife of mine is going to strip for a living.' As if delivering singing telegrams is the same as stripping in a bar! And he went ahead and signed up to leave on a certain date. The last couple of weeks before he shipped out, I was swallowing birth-control pills by the handful. I swear to the good Lord, I was praying I didn't get pregnant."

Stevie Rae belted back the last swig of her shot and chased it with a chug of beer. She rubbed her right temple with her cigarette hand. "I went down to see him off at Pensacola, and they took all the wives on a tour of the sub? Brother, I'm telling you right now, you'd never get me out on one of those things in a million years. You know where the crew sleeps? On sling beds strung between the missile silos. You tell me they don't have to smoke some potent shit to get to sleep at night! I slept some strange places in my life, but *nooo thanks*! And all the security around? I declare, I was wearing a pair of high heels that day, and coming across this steel grate during the tour, my heel got stuck in the grate. So of course, being a mainly aquatic type of person, I twisted my knee real bad and I staggered. Those security guys grabbed me like it was suddenly Red Code High Alert or something, rushed me into this little room there, and said, 'You're drunk, we're throwing you off the vessel. You can't come on a missile sub inebriated.'

"I told them, 'Deed I can! But if you-all think I'm drunk you are admiral-sized assholes, and I don't want to spend another minute on this damn seahog anyway.'

"I'd only had a few beers before we got there.

"Came time for Jack to leave, he starts blubbering how he'll be home soon's he can, he's gonna be faithful to me, how he'll write to me and call every chance he gets, and all that sort of song and dance. I was thinking, Tell it to the Marines!

Puts me in mind of a story my daddy used to tell about the Civil War. What happened was that when Colonel Ashley went off to fight the Yankees, he wanted to make sure his wife, Lady Gwenn, remained virtuous? So he'd read about chastity belts in the old Walter Scott novels about the Crusaders, and since he imagined himself a knight like that, he had the plantation blacksmith forge him an iron belt. He put his wife in, locked her up, and gave the key to his best and most loyal buddy-friend, Malvis Riddley, and he told Malvis that if he died in battle, that Riddley should release Lady Gwenn.

"Well, what with his mind at rest, Colonel Ashley packed his things, mounted his fine horse, and paraded away. But he hadn't got t'other side of his plantation when he looks back and there's a horse and rider galloping after him, trailing a cloud of dust. And it's Malvis Riddley, coming after him at a gallop, crying, 'Why, Colonel Ashley, Colonel Ashley, wait! You left the wrong key!' "

One drunk who got the joke started laughing and the rest laughed too, though most were too drunk to remember what they were laughing about. After the laughter, Salty announced last call.

"I didn't hear from Jack for three years after that," said Stevie Rae. "You think he ever wrote? I never got word one. I didn't know where he was, Veetnam or under the South Pole, like Admiral Bird o' the Antartics or something. I missed him real bad sometimes, but I was glad to get rid of him, too, in some ways."

Stevie Rae closed her eyes. "Like I said, most of the time I didn't miss him at all, I just found out there was a lot more space in my life without him. I could go water-skiing or fishing after the show, instead of waiting for him to come home from the base. But there were nights when I missed him so bad, I used to play this evil little game. I'd lie in bed, concentrate real, real hard, and try to conjure him into, you know, coming in his dreams, wherever he was. Ain't that the wickedest damn thing you ever heard?"

"How'd you know he was even in the same time zone, Stevie Rae?" someone heckled.

"I never did find out if it worked or not," said Stevie Rae, chuckling. "Anyway, during that whole time Jack never called once. Then about three years later, he called one night, drunk as Cooter Brown and bawling tears to beat the band. He said he was in Manila in the Philippino Islands on shore leave and had to get married to a girl there he'd knocked up on shore leave the year before, and she had a baby and her father was, like, threatening to cut Jack's head off with a machete and boil it in coconut oil or something if he didn't marry her. Poor ole Jack, he wanted to know what to do."

Stevie Rae sniffed back a tear. "I told him, 'You got one helluva nerve asking me!' I was so mad I spit at the phone. The connection was real bad. Like someone was down there under the ocean shaking them wahrs for a prank. I guess I called him every name in the book: 'You lousy-two-timing-goddamn-selfish-sonofabitch-slob-asshole-bigamist-traitor-jerk! Don't you ever call me again. And don't you *never* darken my doorway.' Then I put the phone down—didn't hang up—and went at his collection of rum bottles real slow. I smashed more'n fifty of 'em, one by one, so he could hear it all the way over there on the other side of the world. 'Course, by the time I was finished, he'd hung up."

Stevie Rae twisted her smoke out in the ashtray. "I packed up my collection of early Navy furniture and moved back in with Daddy after that, and we went into the shrimping business together. Daddy said, 'Honey, you want to make some real money and forget that jerk, let's get us a shrimp boat.' So we did."

"You know, you can catch two thousand pounds a trip at it. You hear them old shrimpers bitchin' and moanin', either it's all fished out, or the water's getting too cold, or it's the Veetnamese, or how shrimping is hard on a family man. Shit, it don't make no never mind! You got to fish by night cuz that's when the shrimp come up the surface to feed, thirty-five, forty miles out, where you set yur nets. Sometimes you got to stay out five, six days at a time. Sure, it's hard work! But it ain't no different from anything else: you can make good money if you work at it."

"You conjure them shrimp into yur net, too, Stevie Rae?" said someone down the bar.

"Oh, yeah," she said. "I sure did. I call it soul fishing, and I am without doubt the greatest at it. First, you got to know your astrology, yur stars. Best shrimping is at full moon. Moon controls jes' about everything round here, I guess. You get a full moon, fish and people go crazy. It's a proven fact. They kill themselves or someone else. Happens all the time, sometimes. One time I planted out some watermelons in my garden when the moon was full? Well, they say you oughta plant at full moon—or maybe it's new moon, I can't keep it straight. Huh—whatever! And you know what? Those watermelons all turned over and rotted, every last damned one. Wull, it's just the same way with shrimp.

"So we had the *Good Times*—that was the name of our shrimp boat—docked over at Bayou La Batre on the Alabama side, till Hurricane Frederic hit the coast in seventy-nine. It was bad because it was the first hurricane I'd ever seen hit during the day. Usually the ones I remember have mostly hit at night. The winds from Freddie was only around a hundred miles an hour, but it all seemed so much worse 'cause you could see it all happening. That wind don't blow, it slams, hammers. It's like—hammer of the gods! Things don't just bend over and break off, like you'd expect. They explode! Trees and buildings and stuff just shatter, more like they're being bombed than blowed down.

"They evacuated Bayou La Batre—'course we didn't go, afraid we'd lose everything on the boat to looters if it survived the storm, but it didn't. I put in plenty of beer and batteries like you're supposed to. Daddy and I were playing cards when it hit, and I was listening to my mentality tapes on a Walkman—they teach you how to stay calm and set goals and stuff. There was like a humungous pop, then like the whole side of the boat caved in. We ran outside and got onto the wharf and in, like, five seconds she totally smashed up and tore apart. I mean, there warn't nothing left to salvage. *Nada!* That Hurricane Freddie was a holy terror, all right.

"Afterward, when the hurricane had moved on, the thing was, you saw what's been hit and what not. You'd see the docks and there'd be maybe fifty slips. Forty-nine of 'em the boats'd be just completely fucked, total destruction, and then one boat'd be sitting there 'thout a nick on it. Scratching yur head, wondering, now how the hell did that happen? You'd go down a street and one house would look like a war zone, the one next door hardly touched, maybe just a tree limb down, some roof shingles off, or something like that. Nobody don't know why, but that's the way it is with hurricanes, they're fickle."

"That's why they shoulda kept naming 'em after women," said someone down the bar.

"How come you never had a hurricane named after you, Stevie Rae?" said a drunk.

"You can say whatever you want about hurricanes," said Stevie Rae, "but I always believed what Daddy said about 'em. Daddy always said you could see the hand of Providence in how a hurricane touched different folks. He'd see how a hurricane damaged some church real bad, and he'd say, 'Yes'm, that church was where the hypocrites prayed.' Then he'd see how somebody lost their roof, and he'd just say, 'Yup, look how old Elena done them. Now, I'm the devil himself, and Elena didn't do me near so bad, so they got to be hypocrites in there! Lord sent old Elena to clean out them hypocrites, and she caught them up good, sure did.'

"Course, Daddy never said a word after Freddie destroyed the *Good Times*.

"It was just around that time when Guess Who? showed up. He arrived late one Friday night, in a haze of booze and God knows what-all else. No word he's coming or anything, just shows up, and to make it all as tacky as possible, he's driving a stolen Porsche from Miami. Jack liked surprises.

"I just said to myself, 'Uh-oh, Stevie Rae, this means trouble.'

"After Freddie wiped us out of shrimping, I had went back down to Weekee Wachee to ask for my old job back swimming in the show, but everything had changed. They had a new manager there because the theme park had been sold out to some big conglomerate from California. The new manager, Mr. Murphy, he was a real California slick—BMW, hundred-dollar sunglasses, the kind of guy, if he fell down, he'd break his hair. He didn't make *nooo* bones about what it would cost if I wanted my job back in the show. I was seeing other guys by then, but this Murphy wa'n't my type at all. I thought, shit, I'm the only woman I ever heard of is sleeping her way to the bottom. But, hell, swimming around that tank a couple of times a day, it ain't a bad way to pay the rent, and finally I said to him, 'Okay, you're the boss, anything that cranks your tractor. But I ain't going to no motels. This is just a perk of the job to you, but I was born around here and purty near everybody knows me. Long time after you go back to California, I'm gonna still have to live here. I ain't hanging no dirty laundry out where people knows me since I was knee-high to a mullet can see it. If you want it, it's gonna be in my bed in my houseboat.'

"See, because I was staying with the same friends who had rented the houseboat after me, while they were over working in Pascagoula at the Sea World there. So we drove back to my place, and we stopped on the way, picked up a case of wine coolers—Mr. Murphy was getting ready for a real yahoo, but I figured that I would bring him back, get him so loaded he wouldn't be much trouble, and then afterward go into the bathroom and say, like, you know, 'Oh, shit, can you believe this, I'm starting my period,' and he'd get out of there fast. But any way you look at it, he didn't expect to meet my ex-husband, Jack, there.

"You ever try to jump out the windows of a houseboat?" said Stevie Rae.

Everyone at the bar cocked their heads.

"Jack came in like a herd of buffalo on the rampage. Right into the bedroom—he actually remembered where it was. He sees the guy, Murph sees him. Mr. Murphy turns to me and says, 'You set me up, you little bitch!'

"I thought, Oh, shit, there goes my job in the show! Meanwhile Jack is, like, pounding the shit outa this guy from four directions. He hit him in the face, Murph crumpled. Jack couldn't wait for him to hit the floor. Slugged him twice in the body on the way down.

"I just lay there in bed takin' it all in. It was a lot like watching one o' them Chuck Norris action videos, because I didn't really care which one got hurt worse—screw the pair of 'em, you know? Finally, when he stopped kicking Murphy, I said, 'Good work, Jack. What now? Rape me and shoot yurself in the haid?'

"You know what that asshole said to me? He goes, 'I don't have no gun.' I told him, 'Well, you still got plenty time before the cops get here. I'll loan you mine, you can get started. You are a real piece of goddamn work, ain't you?'

"Well, by this time his frenzy had passed. He was so shit-faced drunk he couldn't hardly stand up, let alone talk. I guess I was real lucky that night, if you call that luck. Because by the time the state rangers came to assess the damages, Jack had been passed out on the floor a good forty-five minutes. They had to slap his ass awake just to read him his Miranda rights.

"You get yur old job back, Stevie Rae?" asked a stranger at the bar.

"I surely did," she said, twisting the fine ash off her last cigarette. "Just lucky for me Jack passed out like that, since it gave me time to help Mr. Murphy, and I explained the whole thing to him, and he left before the cops came. He wasn't such a bad guy, after all. But I'll tell you one thing. That manager left me alone after that.

"I been back in the show 'most ten years now," Stevie Rae said. "Two more years, then I quit; since you can't retire from being a mermaid at Weekee Wachee, they got a special agreement with the state to let girls go when they reach, um, a certain age, so that the mermaids will always be fresh and appealing? It's changed completely, working in the show. You have to swim three shows a day now instead of two, and the season's longer, and you don't get hostess points for the photos with the snowbirds anymore. It's a different show now, too, about Carnival in Rio, and my part is, I drink a bottle of Coke underwater to international friendship while they play the Coke jingle:

> *I'd like to teach the world to sing in perfect harmony*
> *I'd like to give the world a Coke, and keep it company*

Whatever that's supposed to mean!

"The worst part of the show now is, since the alligators made a comeback 'round here? We got some of them big ole bohonker gators swim right into the springs during the show. Scares all the girls to death. Me, I ain't really as afraid of them gators as I am of lightning. If I see one of them gators coming toward me while I'm doing the show, I just look him straight in the eye and say, 'Hey, some o' my best friends been reptiles—and darling, I speak-a you language'!"

Prince Hamlet of the
Florida Territory

Florida Territory
February 12, 1838

My dearest darling wife:

Having had no word from me for so long, you must by now
think I have met some terrible death facedown in the mud,
my anonymous body ravaged by vultures. Since the date of
my last letter I have been wandering as usual. I returned to
Florida Territory in the summer months, then traveled several hundred miles back to Fort Moultrie near Charleston.
How I regret the ordeal that I have put you and our beloved
baby daughter through, to come out with little more to show
for all this travel than a bundle of unsalable pictures—and
very likely, a larger bundle of unpayable debts.

Have you had word from Mr. Peale on whether his museum will take any of the landscapes I shipped in June? I can do seventy-five more for him without trouble. The weather is so fine and predictable here, I no longer bother to sketch outdoors and paint in, but carry my paints about everywhere I go in a backpack and set up an easel from cut branches wherever I please. I can do two or three small paintings in a day. Here the warm climate makes outdoor work possible throughout the year, and the light is always enchanting. There is one among the last batch conveyed to Mr. Peale I am particularly fond of, as I think it captures something of the soul of this land. It is a view at twilight, looking across the shadowed prairie toward a grove of tall palms burnished golden by the sinking sun. These groves are to be found everywhere: they grow up above wet sinkholes they call hammocks, which must all communicate by water deep underground. The plains are cut by these hammocks, always identified by thick clumps of cabbage palms with a dark and humid underlayer of saw palmettos. From a distance, the palm trees stick up out of the prairies like pins from a cushion, some only a few hundred feet across—just about right for a single tom turkey and his harem. But other hammocks follow subterranean creeks for miles. In the rainy season, the hammocks fill up quickly with cool, transparent water. Then the prairie grasses around them are rapidly transformed from a dry brown to brilliant green, like a sudden resurrection of the world.

It was on just such a day of earthly transformation that I painted the aforementioned landscape. I established my perspective looking west a few hundred yards toward the hammock, set up my easel, and commenced work about nine o'clock in the morning. It was not long before I found I had company: a newborn cow's calf poked its head above the short grasses; later its mother ambled along to provide milk. Silver-plumed herons fished round the edges of the ponds. Then a handsome pair of young bald eagles engaged talons at several hundred feet of altitude, locking claws and tumbling down together, over and over, lower and lower, until at last breaking free just before striking the earth. By the middle of the stifling hot afternoon, a black sky in the east was hung with hundreds of pale white, round clouds. Until at length the slanting sun sank behind the hammock, coating it like a mysterious golden garden. They say the word *hammock* derives from the Seminole tongue, and means "garden place." But I have heard the Indians use it more to mean refuge or hiding place. On that day it seemed to me a haunted place, where the Seminole's secrets clung close to cooler, dark air.

I moved on south again in early autumn. Not a day goes by that I don't find myself wishing this restlessness had never led me from our happy hearth in Philadelphia. To rest at ease in the bosom of one's family should indeed be a privilege guaranteed by the Constitution. I miss you both so much that I sometimes feel on waking in the morning that half of my body is missing. What will our dear young Clarissa think, when she grows up, of her itinerant papa? I wonder. Will she see at least something worthwhile in his endless journeys? Or will she hold him in contempt for caring more for his art than his own family?

Yet against this bitter loneliness is the duty I feel to use the small talents God has given me to paint and record something of this Florida Territory and her Seminole natives before such events as are now taking place irrevocably change the former and banish the latter from the face of the earth forever.

I believe an American artist's task, after all, is to try to preserve for his countrymen and future generations the places and ways of life we are at this time hellbent to crush, obliterate, or make over, albeit in our darkest image. In the case of Florida, a noble people now on the verge of extermination. We wandering scribblers and scratchers have to represent these vanishing souls with all the energy of our hearts and the strength of our hands. For no one else will represent them, God knows!

At no time since first arriving on the southern frontier have I felt with greater intensity the purpose of my project as within the past several weeks. For the war being waged to dispossess the Seminole and remove them west of the Mississippi River has taken a decisive turn with the capture of the infamous warrior Osceola, whose death occurred at Fort Moultrie only last Friday. This young man was an extraordinary fellow, looked upon by the Seminole as their master fighting spirit and war leader of the tribe, although not himself a chief. I am convinced from what I saw of him and learned from his lips, and from the high regard with which the captured chiefs treated him, that he was held a kind of prophet to his people; he was certainly the most powerful and uncompromising figure of Seminole resistance to the Americans.

I was able to accompany the Seminole prisoners from St. Augustine in Florida. At Fort Moultrie the commanding officer of the post, Captain Winston, was good enough to allow me use of one of the provisioning stores to work in, and further permitted his captives to pose before my easel, even though my sympathies are not a secret; a guard was stationed constantly at the door to prevent my assisting the Indians to escape!

Working swiftly, I accomplished several likenesses of each man, including portraits of Micanopy, the head chief of the Seminole tribe, his brother-in-law called Ematla, or King Philip, said to be part Spanish grandee; a distinguished personage called Yehowlogee, or Cloud; and two pictures of that brave warrior Osceola, the first at full length, posed in the costume he wore at the time he was attempting to make contact under a flag of truce with General Jessup.

In stature he was not above medium height, but compact and energetic, muscles hard as stone from living long in the swamps and forests, but with the elastic and graceful movements of a panther.

His face was so animated that you could ransack the whole world without finding another so intensely emotional. His dark eyes blazed, yet seemed set far away, as if he were already viewing some other world; perhaps the happy hunting grounds that Indians say are found among the trails through the stars they travel after death. His high cheekbones and lanky black hair were those of a full-blooded wild Indian, but his jaw was square as an Irishman's, and his nose as straight and long as any of the Caesars. To look at him, you might easily guess he was in part a white man. Indeed, the army officers referred to him contemptuously as the half-breed Billy Powell, saying his father was an English trader. Osceola hotly rejected this name, but had few words for his captors in any case. As a warrior, he considered his capture and his death as one and the same. The connivance and trickery employed to apprehend him did not increase his regard for his white enemies.

He accepted me, undoubtedly as a result of my knowledge, far less than perfect, of the Seminole tongue. I was able to explain to him and the other chiefs my purpose, to record them for future generations, and as a nonofficial win their approval. I painted Osceola precisely in his full ceremonial costume. Three ostrich plumes rose from his varicolored cotton turban, and a red bandanna was knotted at his neck, below which hung a breastplate of three gold crescents and necklaces of pearl, coral, and jade. His dress and skirt were chiefly of printed calicos, with a handsome beaded sash set diagonally across his chest and a wide red belt around his waist. Below was a buckskin jerkin, fixed at the wrists by golden bracelets, from which hung loose buckskin strings. He wore similar leggings wrapped in beaded lizard skin at the knees.

In this princely regalia, with his melancholy expression, he seemed not like some desperate savage but rather the very figure of Shakespeare's Hamlet, Prince of Denmark, his broad knife replacing poor Yorick's skull. Describing this character from a play to the Indians, I was amazed to hear Osceola and the other chiefs laugh, then admit that several of them had acquired elements of their clothing accoutrements in a raid on an army encampment, where the Indians had watched from the woods at night as a band of traveling actors entertained the soldiers. When they attacked, the Seminole took the unguarded boxes with the handsome costumes and made them their own. I tried then to recount for them the tragedy of the ill-fated Prince Hamlet, but I doubt I made myself understood.

The second portrait of Osceola I executed after his final breath, when by custom a great horned owl was placed upon his chest, since the Seminole believe that their spirits travel by night and often assume the body of the owl to make their final journey. The Indians say that the Milky Way is the pathway to the spirit world in the western sky, and that the stars shine brightest following the death of one of their tribe, so that his journey may be lighted. In the event, the sky was brighter than I can ever remember seeing it the night after Osceola's death. I rose from my bed as if sleepwalking, and added that nocturnal sky as background to the death portrait.

I was with Osceola much in his last days, for every evening after painting all day, I had him and the others in my room until late hours at night, where he obliged me to sketch scenes of his life while he gave me a full account of the war and the disgraceful mode in which he was captured—or rather betrayed, as I shall presently relate. Although only thirty, or perhaps thirty-five years of age, Osceola was wasting away from the swamp fever so prevalent in this territory, complicated by severe quinsy, and very emaciated, as he also refused all nourishment. Fully aware of his condition, he spoke only of his broken heart. When I made bold to ask him about this, he said, "The day and manner of man's death is given out. Whatever I encounter, I fear nothing. When death comes, I will die like a man."

And so he passed, little interested in extending his life, preferring death to defeat, but meeting both with the same tranquility. Whether his shade has now transited to the spirit world or returned to the glades and swamps of his people, I pray he has found some measure of the rest cruelly denied him by our government and army in this inglorious affair. The story he related to me in our several conversations serves only to confirm my deep doubts that this military action in Florida against the Seminole and their Negro exile allies is either just

or necessary, but rather the greatest calamity for our nation. President Jackson has usurped a slack Congress's power to make war, and Congress has returned such good service by appropriating some 20 million dollars for the Florida campaigns, whose only purpose is to punish the Seminole for protecting the ex-slaves among them.

This precedent bodes ill. I have the greatest fear that once done, this tactic will be used again and again, until military interventions against our neighbors will become our national trademark. Those who counsel peace or nonintervention will be termed traitors. To oppose the president will become regarded as opposing the nation itself. And with each expansion, there will be a new border threatened, new settlers to protect. The Georgia and Tennessee slaveholders, who have tirelessly campaigned to promote this warfare in Florida on the grounds that they cannot maintain and control their chattel when Africans can attain freedom and lands across the Florida border, have prevailed. The government's intent to remove all the natives west of the Mississippi, return the escaped black freemen and exiles to slavery, and open Florida to settlement by whites and planters is now on the very brink of success.

An artist's opinion counts for little in the affairs of history. But I feel compelled to tell you, my trusted confidante and mate, that when I pick up my brushes to paint the savannahs and primeval swamps of Florida, I can no longer see the American frontier President Jackson speaks of, nor yet that extending zone of liberty President Jefferson dreamed of, but rather an empire, rising, as all empires do, on the crushed bones and bloody corpses of those in its way.

One evening when visiting my room, Osceola picked up several books I have with me here, turned them over in his trembling hands, opened them, and stared at the pages with the most amazing expression of puzzlement and regret. He said he had often as a young child seen white people employed in reading, and as a boy had a great curiosity to "talk to the books," as he thought whites do, and so to learn "the beginning of all things." For that purpose he had from time to time acquired books, either through trade or discovered during his travels and raids through Spanish and white settlements.

Osceola said he had spoken to them when alone, then put his ear to the page, hoping they would answer, and became very troubled when he found the books remained silent. Later he became angry when several of the Seminole chiefs signed the treaty at Payne's Landing, promising that the Seminoles would remove out of Florida, as the Georgians, Tennesseans, and Carolinians have ceaselessly demanded. Osceola claimed that those Seminole representatives present at Payne's Landing could not read either, had been tricked by their own chosen Negro translator Abraham, and did not understand the document they were obliged to sign. Further, he said that those chiefs had no right to sign such a treaty, as they did not constitute a negotiating party, let alone a council elected by tribal law. From that time on, he despised the "black seeds sown on the little white fields" as nothing but lies. He demanded I take his story down, not with black ink and quill pen, but rather in red vermilion from my palette, which I consented to do in order to ease his troubled mind in his final days.

There only remains to tell you the manner of this Seminole warrior's death. He refused all treatment from the Army doctor Weedon, who made it known to the Seminole prisoners that he was brother-in-law to the agent Wiley Thompson, whom Osceola had considered his greatest personal enemy. Instead, Osceola asked a Seminole medicine man imprisoned there to help him prepare for his journey to the other side.

About one hour beforehand, he seemed to know that he was dying. Although he could no longer speak, he signified that he wished me to send for the chiefs, and for the officers of the fort, which I did. He made signs to his two wives, whom the Army had permitted to join him at Fort Moultrie, two fine little boy children by their sides. I did not understand all the sign language, but it seemed to me he may have been releasing them from a solemn tribal duty for the wife to die along with her husband. Then he asked them to go and bring the full dress he wore in time of war. As soon as the women brought forward his raiment, he slowly rose up from his deathbed on the floor, which momentarily caused alarm among the officers and guards. But he was only drawing on his shirt, his leggings, and his mocassins. Then he girdled his warbelt around his waist, put on his bullet pouch and powder horn, and lay back down on the floor, placing his warknife by the side of him.

He called then for vermilion paint. His looking glass was held before him. He arranged his hair and war bonnet with the greatest deliberation, painted one half of his face, his neck and throat, his wrists, the backs of his hands, and the handle of his knife, a custom practiced when the irrevocable oath of war has been taken. His scalping knife—not long, but quite thin, like the knives used on the Philadelphia wharves to filet fish—he then placed in its sheath, under his belt.

Then lying down on his pallet, resting a moment, Osceola rose again, half-sitting. And with a broad smile he extended his hand to myself and to all the chiefs and officers that were around him, and shook hands with each in dead silence. Also with his wives and little children. He signaled them to lower him down for the last time on his bed, which was done. The wives made him comfortable. Slowly and with great dignity he drew his scalping knife, grasped it tightly in his right hand, and folded his arms across his chest. Finally, he signaled the chiefs for his Spanish shotgun, and the medicine man for the dead owl—the companion he would take to the next world. I was incredulous how any man could so magisterially direct his own death ceremony. But fixing his look on his wives and children, Osceola passed from this life without a struggle.

In addition to the death portrait, I was to have undertaken a death mask of Osceola by request of his wives. But before the body was quite cool, Dr. Weedon came in and severed Osceola's head with a surgical lancet, no doubt as a medical souvenir of the war against the Seminole. I couldn't help but think he was exacting revenge for Osceola's killing his kin, the Indian agent Thompson. I tried to stop him and a strenuous argument ensued. But in the end I was powerless to prevent this officer's outrageous and perverse mutilation of the Indian's corpse.

He was then given a full military funeral ceremony. General Jessup himself attended, a laconic man who spoke only a few words in self-justification for seizing the Indians under the truce flag in abnegation of every rule of civilized behavior. General Jessup said, "If it was lawful to remove them, it was lawful to seize them."

Who could dispute such logic?

Time is short. I shall try with what is left of this night to set down as many of Osceola's words as I can, as faithfully as I can, while still fresh in my notes and my memory.

—

I am Asi-Ya-hola, the Black Drink Crier, the singer of morning. I am of the Muskogee people, of the Tallassees, of the Red Stick Clan—we are those who make war. I was born at the River Cha-ta-hoo-chee. My mother delivered me on a bed of stones, in the deep, cold waters, that I might grow up strong and fierce, in the way of the Red Stick Clan, to swim the streams and leap over the logs of the forest in pursuit of game. That I might stalk and chase the bear, deer, and wild boar, furnished by our great Mother Earth, instilled with life by the Master of Breath. That I would show courage on the warpath and lead in the attack, never knowing fear of man or beast, nor the taste of cowardice on my tongue.

We are called the Seminole—those who camp at a distance. We are a wild and scattered people. We are the exiles, the wanderers: Muskogee, Hitchiti, Mikasuki, Yamasee, Yuchi, Eufala. All those set in motion by the coming of the white people were welcomed into the Seminole nation. Like the crane that makes its nest at night far from the spot where it dashed dew from the grass in the morning, so did our people travel near the shores of the Great South Sea.

I was still a baby sucking at my mother's bubby when my father died in battle, defending our village against the whites. I was taken captive with my mother. Our village was burned, destroyed. The troops released us but made us leave our home, where the whites wished to settle.

So we wandered many nights and days, many moons, many seasons. Women and children, the old ones, staying ahead of the invaders, with no one to protect us. We passed Fowltown on our journey, a Seminole village where fugitive Negro slaves had found shelter. The whites burned it to the ground.

All slain—the men, the women, the children and elders. Then we knew we had not gone far enough.

We saw the vultures at Negro Fort feeding on the bodies of the three hundred blacks there, slaughtered in the Army's attack, left to rot in the sun. And there, too, the women, the children and elders. Still we had not gone far enough.

Then the Tennessee slave raiders came with General Jackson, killing and maiming. Again we were taken captive. That time my grandmother spoke with this demon Jackson and persuaded him to release the women and children.

We scattered and hid in the forest, under the palmettos, deep in the hammocks. We crossed the River A-pala-chi-co-la. We went beyond the River Och-i-ok-nee, into the great swamp O-ke-fe-no-kee, and again beyond the River Suh-wa-nee. Till we came to a place called A-la-chu-a, a great swamp of big cypress, where the River Whit-la-coo-chee twisted and turned. There we met the survivors of our band, and built our chickees at Peas Creek.

So we entered the Land of Flowers, where the earth is cut and divided into islets, knolls, and prairies, scored by rivers without number, creeks, lakes, and swamps. We saw so many secure retreats and safe dwelling places. The hammocks to protect us from invasions. The swamps to secure us from attacks by enemies. On the savannahs and marshes, we could hear and see far. We felt safe. Then the elders said, "Let us consecrate this place. Let us be buried here. Let us rejoice, celebrate, and enjoy ourselves. Let us shoot arrows into the sky, and call the Land of Flowers our home, furnished with all things beautiful and useful, by our Great Mother. And abounding in game and fruits, provided by the Master of Breath."

So we buried our dead, those who did not survive our wanderings, and consecrated these lands.

We needed no government to tell us what to do. We needed no treaties to mark our lands like fences. We lived in freedom, till the whites came again, this time in multitudes like angry wasps, with lies in their mouths, always seeking Seminole lands.

When I was a boy, the Land of Flowers was my home. The Muskogee worked for no master but himself. The Muskogee never labored for money. We did not know these words: *property, cession, removal, reservation.* Our women had only to throw seeds upon the earth, and something good to eat grew there. There was always plenty of coontie and yams. We planted maize, squash, and beans, the three sisters of our gardens. We gathered the acorns, the peaches, and persimmons. Oranges we planted by our chickees, also May apples and shattucks. An abundance of melons we cultivated in their season, to slake our thirst in the burning days of summer.

In the Land of Flowers, the sun never failed us. The rains came always in their season, as the berries come to fatten the bear before winter. In the shade of the tall oaks the Seminole rested. How well I loved to hunt there with my brothers. To chase the deer, the bear, and the boar, the turkey, the panther, and the alligator. We cast our nets into the rivers for mullet fish. The eggs of the turtles were our boast. Honey we took from the diligent bees.

Our spirits were gladdened by all these gifts, the wealth of our domains. We know the white man measures his wealth against his neighbor's. To have more than the next is his greatest desire. Thus he permits himself to take wealth from another. Thus he permits another to take his labor from him.

The Indian will never understand this. The red man is wealthy when he has what he needs. In the Land of Flowers we always had plenty. We felt happy.

We knew all the swamps, the hammocks, and the resting places. There was open ground where my brothers and I could linger under the stars, telling our stories. Time was not the Seminole's master. We shared our hunt in every camp with the widows and the elders. Among the many branches of the Seminole I would visit, and found welcome everywhere. I danced with my cousins late into the night, wild as the buck, which knows no bounds in leaping.

But the winds of change followed the Wandering People into the Land of Flowers. We could not see the winds, but they were evil, blowing from the north of our borders.

When I was still a boy I saw the white man from far off. I did not know if he was my enemy. Some said the warrior should not use his prowess on white people. They said teach the white man the joy of breath. When they are taught of the abundant life, then they would have compassion on the fields. They would honor the glades. They would bury their dead here, to consecrate these lands for them. And they would learn to take what they need and leave the rest. Then we could live in peace together.

I did not know what to believe. Then Chief Tecumseh came to us from the Shawnee. Came to smoke the council pipe with our *micos*—our chiefs. He told the assembled Seminole:

"Brothers! We all belong to one family. We are all children of the Great Spirit. We walk in the same path. We slake our thirst at the same stream. We smoke one pipe around the same council fire. We are friends, we must assist each other.

We are all threatened with a great evil. The white men want more than our hunting grounds. Nothing will pacify them but the destruction of all the red men. My people wish for peace; the red men all wish for peace. But where the white people are there is no peace, except it be lying dead on the bosom of our Great Mother.

"Brothers! We must be united. If we do not unite, they will first destroy my people. Then you will fall an easy prey to them. They have destroyed many nations of red men already because we were not united. Because we would not help each other."

Still the white men came upon us. So I joined the dance, and became a warrior. I was old enough. I learned the way of Asi, the black drink. I drank the black drink with my brothers till I retched and heaved. The powerful medicine purified our spirits and gave us courage. It purged our guts, made our muscles taut like bow strings. Our bodies were strengthened, our aim always true. Then we fought as one being, made of stone and leather. Or played the ball game, the little brother of war. Or galloped across the prairies, heedless of all dangers. The Spanish had left many horses behind in the Land of Flowers. I learned to ride like the wind.

The black drink scoured our stomachs of evil, banished all weakness and hesitation. I could drink more than anyone. I could spew farther than all others. So they chose me *tu-ste-nu-ggee*—war captain.

Then we went on the warpath. The Indian does not make war for gain like the whites, to take something from someone else. We do not make war to steal land or goods, pretending the enemy has threatened or insulted us. The Indian fights to test his strength, to run risks with his brothers, to prove his courage, and to taste his victories. I counted many scalps. I spared always the women and children, the old ones. It was not upon them we made war or drew the scalping knife. But only upon men. Before this dirty war of the whites came, we did not fight like squaws, murdering women and children. We are men, always acting like men in the eyes of the Great Spirit.

I took my name and became the singer of the black drink— Asi-Ya-hola! I brought the warriors together with my songs. We spewed together and far in the four directions. We purified our spirits and cleansed our bodies. We prepared for the warpath.

The Spanish had left many cattle behind when they left the Land of Flowers. At first we Seminole would not tend them. We are hunters, following the game like our fathers before us. Then we, too, began to tend herds on the prairies. We learned the ways of the cattle from the black men. They were escaping slavery in Georgia, Tennessee, Carolina, Alabama. They came into the Land of Flowers to live, even as the Seminole had found sanctuary. The Negro exiles said they had been taken by force from Africa, across the Great Sea.

In Africa they had tended cattle, and knew what to do. They paid us tribute in meat and fruits. They taught us well the way of the cattle. They became our vassals and allies. Their children married into our clans. They did not desire to take our lands away, but only a place to live in safety for themselves. We lived in peace, side by side, no troubles. Our children grew up together. I took my second wife from among them, she who is called Che-cho-ter, Morning Dew, mother of my children.

The Negro exiles said they would rather die than return to the white man's yoke. In the Land of Flowers their cattle farms prospered. Who were we to deny them?

Then the Spanish ceded the Land of Flowers to the whites. It was the first we heard this word *cession*. So said the Americans: "We have purchased the Land of Flowers." They buy and sell the air, the water, the warm sweetness of the land itself. That is difficult for the Indian to imagine. They said we should return their property to them. We did not own the Negro exiles. We do not own the lands the white men want from us. He may drive us from these lands, but he cannot buy them from us. Each oak tree shining in the sun. Each wave that breaks upon the shore. All morning mists hanging over the rivers. Every beetle that crawls in the night. All the stars in the sky, every part of Earth is sacred to us, holy in our memory and experience. Now even this small land, which the Great Spirit had given us, the white man wanted also.

Soon the Army came to the Land of Flowers, ahead of the white settlers. The soldiers were hungry and weak. They had no place to spread their blankets or kindle their fires. They were feeble. They could do nothing for themselves. Like newborn serpents, torpid and cold, without a mother to protect them or give them food. We shared freely with them, whatever the Great Spirit had given his red children. We gave them food when hungry, medicine when they were sick. We spread skins for them to sleep on.

I went to work for the Army at Fort King. A scout, I led them through the Land of Flowers to the places where the Spanish had been. I showed them where to ford the rivers. I showed them how to cross the prairies. I drove the bellowing alligators away from their camps at night, and provided their regiments with the meat of many deer and boars. I protected the white officials, guarded them from harm, when they met with Micanopy, the head chief at Payne's Landing.

The agent Wiley Thompson was with the Army at Fort King. He said he was my friend. He gave me a good Spanish rifle, telling me to use it well. He offered his hand in friendship. I could not shoot him, as I would a wolf. I took his hand. But he had a snake in the other. His tongue was forked. He lied and stung me.

The white masters sent their slave hunters into the Land of Flowers. Armed posses came, demanding the Seminole to return the black people to them. As if we owned them. As if we could hand them over like a dog on a tether. The American slave hunters roamed our country, clashing with our villages, burning and marauding. Massacres again, as they had done at Fowltown and at Negro Fort. Families killed—old ones, children—provoking the Indians to retaliate, to break the white man's laws. The Army punished us for the crimes the whites themselves committed. For what is the crime of protecting a Negro compared with the crime of owning a Negro? Are they not children of the Great Spirit, too?

The slave hunters came to Fort King. I brought Morning Dew to Fort King with me to trade there. The slavers called me half-breed. They called me Billy Powell. Their insults were like the bites of the smallest insect. I saw how the white man tears someone down to build himself up. How the weak ones hold the strong in contempt. I ignored their curses and their squaw's gossip. But when the slavers called Mountain Dew "runaway," this I could not turn away from. I said I would kill them if they touched her.

If I speak, then what I say, I will do. The slave hunters seized her, carried her away. The agent Thompson signed the papers to take Morning Dew to Georgia, sell her to a plantation. With my broad knife I made the white slave hunters red with blood. Then the agent Thompson ordered my arrest. Four soldiers seized me. They put me in irons, made me prisoner in their stockade.

At night I cried, keen and loud, so Wiley Thompson could hear. Was I, too, a Negro, a slave? I am an Indian, a Seminole! I told him I would use my rifle well to blacken him in the sun and rain. To leave his carcass where the coyote should gnaw his bones, and the buzzard should live on his putrid flesh. Did he think I am like the bat, that hangs by its claws in a dark cave, that I could see nothing of what was going on around me?

The white men were coming into the Land of Flowers. As thick they came as the leaves of the hammocks. They came upon us thicker every year. They stole our cattle, our horses. They cheated us, took our lands. Invading gangs of whites kidnapped our exile allies, shot us for sport, burned our homes. They stole my beautiful wife from me, my favorite, the mother of my children. They chained my hands to the pillory. They chained my feet to a cannon ball. They put an iron collar around my neck.

The demon Jackson became American president. He called himself Great White Father. But we knew well how Jackson hated the red people. We knew he despised us like insects, he who called himself our Father, our friend. We knew how many were the corpses of our relatives, killed at the hands of General Jackson's troops. We knew of the law made far away in Washington to remove all Indians to the Great Desert west of the river called Father of Waters.

But my heart they could not steal, they could not chain, they could not remove. No! The red man's heart will always be free. From that day on, I was the white man's enemy. The time of smoking the pipe was over. The way of peace was lost. Now was the time to sing the black drink songs.

The micos had grown too old. Old men, spent by the years, shoulders bowed—they were finished in the villages. The demon Jackson sent them a message through the Army. They were called to Fort King to council with the agent Wiley Thompson. He talked the demon Jackson's talk. I stood outside the council ring, where I heard every word. Jackson addressed the chiefs:

"Three years ago, at Payne's Landing, you agreed to cede your lands in Florida, and to remove to the country west of the Mississippi. I now learn that you refuse to carry into effect the solemn promises made by you. You have stated to the officers of the United States sent among you that you will not remove to the western country. I tell you that you must go, and you will go. The tract you have ceded will soon be surveyed, sold, and immediately afterward occupied by a white population. Lest some of your rash young men should forcibly oppose your arrangements for removal, I have ordered a large military force to be sent among you. I have directed your friend Thompson that one third of your people be removed during the present season. Should you listen to the bad birds that are always flying about you and refuse to remove, I have then directed the commanding officer to remove you by force."

The chiefs then lost their tongues. They were overcome. Hola Amathla asked time to council, to reconvene next morning.

Then I spoke in council: "My Brothers! The whites got some of our chiefs to sign a paper to give our lands to them. Our micos did not do as we told them to do. They have done wrong. But we must do right. The agent tells us we must go away from the lands we live on—our homes, the graves of our fathers. He wants us to go across the Father of Waters among the bad Indians. When a man has his country, has his house and his home, where his children have always played about his yard, it becomes sacred to his heart. It is hard to leave it. Our people are not hungry for other lands. When the agent tells me to go from my home, I hate him.

"My Brothers! If the Great Spirit tells me to go with the white man, I go. But he tells me not to go. The white man says I must go. He will send soldiers to make me go. But I have a rifle, I have some powder and some lead. We must not leave our homes and lands. If any of our people want to go west, we must not let them. I tell you they are our enemies, and we will treat them so, for the Great Spirit will protect us."

Sore was the disarray of the micos then. Micanopy could not sit at the council ring next morning, for the Great Chief of the Seminole must speak for all, or not speak. The agent Thompson asked the Seminole's answer. Then Otee Amathla, who is called Jumper, spoke: "We never gave our consent to go west. The whites may say so, but we never gave our consent. What we said yesterday, we say today. We did not sign a treaty at Payne's Landing."

The agent Thompson grew angry at this. He called for Micanopy then, to have the Great Chief's answer. Micanopy could not enter the council ring: to speak from divided council is against tribal law. He sent his word back: he could not accept the terms of treaty. He did not agree to cession. He would not remove.

Then the agent Wiley Thompson informed the chiefs, saying that Micanopy was no longer head chief. That he had lied, that he had signed the paper at Payne's Landing, that the

American Father Jackson had decided to remove him. Again he demanded the chiefs make their marks on the white field with the small black seeds, where grow these harvests of lies.

I could wait no longer. To me Micanopy delegated the right to speak for all the micos. I entered the council ring, drawing my broad knife. I brought it down from above my head, pinning their treaty to the table.

"That is your heart, Thompson!" I cried out. "And that is my mark! That is the way I will sign all such treaties! The land is ours."

I raised my eyes to Wiley Thompson. He quaked in his boots. I spoke thus: "The sun is high. I will remember this hour. You have had your day. I will have mine."

I withdrew from the council ring. All the micos left the council with me: Micanopy, Jumper, Holata Mico, Coacoochie the Wildcat, Chalo and Hola Amathla. We left Fort King. No one dared lay a hand on me.

Then we organized our resistance. To the villages I went, singing the black drink songs, gathering our warriors. I traveled to the farthest camps of the Wandering People, far into the swamps, into the distant glades, where the red heron fished silently in the ponds. The old chiefs were gladdened. They did not oppose me but welcomed me as their son. I sang for them. We drank together. Our minds clarified. Our spirits purified. Our bodies cleansed for battle. In every village and camp, each brave took the oath to fight till the last drop of Seminole blood moistened the dust of our hunting grounds.

Then the micos met in council. Long and long they talked together, till all agreed to resist removal. A death sentence was passed on any that should flee to the white agencies, or sell their herds to the whites, or make preparations to remove.

They chose me, Asi-Ya-hola, to enforce the council's policy. Only one chief, Chalo Amathla, favored removal in secret because he had no stomach for the fight. The white men gave him money to sign their treaties. He brought his herds to Fort Brooke. He took the white man's money. In his palm he held it, filthy green fields, greasy black seeds. Money whose name was "traitor." Money whose name was "death." In his belt, below his garments, he tucked his death and began to ride home to his village.

I waited beside the road, under the palmettos, under the pines, crouching like the cougar, my knife sharp and at the ready. The traitor Chalo Amathla came nigh. I pounced from the bushes. I delivered the big medicine of the micos' war council. I drew my blade across his throat, left him facedown in the mud to rot. I cut the money belt from his waist. I looked at the money, the price of the red man's blood. The tears flowed down my cheeks. Tears and blood, mud on the money. In anger I threw it to the winds, to the four directions, to warn the people not to take the white man's money.

The word spread then that the name of money was "death," and none dared take it. Chalo Amathla's warriors did not dare bury him. They joined us on the warpath. The people feared that spot. His bones lay bleaching two years there, until the white soldiers buried them.

We sent the women and children, the elders, to hide deep in Opa-loka, the Green Swamp, where the whites could not reach them. And to Pa-hay-okee, the River of Grass in the south, we sent them, that they might be safe from the white depredations and reprisals. We bought guns, collected ammunition. We were well armed—English rifles, Spanish muskets.

I cried for the dance of war to begin, sent runners to all the villages. Four hundred warriors spewed the black drink till dawn. I sang to the warriors:

If the hail rattles
Let the flowers be crushed
The oak of the forest
Will lift its head
To the sky and the storm
Towering and unscathed!

Then we spread flames of terror across the Land of Flowers. This was our battle plan: to disperse in small bands so the Army could not track us. Our war parties moved swiftly toward the four directions. All at once we struck, from Suh-wa-nee, the River of Reeds, to the church the Spaniards built at St. Augustine. From Fort Brooke in the south to the Big Water O-kee-cho-bee in the east. We hit on all sides, everywhere at once. At the edge of the forests we hid, we waited to emerge at night, burning the plantation houses, burning the slave barracks and the sugar mills. We killed the whites, set free the Negroes. Whites fled in panic to the stockades. We made no attempt to secure our borders but rather melted back into our forest strongholds. The Army could do nothing against us. They could not engage us, could not find us. They had to keep to the roads. They had to stay in their fortifications. They did not have us to guide them anymore. They were lost in the Land of Flowers. We fought on our home lands. The terrain was as familiar to us as our mother's bubby. Naked in our war paint we were invisible, like the owl that roosts on a stump by day to emerge after dusk to hunt his prey. When they marched out we awaited them, lying so low our guns spoke to the pitcher plants. In the dense hammocks we hid in silence, never firing till they were so close we could nearly touch them. They marched into our ambushes in columns. Then our guns thundered. We sent our volley of death into their front ranks. Their officers tasted death first. When the rest fell back, we fired into their flanks. They ran away in confusion, in fear. We took many scalps. We collected many weapons. Like ghosts we appeared, then vanished into our maze of streams and hammocks, leaving no trail behind us. We waited high in the trees, low in the scrub. Their columns came to the Whit-la-coo-chee River. The regulars tried to cross. The militias were on the far bank. We opened fire, cutting off the regulars from the militia. The militia shrank back, refused orders to cross into certain death. The militia deserted. We picked off the regulars with our guns and long bows, one at a time or in pairs. For ten days we pinned them. From desperation they ate their horses.

We sent our spies to the forts to guide the Army columns. We had prepared a surprise for them. We led them straight into the trap we set. Our snipers dealt death to stragglers. They tightened their columns. All in a mass, like hornets at a nest, the white man makes an easy target. Fat, clothed, encumbered with equipment, he falls like a sack of meal. I shot plenty of them, slipping around the troops, striking suddenly at the rear, moving swiftly back into the swamps, into the hammocks. Always staying out of range of their big medicine, their artillery. That is how our bands of thirty defeated Army regiments of five hundred.

Our runners linked our war parties. Our scouts informed us that General Clinch would move his units from Fort King to protect his plantation Lang Syne. Major Dade left Tampa to reinforce Fort King with 110 men, guided by the Negro Louis, a slave the Army paid with money. We offered to pay him with his freedom. He became our ally, leading Dade's column into our snare. Alligator, Jumper, Micanopy, and their warriors went to cut off Dade. They killed 107. Three whites escaped. I took my warriors to Fort King the same day. We hid under the palmettos and pines until the moment was right. Black night fell. The soft winter rain dampened our faces. The mist of dawn breathed upon the land. Still we waited, hidden. It was the afternoon when at last I saw Wiley Thompson. He strolled outside the stockade with Lieutenant Smith. The gentlemen had dined. Their bellies were heavy. They were smoking cigars. They dropped their guard. I was ready there with my braves. They came near the thicket. I stood: my war whoop broke the silence, keen and shrill. He reached for his sidearm, but I used my rifle well. I sent my ball into his chest. Thompson fell, pierced by my ball. I leaped upon him with my broad knife. I stabbed him in the heart. His blood gushed out. I painted my eyes with the warm blood of my enemy!

His life drained into the dirt. With my blade I took his head. Then raising it to our brother the sky, so that all the warriors could see, I stirred our braves to the attack. We took the weapons from the store and disappeared swiftly into the forest. Took the path for the Wa-hoo Swamp. We arrived with the darkness to reunite with our brothers, the warriors of Alligator and Jumper, victorious in their battle against Dade's column. All rejoiced to see the head of the enemy Thompson, the gift of the Great Spirit. We all gathered together and drank whiskey, told our stories. That night we celebrated our victories. We danced a magnificent dance, thrusting our spears into the sand around the agent Thompson's head.

At last Micanopy addressed our warriors: "I say to you our fathers have given us courage and strength. Let us go to work, my brothers. We have not come to stay here, huddled in the forest like renegades. Let us drive the whites from the Land of the Flowers forever."

Thus spoke Micanopy. The dawn was red when at last we slept.

Then war waged without quarter. Battles in the north, in the east and the west. The army troops poured into the Land of Flowers as many as the grains of sand. We had to keep our distance. We could not crush so many. Their columns trudged on, keeping to the roads through the pine forests. In the dust, in the mud, sick from fevers, hungry, without spirit. Yet there was no end to them. Never was there an end to them. Year after year they came, new armies, new officers, new campaigns. We could not win against so many. Nor could they win against so few. It was war without end, easier to start than to finish.

Our people remained hidden deep in the swamps, in the hammocks, under the palmettos, in the high grass. Our people suffered much. The troops could not find us, could not confront us. So they burned our crops, captured our horses, stole the Negro exiles, killed our cattle herds, denied us food. We were hungry, tired, and sick. It was not a good war, as the warriors of old knew. It was a dirty war, proving nothing. We grew tired of fighting. I was wounded, scarred many times. The fevers found me, too.

Then the micos met in council. The hour to treat with the white man had come. Micanopy sent word he desired to know General Jessup's heart. They arranged a truce. Jessup promised the chiefs that all Seminole would receive fair consideration—the red, the black, the mixed blood, all part of the Seminole nation. He promised protection to all from the slave hunters on the long road west. Then the Head Chief called the people to emerge from their hiding places, to travel to the forts, to gather at Tam-pa, near the Great South Sea.

The people came out of hiding, from under the palmettos, from deep in the swamps, the women and children, the old ones. At Fort Mellon we rested in our camps, naked, tired, and hungry. There came to us reports of Jessup's treachery: he had allowed the slave hunters to circulate among Micanopy's people, claiming black as well as red, abducting our people. Jessup gave no protection; his tongue was forked. He lied and stung us once more.

I asked permission of the commanding officer Call to visit my village once more before taking the long road. This was granted. I left Fort Mellon with two hundred warriors. Swift as the stream in spring we rode to the bay of Tam-pa. Under cover of night we circled the camps of Micanopy and Jumper. I plunged in and called the micos from their chickees. I told them they must come away with me. Jessup's pledge was broken; the truce was ended.

Micanopy objected. He was old, spent, worn with care. He had given his word to emigrate, to take the long road west. He urged his braves to kill him there. But I forbid them to kill the Head Chief. None raised a hand against him. I had his horse brought forward. I made him ride at the head of our party. In darkness we led seven hundred of our people from the camps back to our strongholds in the swamps and hammocks.

We made for the source of the five rivers. Our situation was desperate. We had no crops, no food. The summer was dry; even the pig hickory nuts failed us. The men could not hunt; the villages had to be defended. Our people were starving. I grew feeble with fever. My strength ebbed from me.

The medicine men could not gather herbs. In their dreams were evil omens. In autumn, war commenced again. With four thousand fresh troops Jessup marched from the west. From the east came General Hernández with nine hundred militia. Hernández came upon several of our villages, took them prisoner almost without a fight.

Jessup released two captives as messengers. They came to our camps with bad words. New orders had come from the demon Jackson to exterminate the Seminole. To hunt us like animals, to shoot us like dogs. To leave not one of us alive.

The fever laid me low. Black clouds descended over my eyes. My journey toward the shades of my fathers began, my journey toward the setting sun. I had not seen my wives or my children for several years. I loved them, and I wanted to be with them at the end of my life.

I sent the captives back with my message: I wished to meet Hernández, to treat with him under the white flag of truce. Word came back by runner; the truce was arranged.

With one hundred warriors I set out on horseback. We advanced with the white plumes and pipes before us. We marched slowly, no need to go fast. I looked once more and well upon our Land of Flowers till we came to the place called Pelican Creek, where I pitched my chickee and made my camp.

General Hernández arrived next morning, with his staff in full dress, and followed at a distance by a mounted regiment.

The American officers came under the great oak trees; then they dismounted. I stood with my chiefs, my warriors, my Tallassee people around me. The white flag of truce flew from my spear. We greeted them and offered our hands. We invited them to join us at the council ring.

Then Mico Co-Hadjo spoke: "We invite you, General, to council under the white flag of truce. We do not come to surrender. We wish to make peace with the Americans and to end the killing. But we do not want to remove west of the Big River Mississippi." Thus Co-Hadjo spoke.

Then Hernández stood. Said he had a talk from General Jessup for us, a question to me from Jessup: "Are you now prepared at once to deliver up the Negroes, taken from the American citizens? Why have you not surrendered them already?" he said.

I thought my ears deceived me. I thought the fever robbed me of sense. I was overcome. To Co-Hadjo I whispered: "Brother, you must answer; I am choking."

Then Hernández signaled his regiment. Swiftly they surrounded our camp. They dashed our white flag of truce. They had never meant to treat with us Seminole. They took away our arms and made us prisoners. They shackled us and marched us away in a double column. One more deceit. One more trick. One more lie. What could I expect from the white man?

———

Now hear my last words. All I asked was a small piece of this great land, enough to plant and live on, far to the south. A spot where I could place the ashes of my kindred. A place where my wives and children could live. This was not granted me.

Now I have left the Land of Flowers forever. I have done nothing to disgrace it. It was my home and I loved it.

To leave it is like burying my wives and children. I know that the white people call me killer, outlaw, savage. I know that soon I will be forgotten, along with the rest of my people. The memory of my tribe will become a legend among the tribes of white people.

But one day the white man's hunger will eat the Earth bare and leave only a desert. He will always be a stranger who comes in the night and takes what he needs. Always he will move on. Because to him one piece of land is like another. He treats the Earth his mother and his brother the sky like merchandise. When he has killed all the Indians, hunted all the animals, felled all the trees, burned all the forests. When all the streams run dry. When the mountains are ground to dust and the Great Sea cannot heal, then the white man will die of a great loneliness of spirit. For whatever happens to the Indians, to the animals, to the forests, to the rivers and the prairies will happen soon also to all human beings. Whatever befalls the Earth befalls also the children of the Earth.

—

Postscript. My dearest: The stars are extinguished from the sky one by one. And so, one by one, the American Indians are extinguished, until their people are an empty darkness to us. Even as I dash these last lines the bugle sounds "Boots and Saddles." Reinforcements of regulars have arrived from Georgia by sea, numbering three thousand; also irregulars and hired militias—mainly slave hunters—from Tennessee, Alabama, and Carolina. The Army has brought in bloodhounds from Cuba to root the last resisters out from their deepest hiding places in the vast green swamp north and east of Tampa Bay. The barges are lying at anchor here, ready to take those Indians who give themselves up voluntarily to the trans-Mississippi "homeland." The army has issued orders to shoot to kill all others. A $200 bounty has been offered for each Seminole brought in dead or alive. If only Jefferson were still alive!

The dawn is nigh: I leave again for the interior. One of the old soldiers here, a rough-and-ready fellow none too smart, asked why I should go where there can only be desperation and suffering. How can you help the Seminole? he wanted to know. On the contrary, I told him, only the Seminole can help us now.

As soon as you can, take this memoir of the Seminole prince to the American Philosophical Society Library and consult with Professor Bowden there or at his residence on Baring Street. He will know how to transmit the document to Congressman Giddings.

Adieu, *mon chéri*. I kiss your sweet lips.

Your loving husband,
Benjamin Coughlin

The Journal of
Jean Lafitte, Corsair

Ever since my bold assistance to the Americans at the Battle of New Orleans helped banish the British from the United States, I have repeatedly been urged to write my memoirs, so that I might leave a true account of the events of my life. Previously I have always refused to reveal my past, which is a private matter and concerns no one but myself. But I have now decided to do so, for the reason that only in this way can I hope to expose the many deceits and falsehoods concerning myself, my brothers, and my communes at Barataria and Galveston Island, the latter which I have now regretfully abandoned to the flambeau upon orders from President Monroe. If it is too late to convince the American government in Washington of my loyalty to America, which has never wavered, then perhaps I can still prevent others yet to come

99

from multiplying the slanders and fairy tales that swirl about the head of Jean Lafitte. There will always be those who call Lafitte a pirate and brigand, spreading false legends to increase their own petty worth. They are like the frigate birds that scavenge in the wake of the great hunters of the deep. In short, I take up the pen to annihilate this badge of piracy affixed to me by poisonous liars.

Of the treasures and fortunes I am presumed to have buried along the shores of the Gulf of Mexico and the many islands of the South Seas I have visited, I may state here and now that even if I knew the exact places where I was forced to throw valuable objects overboard when being pursued by warships, I have no interest whatever in recovering those objects. I never marked the places where bars of gold or silver ingots were dumped when we were under fire, nor did I know the amount of value of them. It would be useless to spend time seeking buried treasures. The sands constantly shift and change along the coastline in the eternal struggle of sea and earth. Only a fool believes that what was there yesterday will still be there tomorrow. Moreover, I have lived on little and been as much content as when my stores and warehouses bulged with riches. It is just as wrong to spend one's time with no other end than amassing wealth as to waste one's life in idleness and decadence. All my adventures and the many dangers that I have undergone had little to do with profits. Hang profiteers! I was ever a corsair, harassing the ships of Spain and Britain under letters of marque from those young and free nations, conceived in justice and the rights of man, and born into the blood of imperial struggles. When I reach my grave I wish to be remembered as a man who loved freedom above all other things, an errant liberator of mankind.

Nothing else matters in this world but that a man honor his family and assert his liberty.

Now that I have been forced to break up my commune on Galveston Island, I have resolved to withdraw but not surrender, awaiting that time and place to come when such doctrines as mine may shake the foundations of the highest dynasties and leave them to be devoured by the lower masses.

I was born on the island of Santo Domingo, April 22, 1782, into a world of wars and revolutions. I have played the part I was born for, causing chaos to the commerce of England and Spain. And I will die confident in knowing that humanity will finally be loosed from the strangling coils of the old European empires, though millions will perish in these terrible conflicts.

My mother died before I can remember, and my maternal grandmother, Zora Nadrimal, became a mother to me and to my brother, Pierre, three years my senior. Everything I am I owe to the great intuition of my grand-mère, a Spanish Jewess, who told us how our family suffered at the hands of the Spanish Inquisition. The patriarch of the family on my mother's side was Abhorad Nadrimal, who had been an alchemist in Spain, with a good practice in potions, medicines, and chemicals. He was a free-thinking Jew with neither Catholic faith nor traditional adherence to the law of the Jewish synagogues. Grandmother told us repeatedly how the Inquisition had decreed life imprisonment, exile, torture, and death by burning for many of our family. Abhorad Nadrimal died in prison as a heretic who would not embrace the so-called "true faith" and stubbornly refused baptism. His grounds? That if heaven was full of Spaniards, he would rather rot in hell! Grand-mère instilled in me his last words, which became my lifelong credo: "How can man profess to love God, whom he has never seen, yet not love his brother, whom he has always seen?"

Grand-mère knew that a child is formed by family example. She was very liberal-minded, imposing obedience through recourse to reason rather than by scolding or punishment. She never once raised her voice at us, yet always demanded physical endurance and mental fortitude. I learned from childhood to control my temper, assess a situation completely before determining my course of action, and to always express my opinions with calm and confidence. It was from her that I inherited total concentration upon a given course, and staunch resolution to surmount any obstacle.

My seven brothers and sisters were all taught to expect and receive affection, attention, and succor, to feel ourselves an important part of the family, with no feelings of inferiority or rivalry among us. Thus my brothers and I stuck together through the challenges and changes that life brought. The Lafittes have always had the reputation of creating around us an atmosphere of contentment, harmony, and well-being. We never held power over others by force or intimidation, but always served at the pleasure of our crews and communards. For we learned at Grand-mère's knee that men are best organized, motivated, and led by courage, demonstration, persuasion, and honor. Thus Grand-mère taught us that all humanity is our family, and the entire world our home.

Nevertheless, the horrible scenes of slaughter I witnessed when the Spanish smuggled arms to the black slaves of our island, making it possible for them to revolt against the French, served to redouble my hatred of the Spanish Crown and all the persecutions for which it was responsible—not only against the Jews, but also against the poor and ignorant people of all races in the New World.

My brother Pierre and I received the same careful upbringing, the same lessons and good education from our beloved Grand-mère Nadrimal. We were close in age and by temperament congenial and very fond of each other. Our views on all subjects developed alike, and our speculative thoughts sailed the same channels, borne aloft on the same strong winds. We burned with youthful desire to throw off the yoke of Spanish despotism, strike off the tentacles of the British octopus, and establish the reign of liberty in all the Americas. Jefferson, Paine, Lafayette, and Napoleon Bonaparte were our boyhood idols. In all this and more we were inseparable.

Alexander, my oldest brother, was eleven years older than I, a splendid sailor and an expert cannoneer on seagoing vessels. We had never seen any other Jews and had no idea what they looked like, but Grand-mère Nadrimal told us that Alexander and my sister Anna had certain Jewish features. He was short and had a curved nose and large black eyes which sharpened and glittered at the slightest sound or movement. Although very busy with his life as a sailor on the high seas, Alexander took a deep interest in Pierre and me. From time to time he came home to spend several days with us between voyages, and always had a good fund of stories to tell. Pierre and I always liked to share the same room with him because he would keep us awake until midnight with tales of his adventures as a corsair during voyages to Cuba, Mexico, and South America. Late into the tropical nights he described for us the natives of those countries and their curious customs. He told us how the Indians, witnessing the respect and deference that European commoners pay to their so-called superiors, despise whites as abject slaves, wondering how any man can be so base as to kneel before another man. Most of the natives, he said, were pressed into forced labor on the Spanish plantations or in the mines, or in loading vessels with all sorts of merchandise, including gold and silver, all destined for their Spanish masters.

We two boys were fascinated by what our older brother Alexander told us, and little by little we decided to become sea rovers, too, carving our fortunes with our swords and choosing the sea as a life that abounds with variety and would afford us opportunities to gratify our curiosity by a change of countries. For we two brothers were never like other people, content to live within four walls, never interesting themselves in what lies beyond. Our breath quickened at the mere thought of the travels and adventures we could have past the blue horizon.

Whenever he landed at Port-au-Prince, Alexander invited his captain, Jacques Misson, to stay at our home. This Captain Misson was an impressive character, an old seadog with a great black beard and a patch over his left eye from a sword wound sustained in battle. I remember distinctly Captain Misson's last visit, when I was eight and Pierre eleven. We kept begging him to tell us his adventures. Our imaginations simply could not contain the dangerous exploits that filled his memory. His visit lasted three days and two nights, during which he told us all about the way he had conducted his privateering activities against the Spanish, whom he had always detested and deceived in countless ways. He said that neither the English, the French, nor the Americans had ever discovered his true identity or birthplace, and he advised us never to reveal our true names or origins when plying trade as privateers for or against any nation at war.

I was still a boy at the time, but Captain Misson's tales filled my mind with thoughts that still stir my blood. Pierre and I regarded his sea stories as prophetic glimpses of our own destiny. A cold, steely look came into his eyes when he told us that all religion was nothing more than human fantasy, and that the Law of Moses was the only religion necessary for the governing of people. In his own youth, Captain Misson had visited all the shores and islands of the South Seas. Seeing there for himself the licentious lives of the Spanish clergy, he decided that religion was no more than a trick foisted upon the minds of the weak. He taught us his maxim, that "Religion and government should never set up in one house." Thus the monarchs and churches can have no divine right to pursue secular power, to oppress the people and aggrandize their own class.

Captain Misson next fell upon government, and preached that every man was born free and had as much right to what would support him as to the air he breathed. For the Deity brought no man into this world to pass a life of penury, nor did he create the estates of human society. The vast differences we see betwixt man and man, the one wallowing in luxury and the other in the most pinching necessity, owes to no law of the Divine, but rather to the strong enslaving the weak, usurping the prerogative of God over his creatures, which is a privilege no man has.

He also taught us that war is the common harvest of those who participate in the division of public money in all countries, but that war is allowable by the law of nature for the preservation of our own lives. But that no war ought to be undertaken except in defense of our natural rights, which include such a share of earth as is necessary for our support.

When Captain Misson departed, I knew I should never forget his brave fellowship of the seas, bidding defiance to the ancient regimes of Europe. With a ship underfoot we would make war upon the monarchs, aristocrats, and clergy, lawfully claiming that liberty to which men have a right by nature. Pierre and I swore an oath in blood that when we grew up we would capture all vessels flying the Spanish flag in order to establish that liberty founded on those two most sacred documents: the Declaration of Independence and the Universal Rights of Man of the French Revolution. We had no thought of gain or compensation for ourselves.

Our father, a tanner by trade on Santo Domingo, never once objected when Alexander was telling us the customs of the coast—the duty of privateers to share all their prizes taken against nations at war among the captain, officers, and crew. Grand-mère, on whom Pierre and I relied fully, never once said anything to us against our intentions of becoming privateers. At times she silenced Alexander when he would recount stories of crews thrown into the sea when their vessels were captured. Grand-mère's intention was that Pierre and I should use a pen instead of a sword to unchain humanity and emancipate the poor from suffering and exploitation by the beasts who reigned in power over them. But her wishes for our future were not to be, which Grand-mère recognized when she told us, "Scholars perish in times of war." In our young hearts the hope burned bright that some day we two Lafitte brothers would strike a final great blow on the sea against those two Hydra heads, Spain and England.

When I was sixteen years old, my brother Alexander took Pierre and myself on our first voyage, from Port-au-Prince to New Orleans, Louisiana. We left on the nineteenth of January 1798, and although the voyage was uneventful, we saw much sickness during the three months we stayed in New Orleans because fevers were raging. We returned home in March of the same year. Pierre and I then signed on and prepared ourselves to become sailors. We were always first on the yardarm, either to hand or to reef, and inquisitive in the different methods of working a ship. In fact, our attention and conversation turned upon no other subject, and we would often get the boatswain or carpenter to teach us the constituent parts of the ship's hull and how to rig her.

We sailed to the islands of Nevis and Saint Cristophe, hence to the fortress of Cartagena, where we met many sailors of French, English, Danish, Dutch, Jewish, African, and Indian descent. Pierre and I witnessed many tortures and executions under the Spanish regime at Cartagena. We saw the breaking of men and women upon the rack, and the drawing-and-quartering of offenders against the Church or Crown. Once we watched the Spanish authorities hang a man alive by the ribs, between which they first made an incision with a knife and then clinched an iron hook with a chain. In this manner the man was kept alive for three days hanging with his head downward and catching with his tongue the drops of water, it being the rainy season, that were flowing down his bloated breast as the vultures picked at the putrid wound. His crime had been speaking without permission to one of the Spanish officers.

Another time we witnessed the flagellation of a female Zambo slave, who was lacerated in such a shocking manner, receiving two hundred lashes of the leathern whip, that she was literally dyed with blood from her neck to her ankles. Yet her only crime consisted of refusing to submit to the loathsome embraces of a Spanish priest. These bestial sights made my blood boil with rage.

Pierre married at the age of nineteen and already had a son when Alexander went to France to enlist in the service of Napoleon Bonaparte, leaving his six ships under the command of our uncle Reyne Baluche. I, too, was married, at the age of eighteen, to Christina Levine, who was born on the island of St. Croix and was of Danish-Jewish descent. Pierre and I were now old enough to begin service as privateers under the orders of Uncle Reyne, in spite of the protests of Grand-mère, who held that we were still too young to take charge of a vessel on the open sea. Grand-mère was seventy-two years old in the early spring of 1801, when we set sail on a privateering cruise in two of our boats. She wept when we left the wharf, as she would do every time we returned.

Alexander had sent to us from Paris his letters of marque and reprisal, commissioning us under French authority to capture the merchant ships of enemy nations. As soon as our documents arrived, we weighed anchor. Uncle Reyne commanded a vessel of 350 tons, while Pierre and I together received command of a 300-ton vessel. Our two ships sailed along the coast of Yucatán without any incident of more importance than an occasional encounter with Mexican fishing boats.

Then on Wednesday, April 22, at dawn, we discovered through our spyglass a sail far out on the horizon. The vessel could not have been more than twenty-five leagues away, sailing eastward away from us. Immediately we hoisted up our sails and, fully rigged, took off after the boat.

As our vessels, moving at high speed, closed the distance, we started giving all sorts of signals, flying colored sails as high as our masts permitted, trying to draw their attention by firing our big cannons. But evidently thinking that we were determined privateers, they continued on their course. Our vessels were well equipped with compass, telescope, sounding lines, the best reef sails, jib sails, and mainsails, so that with a good wind behind us we were able to keep up a high speed. Within an hour we were within full view of the vessel, which turned out to be a Spanish sloop of the war fleet, named the *Atrevida,* with armed men on its decks. With a big blast of the cannon, we intercepted the vessel at about longitude 88 degrees 14 minutes west and latitude 22 degrees 12 minutes north, if I remember correctly.

Drawing within earshot we could hear that a general outbreak had begun among the crew of the Spanish ship. We could hardly believe that a mutiny would start so quickly, but their cries soon enough convinced us. A few moments later we saw that men were being thrown into the water. A scene of the most terrible slaughter followed, when the Spanish officers commanded that the mutineers be bound and brought up on deck, where the officers then ordered the chef, their Negro cook, to hit each mutineer on the head with an ax and throw him into the sea. That is how the Spaniards make their soup!

Because my brother and I knew how our own people had been persecuted and tortured to death, it was terrible for us to witness this diabolic barbarism committed by the Spanish officers. Uncle Reyne's vessel was almost abreast on the starboard side of the Spanish vessel, while Pierre and I were abreast on the port side with our ship. The language on our boat was French and our conversation could doubtless be heard by some of them who understood it. France was the day's leading light in the young firmament of liberty, and when we were very close, a man on the mizzenmast of the Spanish vessel gave a joyous cry, "*Vive la France!*" The words had hardly been spoken when one of their lieutenants shot his *pistolet*, and the man fell to the deck dead.

Angered by the brutal slaying of the Frenchman, Uncle Reyne took his speaking tube and demanded the surrender of the Spanish officers, that all armed men come out on deck, and that they lower their sails. After waiting a moment we did not have time for further negotiations. A very smart engagement followed.

All our men were at their posts when Uncle Reyne gave the signal to our first and second gunners to fire two shots of twelve pounds and two of twenty pounds. Our gunfire had the most awful effect. The double shots smashed through the lower decks, breaking their fore-topsail at the head of the foremast, killing two of their officers and ten of their men, and hurling at least eight more into the water. The others became so scared they completely lost their heads, running in all directions on the bridges, their discipline shattered. The officers of the Spanish vessel reaped the fruits of their treason to the crew, who were jumping from deck to deck to get to the rafts and had no intention of defending the *Atrevida.*

Uncle Reyne gave the signal for us to take over the boarding planks immediately and force our way aboard the ship. Suddenly a strong breeze kicked, and the sterns of our boats touched. This put us in a most favorable position to throw our lines over their railings and to secure their bowsprit, making it easy for our men to board and take over their boat. We seized the main bridge without difficulty and entrenched ourselves behind the spars, which had been broken by our first cannon volley. Taking great care to avoid the gunfire of the Spaniards still hidden belowdecks, our men fought two hourglasses before the Spanish officers gave themselves up.

When we had disarmed all the officers of the *Atrevida*, and lined them up behind the broken bowsprit, we called up all hands. It was my maiden voyage as a corsair, and now I made my maiden speech. I addressed the crew, informing them we were privateers in the service of France, and offering enlistment under terms that they liked infinitely better than the ones received from their Spanish superiors.

"We force no man," I told them. "Nor will we be guilty of the injustices we blame in others. If any are averse to following his fortune, which we promise shall be the same to all, then only declare yourself, and you will be set ashore."

They one and all cried, "Vive le Capitaine!"

I thanked them for the honor, and continued. "I promise to use the power you have given us for the common good only, and I hope that since you have the bravery to assert your liberty, you will show as much courage in defending it."

Once more they shouted, "Vive le Capitaine!"

I bid them choose their own subaltern officers, giving them power to consult and conclude what might be their common interest. This they readily did, choosing their lieutenants, gunner, and boatswain as representative in council. Among corsairs the boatswain's opinion is like the mufti's among the Turks. The captain can undertake nothing that the boatswain does not approve. He represents and speaks for the interest of the crew.

These newly elected officers were called into the great cabin, and the question was asked, what colors to sail under? The boatswain advised black as most terrifying, but Uncle Reyne strenuously objected that we were not pirates, but rather men resolved to assert that liberty which God and nature gave us, suffering none to grow immensely rich by his rank or his ancestors' encroachments, nor any to be wretchedly miserable, either by falling into the hands of villains, unmerciful creditors, or other misfortunes. He said we should allow nothing but merit to distinguish between man and man, and that if we could not redress our wrongs, then at least we could scorn to yield to tyranny.

Then Pierre spoke. "Such freebooters are we. We make common cause to end the most ancient abuses, which have become respectable over time. And as we do not proceed upon the same ground with pirates, who are men of dissolute lives and no principles, let us scorn also to take their colors. Ours is a brave, a just, an innocent, and a noble cause: the cause of liberty! I therefore advise a white ensign, with the motto A DEO ET LIBERTATE—'For God and Liberty'—as an emblem of our righteous resolution."

The cabin door had been left open, and the bulkhead, which was of canvas, rolled up. The steerage was full of men, who all bent an attentive ear. They cried, "Liberté! Égalité! Fraternité!"

This council breaking up, everything belonging to the Spanish captain and officers was brought on deck and overhauled. I ordered the boatswain to examine who among the men were in want of clothes, and to distribute all impartially.

This was done to the general consent and cheers of the whole crew. They looked a pretty sight, decked out like masqueraders in the costumes of the aristocrats!

When they offered me the captain's chest, however, I demurred. "Our brotherhood seeks to destroy the monarchs and the monarchists, their property, their symbols, and their uniforms. The black sweater and spun breeches of a common sailor I hold more precious than the garments of the richest king!"

Then I ordered the quartermaster to hand out to the men all the wine, rum, and spirits found on board, and told the carpenter to prepare a chest with a padlock, so that the gold and money of our prisoners could be held in common there.

During the celebration that followed, I spoke from the barricades to the following purpose: that since they had resolved to seize and defend their liberty, I recommended to them a strict agreement on harmony among themselves. "For men born and bred into slavery grow incapable of thinking for themselves. Trodden underfoot all their lives, they naturally live in confusion and fear of their fellow man. Ignorant of their birthright, they dance to the music of their chains. Only such toadies would brand such a crew as ours with the invidious name of pirates and become instruments of our destruction. It is self-preservation, not cruelty or greed, that obligates us to declare war against all who would refuse us what necessities we require, and I do now solemnly declare such war. But I recommend to you, my comrades, a humane behavior toward your prisoners, for converts are better made through mercy than by the same cruel means our enemies practice."

Then we sent the Spanish officers past their former crew, who spat in the officers' faces. The Spanish officers were from the upper classes of society, and naturally were hypocrites with arrogant personalities. They were incapable or unwilling to understand the common people of their nation and their provinces in America. They were accustomed to thinking of their government as something sacred, like the Church or Heaven itself, when really all they had achieved was decadence under stupid monarchs with diseased blood in their veins.

Uncle Reyne assigned Pierre to take charge of the wheel of the *Atrevida,* and put me solely in charge of our second ship. Thus all three vessels sailed eastward, transporting our prize to Fort de France. When we had completed our inventories and auctioned off our booty, we left for Port-au-Prince—very happy at having put a small match under the beard of the old Spanish king. Our grand-mère, my wife, and Pierre's wife were the first to kiss us on our arrival in harbor.

As a result of our capture of the *Atrevida,* we now had letters of credit awaiting us in Paris. Uncle Reyne went to France, where he was invited to dine with Monsieur Bonaparte and like Alexander, offered a high rank in the military service. At the same time Pierre and I procured letters of marque in our own names to sail the open seas, engaging in privateering to the advantage of France against the maritime forces of Spain and Britain.

Soon enough, peace disappeared, and the flames of war burst out once more on the Spanish main. The British despot declared open war against revolutionary France, and the Caribbean became a major theater of conflict. During these dark years, Spain took advantage of the imbroglio between France and England to start smuggling weapons to the slaves in Port-au-Prince. We were not opposed to Santo Domingo's freedom, only to Spain supplying arms to the slaves, which accounted for a fearful slaughter of the unarmed French civilian population. We took many cruises during the course of these hostilities and captured seventeen vessels, some loaded with slaves, which we usually took to New Orleans or Mobile to sell. It was a poor business, and with a high customs duty. Twenty years ago I saw nothing wrong with slave-trading, but since then I have changed my mind about this filthy business. Trading for those of our own species can never be agreeable in the eyes of Divine Justice. No man should have such absolute power over another. I did not exempt my own neck from the yoke of submission in order to enslave others.

These black men are distinguished from Europeans by their color, customs, or religious rites, but they are the work of the same Omnipotent Being, and are no doubt endowed with equal reason. I make no excuses, but in those days my enterprise, audacity, and ardor for trade ran as hot as any other young man's physical desires. I could no more forbear to reject a business venture than to reject an illicit proposition from a beautiful woman, no matter that such adventures might be illegal, immoral, or reckless. All sense of right and wrong could suddenly be swept overboard if the reward sounded sweet. To break the rules and yet win the game— moreover, to win the game *by* breaking the rules—seemed to me the perfect prize of the privateer. The scars of my own success needed to accumulate on my hide before I could consider the pain I might be causing others. Wherefore I began to treat Africans as free men, offering them enlistment under the same terms as everyone else. They have made good sailors and officers for the most part, and many have joined my communes without suffering prejudice. Before the mast and the mighty seas all men must be equal. It is those who journey to see the many diverse lands of the world with their own eyes that best learn tolerance, and those who pull together on a vessel who learn the true meaning of brotherhood. Thus I believe that freedom will arrive from the seas upon the lands in every corner of America—the most valuable cargo ever carried by ship!

—

In October 1804, we left Port-au-Prince in order to help French refugees of the Santo Domingo revolution land along the lower Mississippi River. It was on this mission of mercy that we first located Grande Terre and Grande Isle, two sand islands facing the Gulf of Mexico and lying just outside the river's mouth. As we wished to know what was behind these islands, Pierre and I lowered a small bateau and began to navigate the bayous that communicated between swamps and marshes stretching for many miles. We were struck by the many dead cypress trees, rising straight from the waters like the masts of ships, their branches bearded heavily with moss, like tattered sails. A shower of feathery catkins fell from the trees, covering all the bayou but for a single snaking path of black water as opaque and shining as polished onyx, so that it was impossible to tell by eye how wide or deep was the bayou. From the banks large reptiles eyed us. There were hundreds of these crocodiles everywhere, large and small, of all different shades of green. At night their eyes shone red in the moonlight—no doubt a frightening deterrent to spies and traveling gossips. Much to our joy, we found that one of the bayou's channels connected directly with the west bank of the

Mississippi in the city of New Orleans, which spread over a crescent of land following the river's main channel. "*Mon Dieu!*" said Pierre. "We have found the smugglers' alley!"

With deep water before them, and this secluded network of bayous behind, leading to the easy-virtued Creole port, we knew instinctively that these islands Grande Terre and Grande Isle made an excellent base for disposing of the merchandise we captured in our privateering ventures. It was the opportunity of a lifetime, which we two Lafitte brothers could not pass up.

We established our first commune on the island of Grande Terre, and constructed our storehouses along the bay, already known to the Creoles as Barataria, with a previous history as a site for stowing captured prizes. Our first market of goods was held there in October 1805. Our open actions as smugglers notwithstanding, all the leading businessmen of the Louisiana Territory came and bought merchandise there, including numerous members of the Louisiana legislature, as well as American officers stationed in New Orleans. All approved our policy of free trade.

Our project was to organize the smugglers and *contrebandiers*. We provided aid to the fishing boats that shipped our goods up the back alley to New Orleans. Our commune expanded and grew stronger with the addition of the many French refugees and exiles whom we transported there from the Indies without charge. With our profits we constructed new storehouses and a blacksmith shop in New Orleans. By 1812 we had a bustling palmetto-thatched village of more than one thousand persons, with our own police force, well remunerated and disciplined. Among us all titles were abolished, and no church established: our people were free to trade and prosper as they might, according to their own hard work and good luck. We put into practice the maxim of Jefferson that "That government is best which governs least."

Pierre and I were able to divide our time equally between Port-au-Prince and New Orleans. We were happy beyond our greatest hopes. Our transactions were completed behind closed doors; our names were unknown to the buyers of our merchandise. We opened more and more stores within a radius of 150 miles from New Orleans. The officials of the Louisiana Territory were in favor of our community because our stores offered goods of every variety and description direct to the buyer, and were therefore cheaper, without intermediary swindlers. The desire for progress in America was creating a demand everywhere for our merchandise. We saw ahead of us the unlimited future of these so-called *grandes marchés*—great or superior markets—where goods from the entire world could be bought in one spot with convenience and economy. This was all made possible not by any special genius on my part, but rather by the simple fact that the bayous of Barataria provided easy channels for the distribution of merchandise from the entire Gulf, and protection from the prying eyes of officials. The tattered shoreline with its gloomy swamps and broad marshes, though uninhabitable, proved to be the motive force in a new kind of merchant adventure.

Man is not governed by his conscience, but by his surroundings and experiences. My only culpability during this whole time was smuggling contrary to the customs legislations of the United States, after the Americans had purchased Louisiana. My reason for doing this was the conduct of the American customs officers, who asked sums far higher than the regular tariffs to satisfy their personal interests. These dishonest transactions victimized the native Creoles of New Orleans. I continued my policy of distributing French refugees, mulattos, and English and Spanish prisoners along the coastal region from Mobile to Galveston. The members of my crews and my officers and communards were from every nation, assigned to cooperative functions on land and on the vessels in accordance with the merits of their qualifications. In this way we formed a coastal nation, like no other in its equity and impartiality. It was undoubtedly the growing strength of our society that aroused the fears and spite of the Americans. They could not forbear to witness how our commune progressed without the power of officials, the maldistribution of titles and riches, and without the tariffs, taxes, and bribes that keep the governors fat in every land.

Around this time, 1812, the United States encountered a blockade by the British and was unable to ship anything on the open seas, thereby suffering defeats and losses. The capital city of Washington fell into the hands of the English. Cities and ports on the Atlantic were also blocked. Yet when I sent messages of intelligence and offers of assistance, and asked for a commission as privateer against the English and Spanish, my warnings were ignored. My messengers did not return; instead I received insults and threats. Letters written by my hand were spat upon by the Americans. The governor of Louisiana actually offered $1,500 for my capture.

I therefore offered $15,000 for *his* capture.

From that day on, numerous charges were lodged against my brother Pierre and me. We had never been pirates, and had never sought to deal, knowingly, in pirated goods. On common ground, as on open sea, my tribunals always tried and condemned pirates. My commune always acted by authority of letters of marque, furnished by powers involved in struggles with rival nations. I wished only to build a prosperous and free community at Barataria. Pierre and I never intended to be anything but liberators of the suffering masses. So I took the Americans' insults and threats in good humor, in order to continue to fortify my own commune against the British octopus.

However, with my officers accused of piracy, detachments of the American army landed at Grande Terre to make arrests and confiscate our property. My brother Pierre was surprised by a group of soldiers and arrested on June 6, 1814. Accused of piracy, he was put into solitary confinement, his feet and wrists chained. Brought to the lousy prison in the Cabildo building in New Orleans, a grand jury drew up formal charges against him. But Pierre knew the Cabildo as well as his own hand: only the previous week he had been selling our goods in the same building where they now impudently held him prisoner. With little ado, he escaped on Monday, September 5, at two-thirty in the morning. This daring act only brought more repression down on our heads. The American warship *Carolina*, with the 44th Infantry on board and an escort of seven gunboats, landed at Grand Terre the following week, at four o'clock in the morning. When they asked if I knew the whereabouts of Jean or Pierre Lafitte, I answered calmly, "Yes, of course. They are in France."

The Americans intended to confiscate all my ships and sell all the merchandise for their personal gain, but my officers immediately seized torches and set fire to all the vessels and storehouses. Six of my vessels burned, while twenty-six others were confiscated and taken to New Orleans. Later

I learned that the governor, Claiborne, boasted in a letter to General Andrew Jackson that he had succeeded in destroying my colony at Grande Terre. Later he learned that I had many other storehouses filled with rifles, flints, powder, and cannons. The Americans foolishly persisted in treating us as bandits, while I had to hold off the English by guile, for as soon as the English found out that my fort at Grande Terre had been attacked, they understood that easy access to the soft underbelly of the United States was open to them. A British sloop of war landed to parley, and I was offered money, commission, and a full pardon if I would assist the British landing. They informed me that their troops had left Ireland in the middle of September 1814. I put them off temporarily, telling them that I must have my ships back before I could help anyone.

Then I went up the back channel to New Orleans, determined to see Governor Claiborne and convince him of the idiotic folly of his actions against Pierre and me. I strolled into his office without having been invited, or even notifying him of my visit. However, when I pointed out that my men were posted around the building, he did not refuse to admit me.

"I bring the Americans news that fifteen thousand crack, hand-picked English soldiers have left the coast of Ireland for the lower Mississippi, with the mission of capturing New Orleans," I said.

"I do not believe you, Monsieur Lafitte," he replied, "and why should I? You are a well-known liar, brigand, and criminal."

"If the British get past my colony," I answered, "they will easily take New Orleans—I guarantee it. And if they take possession of the lower valley of the Mississippi River, they will arm and incite the Indian tribes to march eastward, crushing the United States as far as the Atlantic Ocean. But you and I can prevent this, Monsieur."

Governor Claiborne reacted in the most stupid manner possible, maintaining silence. I explained and wrote down for him my plans for defense against the British, and described the seriousness of the situation along the coast following the attack on my commune by the very people I wished to help. I tried in a thousand ways to make him understand my genuine feelings of loyalty to the United States, and how these feelings came before my personal interest in the return of my ships and property. Still he obstinately refused to understand the crisis he was helping to provoke with his blunders.

Finally I lost patience with the fool and challenged him to "accept a cup of coffee," as we call it. The coward refused my challenge to duel. But yielding to my menace, he agreed not to make further use of armed force against me and to accept as aid from me 1,100 men, rifles, powder, 362 cannons, and more than 400 skilled artillerymen. With my sword at his chest, he authorized us in writing to be in New Orleans and to construct barricades and ramparts against the inevitable British invasion.

The attacks of the Americans on my commune, however, proved a benefit in disguise in at least one way, for I was able to gain the complete confidence of the English, who were easily deceived into believing that I had no reason to love or assist the United States. They repeatedly wrote me letters, increasing their offers, trying to win me over to their cause. I responded that only a little more time was necessary for me to replenish my forces before we could make common cause. In this way I was kept fully informed of all their maneuvers and the strength of their forces. I advised them to stay away from the channel of Grande Terre on the grounds of the presence of American garrisons on the lower coast of Louisiana—of which there were none! If the English had discovered my deception, pillaged my storehouses filled with munitions, and found their way up our back alley to New Orleans, the city would surely have fallen into their hands. But I proved skillful at playing the double game of cozenage.

While awaiting with anxiety the arrival of General Jackson and the American forces to defend New Orleans, I could not sit still, and so I undertook a reconnaissance of the plantation country surrounding the city. I traveled incognito, disguised as a French salesman of Diderot's *Encyclopédie*, a slightly mad merchant of knowledge with a long black beard and sample volumes under my arm. In this way I was able to gain access to the drawing rooms of every planter, where I revealed my identity. They reported to me that the British had more than fourteen thousand well-trained soldiers from the Napoleonic campaigns already quartered twelve kilometers to the southeast of New Orleans on the plantations La Coste, Villere, and La Ronde.

I had to get this news to Governor Claiborne to relay to General Jackson immediately upon his arrival. But I was loath to go in person, not only because crossing the lines would be dangerous, but because I never knew if that dull-witted fop in the governor's seat might not clap me into irons, as he had done my brother Pierre. Then Heaven intervened.

I stopped for the night at the home of a wealthy Creole family on my way back to Barataria. They were old friends, having purchased many slaves from us. I was especially friendly with the lady of the house, who reminded me in some ways of my dear Grand-mère Nadrimal. I had only just arrived, still in my disguise as the traveling book salesman—though I had revealed my cozenage to my lady—when the servant announced the arrival of another guest. An instant later my hostess was being embraced by her intimate friend Mrs. Claiborne, the young wife of the governor, and the most beautiful, coquettish, and charming of Creoles. With the quick presence of mind that endeared her in my admiration, my friend introduced me as Monsieur Clement, purveyor and representative of Diderot's famous *Encyclopédie* in America, then hurriedly left the room to prepare for supper, leaving her guests together.

As soon as she was gone, I wrote out my information, though I left it unsigned.

"Take this to your husband, Mrs. Claiborne," I instructed her. "It is important that it arrive tomorrow, at the earliest hour possible. The lives of many depend upon it."

"Monsieur, is this a joke?"

"I assure you I am perfectly serious."

"It is perhaps an example of Monsieur Diderot's learning that you send to my husband?"

"Now it is you who joke. It is a report."

"And who shall I say sends this mysterious report to the governor, a book peddler?"

"Encyclopedias," I corrected her. "Say it is from whomever you like. Only get it to him before it is too late. It contains secret military information concerning the British deployments."

"Très bien." Her eyes teased as she spoke. "But, oh, where to hide it?"

She leaned over. I slipped the note into her bosom, and caught the mild scent of oranges floating up on a warm breeze.

The supper went off brilliantly; we departed in the morning, she for New Orleans, I to continue my reconnaissance mission.

The arrival of General Jackson on Thursday, December 2, brought hardly any reinforcements for New Orleans. His appearance and that of his six officers in ragged uniforms provoked general bewilderment. I knew from my intelligence officers what Jackson found out on his initial inspection of the defenses of the city—to wit, that the one thousand local militia were without flints and powder to fire their rifles and pistols, rendering their arms completely useless, and that there were no artillery batteries except the siege guns in the fortresses.

I wasted no time waiting for a chance that would put me face-to-face with General Jackson. With a few officers of my staff, I contrived to come across the General at the corner of St. Philip and Royal streets. There I boldly explained to him that my conduct had always been marked by loyalty to the Declaration of American Independence, and that I was now ready to extend any help to the Americans I could muster. If he did not believe me, in reply to the unfounded insults heaped upon myself and my brothers by the American officials in New Orleans, I then and there challenged General Jackson to a cup of coffee. The idiot invited me to a café.

In spite of the respect I had for his uniform, I must say that the famous American general's intelligence seemed most inferior. Perhaps it was as a result of having spent much of his career slaughtering Indians and putting down slave rebellions. Though I will say in his defense that he was all too evidently ravaged by fevers, a gaunt, emaciated man with hollowed eyes, who looked as though he might collapse and die at any moment.

A room was prepared at the Exchange Coffee House on Chartres Street, and we retired there to discuss the situation. I immediately offered him all the flints and powder necessary for the militia, which were stored at a *chênière*, one of those shell mounds thickly covered with live oak trees along the bayou less than one hour from the city. General Jackson accepted, thanking me warmly, and inquired if we had any information to give him regarding the enemy.

This was the turning point of my career, when I decided once and for all to cast my lot with the Americans. There was no conflict in my mind. I knew exactly what was to be expected in the long run from any arrangements with the British: double dealing, lying, backstabbing, arrest, and finally a walk down the plank, as we say. My reputation as a pirate among the Americans notwithstanding, at least with them there was hope for something better. As my Grand'mère Nadrimal used to say, "Hope may do you harm, but it will not kill you."

"The situation is thus, mon Général," I began. "The British infantry forces possess overwhelming superiority in numbers, arms, and experience. We can only lose if we wait to receive their infantry. We must defend the city as if New Orleans were a ship—that is, by attacking them first with cannoneers, then sending our troops out after the artillery has accomplished its work. I can offer you for this purpose 452 artillery pieces and the most skilled marksmen in the world."

By common understanding General Jackson and I resolved to strike a daring blow: a coordinated attack by a battalion under General Coffee and a battery of my cannoneers, to begin on Wednesday, December 28, at sundown.

The battle lasted approximately three hours. The losses on the English side were eighteen times greater than ours. We lost twenty-four men. As soon as the English became aware of my alliance with the American army, they sought to gain time for new stratagems. However, this also gave time for General Jackson to receive reinforcements. They arrived from Tennessee. Creoles came from all parts of Louisiana. Many Indians enlisted and were well paid for their service. Three generals with five hundred soldiers arrived from Kentucky. New Orleans was fast becoming a garrison city. The new soldiers were miserably clothed and also without flint and powder for their firearms, but my storehouses held enough gunpowder, flint, and firearms to supply an army of thirty thousand.

On Friday, December 30, the English could be seen digging trenches and cutting down trees. We waited until Sunday, January 1, when they had finished their positions; then my cannoneers opened long-range fire, demolishing all their defense work, ruining their fortifications, and killing many of their soldiers, while ours were safe.

On the night of January 2, we prepared a wholesome feast for General Jackson, Major Latour, and my captains, including Uncle Reyne Baluche and Dominique Youx, released from the Calaboose prison, where they had been held for piracy, to command artillery batteries. It was a cordial gathering, with my brothers Alexander and Pierre also both present. On this occasion Pierre had the opportunity to explain the life of the privateer to the veteran Indian fighter, whom they called Old Hickory. "We wear no distinguishing mark of rank, and never need one. We choose only the strong and valiant as our *bos*. We are common men, but we belong to no one—no king, lord, or nation—and we have tasted the finer things of life!"

Alexander, by now an aging veteran of the Napoleonic campaigns, conversed most charmingly in English on technical improvements in long-range weaponry and dazzled the American officers with his knowledge. At two o'clock in the morning, I had the steward bring a bottle of the finest Burgundy and a box of Havana cigars, and proposed a final toast to our victory. General Jackson remained as our guest that night, confident that he could rest, while I left with Major Latour to inspect the lines. My artillery was well organized in a solid, steadfast line of batteries.

I stopped soldiers on the road, inquiring if they were well outfitted and equipped. After a short rest in the morning, I spent Tuesday and Wednesday with the Creole militia removing a large number of the inhabitants from dangerous sectors of the city. From there I went to Barataria to inspect my reserve stores. I then sent word to General Jackson that all was in readiness for the annihilation of the British.

The following morning, Sunday, January 8, I was awakened before dawn. I could hear the roaring of cannons in the distance. I quickly crossed the river. When I arrived at the rear of our artillery, I had been running so fast in the brushwood and mud that I was exhausted and out of breath. My hands were bruised, my clothes soiled and torn, and my feet soaking wet. I could hardly believe my eyes when I arrived at the front lines. My brother Alexander, as the most expert marksman in the battery, had with one shot knocked the English General Pakenham from his horse, tearing off both his legs. He died two hours later.

With Pakenham's death, the British army lost its head. We cut down wave after wave of infantry with our cannons. Never could I have guessed that the battle would be of such short duration. The battlefield spectacle we beheld was horrible. There were three thousand wounded and dead English soldiers on that marshy battlefield, a dreadful and ghastly sight. We had lost only one hundred men, six of them my own. General Jackson himself marveled at the marksmanship of my cannoneers, under the command of my brother Alexander and my Uncle Reyne, who stood covered with mud and fatigued from want of sleep.

The first news had already arrived to the city, informing the citizens that our cannons had vanquished the enemy. By the middle of the afternoon, those who had left the city began to feel convinced that New Orleans was really safe and were returning to their homes.

After all the hardships and uncertainties the people of New Orleans had suffered, they now felt assured of security and began to assemble at the Place D'Armes to celebrate the great victory. When I awoke in the morning, I saw the Place D'Armes crowded with people. An arch of triumph supported by Corinthian columns was gaily decorated with greens and flowers. Bands were playing the "Marseillaise," and the bells of the Cathedral St. Louis rang. Between the arch and the cathedral door stood two lines of maidens, clothed in white with blue veils and sashes representing all the states and territories. Citizens dressed their children as cherubs and gave them laurel wreaths to bestow upon those who had fought in the defense of New Orleans. The church clergy, too, put on festive vestments. Guns were fired, fireworks displayed, and dancing and banqueting were organized in the squares.

Many of my artillerymen were highly praised during these festivities, and we accepted these honors in good faith. My joy was greatly increased to see my two beloved brothers and some of my officers, who only days before had been prisoners in the Cabildo, accused of piracy, marching past me in the parade. Now not only were they liberated, but because of them the British enemy had been crushed. Now they were admired, praised, and honored for their valor as expert cannoneers. Even General Jackson referred to us now as privateers—not "banditti from hell," as my intelligence officers reported he once called us.

The streets were crowded with people until late in the evening. Wine flowed freely, the women of every color were in a lusty mood, and the people shouted, "New Orleans has won the war!" As my Baratarians had distinguished themselves on the battlefield, they now showed themselves second to none when it came to debauchery.

My brothers were hard at their own intemperances, but I was persuaded to attend the victory ball organized by General Jackson and Governor Claiborne at the French Exchange. Unfortunately I attracted a great deal of unwanted attention as one of the most prominent figures. Many ladies began to question me, even in the presence of their husbands. It was the first time that I had ever been in the midst of a large social gathering, and I was not accustomed to such crowds. Therefore I was very circumspect when engaged, and answered questions as briefly as possible because I did not want to reveal my life as a privateer. I was still worried about the retreating enemy, even more so about the continuation of our alliance with the Americans, when no longer motivated by the threat of English conquest. But there was one engagement that evening I could not escape, when Mrs. Claiborne cornered me out of earshot of the rest.

"What a surprise to find you here, Monsieur Clement!" she teased. "And when will my new encyclopedias arrive?"

"I believe the usual wait is nine months, Madame," I chided back.

"Ah, such a very long time to wait!" sighed my lady. "Perhaps I shall use the time to study the handbook of Lafitte."

"What a lady reads is her private matter, don't you agree? You know now who I am. To tell you on the previous occasion might have put you in the gravest danger."

"Mais oui, I know you," she shot back. "You are Jean Lafitte."

"Oui, I am Lafitte, the pirate!"

"My husband has hung you a thousand times in his dreams!"

We laughed, and returned to the others.

—

On the afternoon of January 26, 1815, my brothers and I went to visit General Jackson to discuss the matter of our property, which had been confiscated by the American officials in their raid on Barataria. Also present was our attorney, Mr. Edward Livingston, a distinguished New Orleans barrister, who had also acted as General Jackson's military secretary and translator during his stay in New Orleans. However, nothing was accomplished, as we awaited more information from Washington, which was then in the course of reconstruction from the damage done by the English during their attacks.

At length a proclamation was made by President Madison dated February 6, 1815, as an official warrant of pardon, dropping of charges, and a remission of penalties on the grounds that my men and I had rendered good and loyal service to the country. My men and I appreciated the pardon and accepted it in good faith. Yet to my brothers and me it sounded hollow. No mention was made of the material help I had donated to the American cause, nor a single word spoken about the disposition of the merchandise being held.

Meanwhile General Jackson proclaimed martial law in the city on the grounds of precautions against another invasion by the English, who had probably not yet completely evacuated the country. But the French-speaking population believed that martial law was only a pretext concocted by General Jackson to exercise his authority over them. The prominent Creole businessmen and officials of the city were annoyed and displeased by the many unjust arrests occurring under martial law.

The increasing number of demands for his resignation provoked General Jackson's temper, until he ordered all the French population, including the French consul, to leave the city. When the *Louisiana Gazette* published the British peace treaty on Tuesday, February 28, with the final assurance that all danger was over, General Jackson ordered the arrest of the editor and author of the article, Mr. Louis Louaillier, who was also a member of the state legislature. However, Judge Hall of the United States Court of Appeals granted a habeas corpus to Mr. Louaillier, and General Jackson's anger exploded. He had Judge Hall arrested too, court-martialed Mr. Louaillier as a spy, and had them both deported from New Orleans.

Three days later salvos from cannons announced that the peace treaty had been signed by the president of the United States. The French Council and all the French population returned and openly manifested their contempt toward General Jackson with defiant deeds—and, I may add, vulgar gestures. Bands played and dancers paraded beneath his very windows. A wild celebration such as must have put the stiff general's hair on end followed the removal of martial law, and hundreds of charges were filed in civil courts against the general for scorning the laws and rights of New Orleans citizens. This wave of resentment was so intense that the people haled him from the courtroom and threatened to string him up. I speedily sent my own men into the streets to protect him from bodily harm.

Later, with tears in his eyes, General Jackson assured us that this rescue would never be forgotten. However, he was a weak and vacillating man, inclined to forget past favors. The valuable assistance I had rendered him when his very life was endangered by the mob was soon forgotten. It reminded me of what our grand-mère taught us: you can always form an opinion of a person by his reaction to your own generosity. If a man abuses your generosity, then he is not worth confiding your trust in or associating with.

Although my lawyers carried my suit to the Supreme Court in Washington, I was alert to the possibility of the Americans selling my ships and merchandise. The auction unfolded as a carefully planned game to spread yet again the insulting misnomer of pirate. False claims that Baratarians had stolen American cargo and jewels were lodged against me, designed to provoke the withdrawal of my lawsuit. When this stratagem failed, the auction sale was hastily advertised and carried out in a flash, before the courts could act in our favor.

I began to see that the results of my alliance with the Americans at the Battle of New Orleans would be contrary to my hopes. My men and I never dreamed that those for whom we had fought would treat us so contemptuously and unjustly—that justice could be so deformed in the birthplace of the Declaration of Independence. Whether traveling or at home, I now always hoisted the American flag. I considered myself a citizen of the United States, and had amply demonstrated my loyalty to the nation. But I was left to wonder if any nation state could be trusted. For won't they all sell out the truth for what is perceived as the higher interest of the nation, which is often only the private ambitions of its officials and elites? When I saw how it was with the Americans, I could only recall the words of my dear Grand-mère Nadrimal, when she said, "Equal justice is found only in the graveyard."

—

I had no more time to be involved in legal affairs. I had never desired to hire an attorney, much less to know one. My occupation had always been upon the ocean, cruising the Main with a fast ship under rig. I was powerful on the seas, but on land I had no military forces. Therefore in 1816 I decided to continue my mission as a corsair on the high seas in order to help the revolutionaries of Mexico and Texas in their struggles for independence against Spain. I left Louisiana with the warning fresh in my mind that eventually I would have to deal with American armies led by so-called generals who would endanger my communes, and even my career as a corsair.

After the wars between Napoleon and England, confusion and poverty reigned in Europe. Many who had served loyally in the armies of Napoleon became refugees and had to flee the Continent. After Napoleon's defeat, King Ferdinand of Spain regained his throne, but the Spanish cyclops had very few areas of possible expansion apart from holding its provinces in South America, which were fighting for their independence. The Mexican Republicans were most active in trying to occupy Texas as a preliminary to liberating Mexico.

My Uncle Reyne suggested that my brother Pierre and I should visit incognito the agents of Spain in New Orleans and Havana, in order to gather intelligence on how to establish a new port, where our vessels could sail in and out without risk of encountering the naval ships of royalist Spain. Posing as merchant-adventurers eager to do business at Spanish ports, but worried for the security of our ships and cargoes, we dined with the Spanish vice consul in New Orleans. There we learned that the king of Spain had sent instructions to disperse all *piratas* from the Gulf. But as the king had neglected to send a fleet of war to back up the ouster, there was a need for someone to carry out the monarch's plan.

"Sacre bleu!" Pierre said as soon as we were in the street. "Don't you see? We can play a game of confidence with the Spanish Crown!"

A game of confidence meant cozenage or fraudulent schemes. Pierre was always clever in such stratagems. He had decided to tweak the stupid nose of the Castilian king. We immediately set sail for Havana and offered our services to Spain as determined royalist privateers. We would provide ships and fighting men to disperse the piratas in the name of Spain. To authenticate our good intentions, we thereupon enlisted in the Spanish intelligence service as agents Nos. 13-1 and 13-2. We swore an oath to inform on those conspiring against the Crown and its sickly legislative cortes.

By this subterfuge we got the Spanish captain general of Havana to advance us large sums under the pretext of outfitting a small, swift, well-armed fleet to help the Spanish defend their colonies against the Mexican *independentistas*—and against corsairs like us! We agreed to sail secretly out of New Orleans for Galveston Island on the coast of Texas, where we would lure in the pirates cruising the Gulf one by one, wiping them out.

With the funds advanced to us by the Spaniards, we were nearly compensated for the loss of our twenty-six ships to the Americans. I had built in Charleston the fastest vessel on the sea, fitted with the best and most modern apparatus. It was painted dark brown and named the *Jupiter*. In her I knew I could outrun the fastest cutter or sloop of war.

We left the port of New Orleans on March 16, 1817, in our new ships, and arrived off Galveston on March 23. I anchored the *Jupiter* outside the bar guarding the harbor, and found there six ships, not including Pierre's. Among them, to our delight, was a Spanish schooner captured by the corsair vessel *General Arismendi*. And who was the master of the *General Arismendi* but our own infamous Uncle Reyne Baluche, recently commissioned as a privateer against Spain by General Simón Bolívar in Venezuela, and flying the flag of the United Colonies of South America.

Among the other corsairs awaiting us in harbor at Galveston was our old comrade Jonny Barbe en Feu—Captain "Beard-on-Fire," Redbeard to the Americans—who had been indicted by a New Orleans federal grand jury, along with Pierre, for piracy. Now, however, this same audacious Captain Redbeard commanded the armed sloop *Congreso Mexicano* under commission from the fledgling Mexican Republic.

When Uncle Reyne heard the delicious story of how we had beaten Spain at a game of confidence, he laughed till his sides ached and tears rolled down his face. To make it all the sweeter, our comrade Capt. Barbe en Feu proposed that we should hold a banquet and jointly sign a document of fealty to the Mexican Republic. Luckily his ship *Congreso Mexicano* was laden with fine foods and wines for just such a revel—all captured Spanish cargoes, of course. After our splendid maneuver we felt like celebrating, and stayed there two weeks in riotous rejoicing, for it cannot be wrong in the eyes of the Deity, who bestowed the pleasures of this life upon the earth, to enjoy the same. Many a drunken sailor danced on the deck of the forecastle, and many an African wench gained her freedom dancing for an inebriated sailor belowdecks. Each night the torches blazed and the wine flowed; each day the flies buzzed and the snores rang out as sailors slept off their prodigious drinking bouts on the beach under the trees.

On April 15, 1817, we swore allegiance to the Mexican Republic, formally organizing our new commune under the name Campeachy, with its citizens recruited from corsairs, adventurers, and our French refugees. All our people were gathered on the *Jupiter* for this ceremony. I had the steward open casks of rum and proposed the following toast: "Today we are all comrades together, and we act as one. Our brotherhood is our birthright as free men to associate, assemble, and unite. We will never surrender those rights willingly."

"Vive la fraternité!" they shouted.

"Fraternity," I went on, "means comradeship, friendliness, and the willingness to help one another. It is the very spirit of unselfishness and love for one's fellow men counseled by the world's religions. But those religions revere a God they have never seen, yet deny their brothers, whom they see every day. We corsairs have not only attained that brotherly love, but we also get to drink the finest wines and screw the plumpest wenches!"

"Vive la fraternité! Vive le bos!" they chanted in time.

Meeting in secret, we submitted our document to the Mexican Congress, which commissioned Campeachy as a Mexican port of entry, appointed me as provisional governor, and established a court of admiralty to legally dispose of our captured prizes and to settle disputes. On the faith of our Mexican letters of marque, my accredited vessels became active in Texas and Mexico, bringing back ships they captured to our new commune.

The Spanish royalists were royally deceived. While we were overhauling every Spanish galleon for gold and silver, the captain general of Havana was sending us our pay each month as mercenaries fighting the piratas. I regularly drafted my reports to him in my own hand, signed them "Agent 13-2," and sent them by secret messengers up the back way of Bayou Lafourche to New Orleans. We had agents and many plantation customers along Bayou Lafourche for the slaves taken off Spanish ships.

I could not imagine why, but the Spanish ambassador to Washington, Luis de Onis, became suspicious of us. He sharply asked the American Secretary of State John Quincy Adams about the growing population of French immigrants on the coast of Texas, asserting that Texas was still a Spanish province. We did not find out until later that the United States was claiming Texas for itself. We had no idea that our operations were beginning on American territory.

The Spanish ambassador raised such fiery protests that at length the Americans were obliged to invite the Lafittes to Washington to explain our enterprise. Pierre—wearing his presidential pardon, as it were, on his sleeve—went to Washington on our behalf and met with Mr. Adams. The secretary of state did not make much ado about our commune Campeachy, but he said that there were powerful forces in Washington ready to abandon democratic ideals and pounce on Texas. He informed Pierre that he knew our corsairs were also capturing British vessels, and that this must stop because it violated the American peace treaty with England. Mr. Adams warned that any American forces sent to Galveston Island would undoubtedly enforce the American claim to Texas, and that this would go hard against our business interests.

We surmised that he was telling the same to the Spanish ambassador De Onis, who no doubt also would not desire an American intervention in Texas.

Our vessels were making profitable runs between Mobile, New Orleans, and Galveston, declaring false destinations in New Orleans, then smuggling goods through other ports, cheating the customs of New Orleans. Even after the Americans purchased Louisiana, New Orleans remained the best port for privateers—the easiest port in America, for that matter, and the first city of the New World in my own eyes. Aboard my ship the *Jupiter* every other barrel remained empty, ready to hold gold, silver, silk, and other precious materials, or bronze and wrought-iron articles bound for other ports on the Atlantic coast.

Pierre and I were kept extremely busy by our new enterprise. As Grand-mère used to say, we had to "sleep fast." We captured Spanish cargo vessels coming into Veracruz, Tampico, and other Mexican ports each week, as well as Spanish vessels leaving Havana. Goods flowed into the port of Galveston in pleasing proportions. My captains were bringing me large quantities of money, precious metals, black slaves, and goods of all kinds. They had to fight many battles on the high seas, and some of them disappeared with cargoes rather than share their captures according to the rules of my commune. I let all of them know that I would not accept such treachery. Officers caught smuggling on their own account faced the alternatives of the court of admiralty or a duel with me.

I was thirty-six years old at the time my commune Campeachy began to flourish. I was an expert duelist, and no one alive could handle a sword as well. Many will ask how many duels I have had, and how I have been able to come out the victor in all. I have fought and won seventeen duels. Most were easy. My method in any struggle with a sword is to look straight into the eyes of the opponent, never at the point of his sword. The hands can always deceive the eye, but the eyes are the reflection of the inner self. I always try to determine my opponent's next move by his way of looking at me. All my opponents in duels sooner or later revealed some small inferiority, suggesting to me an opening. I fought my duels as I have led my life—always alert and fearless, ready to grasp opportunities, moving ahead rapidly, not wasting time. I do not always consider it necessary to kill my opponent, and derive no satisfaction from the taking of a man's life. However, as Grand-mère taught us, dead men don't tell tales. In all my duels, twelve rivals have not lived to talk.

By the end of 1818, Campeachy numbered nearly one thousand *citoyens* and serviced corsairs with letters of marque from five nations. Sailors of all nationalities, races, languages and faiths received warm welcome in our harbor. We gave shelter to refugees from European injustice and victims of New World oppression, who had fled their own countries and come to ours seeking safety, prosperity, and progress. With us any man could bury his past and start afresh as long as he always acted with honor among us. We asked no questions, but only bid that newcomers join our loyal band of brothers and live according to natural and divine laws. For we hold that men treated in fairness and equity will live in amity with one another. In this way Campeachy became like the melting pot in a blacksmith's forge, where all varieties of men were wrought into a new man for the New World.

Unfortunately the American officials in Washington were bound by their new treaties with the European powers. They investigated the question of French refugees, not knowing the exact place of their debarkation, because the Texas coast was not officially in the territory of the United States, nor even under its supervision. At this time, however, American merchants beginning in business in the ports of the Gulf were receiving loans to finance their commerce from private banks in England. To protect their financial connections and business interests, these merchants set up a clamor against privateering. Spain was increasing its trade and commercial exchanges with the United States, too, spending large sums of money to persuade the government to get rid of privateers.

The American nation was still young, but the future was already revealing itself. It was the beginning of steamships. Newspapers were being read by a greater number of people, and naturally the papers profited by printing scandalous publicity about my commune.

One false tale in particular did great damage to the reputation of my own home, Maison Rouge. This concerned the wife of the Spanish Count Montefusco, the so-called "Señora Blanca," the Spanish Lady in White. This young gentlewoman was sailing to Peru by way of Havana and Darien to join her husband aboard the Spanish merchantman *Gravitas,* when taken prisoner by one of my captains and returned with the ship to Galveston harbor. Brought to me, I beheld a vision swathed in white. Her years were but few—perhaps no more than twenty or twenty-two—but her beauty was so great that I doubt whether in all Europe any could be found to surpass her perfections. Her long hair shone black as a raven's plumes, while her lips were red as rubies. Her dark eyes sparkled with the most charming and naive anger, for no sooner had she appeared before me than she delivered this resolute declaration: "Monsieur, my life is in your hands. But as to the lasciviousness and concupiscence you practice as a brigand and pirate, why, my soul shall sooner be separated from my body through the violence of your arms than I shall condescend to your bestial desires. Therefore may you imprison me in your darksome and stinking cellar, for God Almighty will bless and preserve me."

"My dear lady, I have no intention of putting you in any cellar," I replied with mild humor, for anyone could see she had been milk-fed on horror stories. "Nor is there need at the present time to consider the separation of your body and soul. For it is not our custom at Campeachy to have designs on a woman's chastity, neither by force nor by guile. Whoever put these wild notions into your head is guilty of striking useless terror into the pure heart of an innocent and charming lady. We do not deign here to corrupt virtue any more than to enforce it, but only to let each one live according to his own private pleasures, whatever they might be. I myself was a happily married man, with daughters who would perhaps be as old as yourself, if a Spanish war sloop had not abducted my wife and children and tortured them to death. Nevertheless, I seek no personal revenge; I guarantee you will be perfectly safe here and treated with the utmost respect."

Then I assigned her to lodge in an apartment in Maison Rouge, giving her a Negress to wait upon her, and commanded she take her victuals at my own table. The afflicted woman begged that she be treated as any other prisoner, for she feared such kindness might prove a subterfuge. She said she had heard from her husband and relatives that we were not men but beasts and heretics, who neither invoked the Blessed Trinity nor believed in Jesus Christ.

I dismissed her with civility, not remarking openly upon the combination of resolute heart, ignorant gullibility, fierce pride, and heedless piety that make up the Spanish aristocrat's character. I had already decided to turn the tables on her husband, who had no doubt filled his young wife's head with so much grotesque foolishness.

In the weeks that followed I saw Señora Blanca at table each day and always treated her with courtesy, despite her habit of praying before meals to God Almighty for "constancy and patience against the cruelties and wickedness of Captain Jean Lafitte." Nor did I fail to keep her informed of her situation, which was that of any other enemy prisoner taken in war. We sent letters to her husband, the Count, apprising him of the bond he should post for her unconditional release. I read these letters to her; like many Spanish aristocrats, my Lady Montefusco was illiterate.

At first this lady kept up her vituperation. I did not demean myself to debate, but instead showed her all the hospitality I could, offering her the most succulent of fresh seafoods and the best wines in my larder. From time to time I entertained her with stories of my sea adventures, or engaged her in conversation. Little by little her intelligence won out, as she saw firsthand the nature of all the false accusations against me. As the weeks and months passed with no reply from Count Montefusco, it began to dawn on Señora Blanca that perhaps her husband was not so eager for her return as he was to blacken my name and the reputation of my commune. I did not have to encourage her in these surmises, but only to befriend her and let nature take its course. As my grand-mère had long ago shown, example is the best teacher. Admitted to my confidence and treated with temperance and truthfulness as one of my own family, the Lady in White succumbed to a conversion so steep that one evening at supper she volunteered herself as my mistress and begged that I never send her back to that cruel master her husband, whom she now despised and reviled. I was careful, as always, to say nothing, but accepted her new loyalty and affection with a bow and expression of deep gratitude.

In order to demonstrate her complete scorn for her erstwhile spouse, Señora Blanca cut her hair short and adopted the new habit of wearing my own white shirts, with a fiery red sash round her waist. By constant urging she ultimately convinced me to give her lessons in the art of fencing, and took to wearing a sword at her hilt, as I do. It was a dashing and different figure that Señora Blanca cut now than when she had first arrived at Galveston Island!

Imagine then our surprise and outrage when we received from our commissioners in Washington word that the American newspapers in the East were retailing the scandalous story of a Spanish lady taken prisoner by the pirate Jean Lafitte. According to the story in the press, this Señora Blanca had been instantly designed for the voluptuous pleasure of Captain Lafitte, whose "false civility soon turned into barbarous cruelty to enjoy the accomplishment of his lusts." The story said that as soon as Lafitte understood the resolution of her mind, he supposedly commanded her to be stripped of her apparel, and allowed her an extremely small quantity of meat and drink, wherewith her life was nearly extinguished before she was forced to accept the many hard and vile usages the pirate thrust upon her chastity without compassion. And all these events were reported as related by an eyewitness, who remained anonymous!

Though I wished to file a lawsuit to defend my reputation in open court, my lawyers advised me instead to release Señora Blanca immediately before the American public howled for military intervention to benefit her cause. This I did, though with regret; she had been free to leave for many months, but had always chosen to stay at Campeachy. Yet when Contess Montefusco traveled to Washington of her own volition, determined to correct the fraudulent impressions spread by the scandalmongers, she was neither allowed to tell the truth nor even received at the offending newspapers' offices. We were entering a new age that would judge a man by the image of his appetites, not by his accomplishments.

—

All these harassments were beginning to cordon my plans and stifle my dreams. But in spite of all obstacles, the commune was flourishing and everything going according to our wishes prior to the hurricane that struck Galveston Island almost without warning in September 1818. The men scarcely had time to make fast the ships in harbor and evacuate all the women and children to the upper story of my Maison Rouge when the storm howled across the waters and smashed Campeachy with terrifying force. When the devastating wind finally died down, we could see that the damage was immense. A number of men had been drowned, some of the women injured; most of the vessels in harbor had capsized and overturned; quantities of food were spoiled, many buildings destroyed.

The ruin and devastation were nearly complete. All my energies had to be directed to assisting the people to rebuild their homes, shops, and storehouses. I felt especially obliged to the many French settlers we had brought to settle there, all ruined by the storm. In consequence I neglected my own interests. My officers, though honest, were too liberal in distributing letters of marque. This opened the way to temptation and corruption. The foolish behavior of Captain George Brown in particular resulted in further damaging exposure of our operations to Washington. He had led his men to capture an American vessel, bringing it back to Galveston.

When word of the crime reached the American schooner *Lynx,* patrolling the Gulf, she set sail immediately for Galveston harbor. The officer in command, Lieutenant Macintosh, came ashore and demanded that I give up Brown and his men for punishment by the Louisiana authorities.

"You may have the men," I told him calmly. "But you are too late for Brown. I hung him."

I led him to the spot where Brown's body still swung from the gallows. He had been tried, convicted of piracy against the United States, and strung up by the neck, according to the laws of admiralty. I assured the American officer that this would be our commune's treatment of all those who defied the ideas of Thomas Jefferson and the deeds of Napoleon Bonaparte. The *Lynx* left Galveston harbor with the carcass of Brown still swaying in the wind, a forceful demonstration to the Americans of how the bos of Campeachy dealt with criminals. I have never feared the Spanish or the English, but I always dreaded a confrontation with the United States, with its vast land forces and the Puritan blindness of American officials to the Latin way of doing things.

Nevertheless, because of Captain Brown, my name was once again before the public in Washington. I was accused of having established a new "nest of pirates" on United States territory. The Spanish representative now complained bitterly to President Monroe about our enterprise, leading the American government to believe that my armed communards constituted a danger to the territorial borders. He urged the Americans repeatedly to banish me to some province in South America. At length I received notice again to come to Washington and challenge the charges against me. Pierre, several officers, and I left for Washington on the advice of our lawyers.

There I immediately went to see the American secretary of state, Mr. John Quincy Adams. He was then about fifty-one years old. He received me with much kindness and consideration. I presented my case on the grounds that no one had ever disputed my possession of Galveston Island. I had acted only to offer refuge to armed vessels of the Mexican Party of

Independence; and to establish a just and secure homeland for the many French refugees forced to flee their homes. I resolutely repeated my continuing intention to come to the aid of the United States, as I had at the Battle of New Orleans, if circumstances again required it. I told the secretary of state that I had promulgated the strictest orders to respect the American flag, but that Mr. de Onis and private bankers were putting American cargoes aboard Spanish ships in order to confuse my captains and create public outrage. I had hanged more than one brigand convicted of piracy at my commune, and pleaded my prior ignorance of the American government's intention to claim the Texas coast from the Sabine River to the Rio Bravo. I said that whatever he decided my fate might be, I gave the government the full assurance of my obedience, and my entire resignation to its will.

To speak bluntly, I failed in my mission to Washington. Perhaps it came too late. Shortly after my return to Galveston, we learned of President Monroe's doctrine avowing the supremacy of American national interest in the Latin American nations, a catastrophe for both parties that will haunt them forever. For when Spain and England withdraw their forces from the Gulf and the Caribbean, as some day both nations are bound to do, there will be nothing to balance the puissance of the American nation. What happened to Greece, what happened to Rome, the Americans will not avoid in Latin America.

On learning of Monroe's doctrine, I knew the United States could never allow free communes like ours to survive. It would set a "bad example" to the whole hemisphere. Better to forget the ideals of Thomas Jefferson and the warnings against foreign entanglements of George Washington.

The hostility of the American government toward Campeachy made it even more difficult to maintain discipline among the corsairs. Many demanded payment in gold. One by one the United States negotiated treaties with the emerging governments of the Spanish Main and South America, revoking rights and duties under letters of marque. Commissioned privateers were becoming almost nonexistent, and the fluid situation in the Gulf was an open invitation to piracy. Then, too, after the hurricane, the French population of my colony decreased as they moved inland along the Sabine River into Louisiana Territory, where they were subject to the laws of the United States. Regrettably, I was finally obliged to recognize that if I did not withdraw from Galveston Island, the U.S. government would deliver an ultimatum and declare war on us. After my experience at Barataria, we could be certain of the outcome.

On Sunday, January 7, 1821, a warship appeared near the port at sunset. At first my officers and I thought it a Spanish sloop. One of my captains went out in a rowboat to ascertain the flag colors of the ship, and returned to report that it was the *Enterprise,* a United States warship. How ironic, I remarked, that a ship so named should arrive to quash the very idea of free enterprise we had fostered at Campeachy.

By early next morning it was evident that either the Americans could not navigate the bars, or else feared a hostile reception. Therefore I sent a small boat to escort the officers into port. Lieutenant Kearney disembarked and was shown to Maison Rouge, which was still under reconstruction from the damage of the hurricane. I shook hands with him. He appeared very cordial, and seemed saddened when he had to read the eviction notice from the American government ordering me to leave Galveston Island. I saluted and bowed my head as a sign of respect for the orders, and displayed no resentment. I had already decided to accept the ultimatum of the United States to leave Galveston. For Spain the game was nearly up in Texas; there was no opposing the American future there. An independent Mexico could in no way defend herself against American encroachment.

As for my family, we moved constantly, like the world on its axis. Pierre feared being arrested again, having received a warning. He left for Savannah and then Charleston, only to leave there again, traveling under an assumed name. My brother Alexander was not in good health because of serious injuries he suffered in 1814, when the vessel *Sine Qua Non* capsized near the Mexican coast. His last voyage had been to accomplish the escape of Napoleon from the island of Elba in the early spring of 1815. Since the failure of that venture he had been providing valuable secret services in New Orleans, where he was still notorious for his expert marksmanship as a gunner when he had killed all those English officers on their horses. Uncle Reyne, twelve years Alexander's senior, was also a veteran of the Napoleonic wars and hero of the Battle of New Orleans. He was still enjoying good health, and now commanded the fleet of General Bolívar in Venezuela.

It was my duty as bos to conclude all our affairs at Campeachy. I stood ready to aid those who needed help, and promised I would furnish them all with vessels and let them choose wherever they wished to go. I began to have all the houses emptied, and placed all belongings such as furniture, or anything else of value, in one place. I divided everything among the people of the commune. I had no intention of leaving anything for the greedy scavengers from New Orleans and Mobile, whom I knew had already made their private arrangements with American officials. Most of our families went north to settle near the banks of the Sabine River.

The greatest part of the work was finished by Saturday, February 24. On Sunday I suggested to all those staying on that we decorate the graves of our comrades in arms who had died in battle. We reduced two bars of gold and scattered the dust over the graves, that it might land or travel with the winds, as nature decreed. I spent two hours on that beautiful Sunday with my people, taking one last walk on the paths west of my commune. During our stroll, I gave my final instructions to the men. I told those staying on in Texas not to plan a revolution until the right moment arrived.

"Texas will be American," I declared. "As for me, I never wish to come back to Texas, nor to New Orleans, Mobile, or any part of the United States. I am more interested in Cuba. Havana is the Spanish base for the suppression of the Mexican provinces. Whatever happens, I will always be at war with the Spanish dogs and the English beasts. Let us travel to all the ends of the earth, to organize the humble and topple despots from their thrones. I will always wish for a universal change of man toward man. My intention is to embrace every cause of liberty, to snatch away kingdoms from monarchs. Vive la liberté!"

"Vive la liberté!" they all cried.

"This Sunday will always remain in my memory," I vowed. "Let's make it a farewell celebration—a souvenir and a promise of our eternal brotherhood. Let's drink one more time, for while this day lasts, we are still comrades together, one for all and all for one."

"Vive le Capitain!" they chorused as of old.

I continued, "Our commune was founded to perpetuate a new form of government, to prevent any one individual from reaching the pinnacle of absolute power, with an assurance of equality for all and no special privileges for any. If anyone knows of one instance when I or any of our officers have abused the popular will, let him now step forward and testify. We all grieve at the disappearance of our utopia, in whose formation we have spent so many years. Our efforts at Barataria and Galveston will remain fresh in our minds for life, even though we know that history will try to blacken our names and pervert our deeds. Hang the historians!" I cried.

"To the gallows with the lying dogs!" the people responded.

"Only idealists know what ought to happen," I said. "In my family we were taught to struggle against the restrictive laws of governments, which use the churches as a tool to subjugate the people. Most of my officers have been agnostics, but others Catholic, Jewish, and even followers of the prophet Mohammed. Harmony has always reigned among us, and religious quarrels are unknown. On silver coins is engraved the motto 'In God We Trust,' but illiterate citizens are easily taught to adore the money and blindly neglect that sacred inscription.

"We know from personal experience that all governments are changed and displaced through cycles of time. A new doctrine or manifesto will some day overthrow England. Spain has lost its grip. Even the United States will learn some day that as the sun reaches its zenith, it is already beginning to descend.

"But where will men like us go if rebels lose their cause? Where will we draw our cutlasses to break the chains of oppression, if the world falls to the scheming bankers and corrupt politicians? Let us never regret the sacrifices or losses we may suffer to bring about the revolutions of the world. May future generations have life, liberty, happiness, success, love, peace, and tranquility to reign over them to the end of time."

The work was finished; the party ended. Next day our communards departed. One by one the ships found the channel, sailing out of the harbor and across the bar. With canvas slack in the soft spring breeze, they vanished on the horizon. I invited Lieutenant Kearney and all his crew on board my ship the *Jupiter* for dinner. My brig was the sole remaining vessel. At table I was asked many questions, to which I replied briefly. I informed them that Campeachy would be burned.

Everyone left the island at four o'clock. The sky brightened and a breeze came from the northwest. Alone, I left the *Jupiter* and went ashore in a small rowboat. I set the torch myself to Maison Rouge. Soon a roaring flame swept Campeachy and blazed along the shoreline. My ships head south, on a mission that must remain secret. Seven leagues out to sea, I can still see Galveston on fire, looking like a sunset.

Africatown, Children

For all her grandchildren and great-great-grandchildren, for the descendants of the last slave ship, *Clotilde,* and all other slave ships, and for the once-and-future queens of Africa who sailed up Mobile Bay, and every other bay, in chains, this is the true story of Africatown, USA, told as it only could be by Mama Lulu, matriarch of one hundred years if she's a day, and still full of piss and vinegar, bless the spacious spheres of her heart. Widow of a railroad man, high deaconess of the Union Baptist Church, stationed on her porch rocker in the eternal Gulf Coast summer of her days, barking orders to the generations of children behind the screen door, who all want a piece of Mama Lulu's cherry pie and a glass of milk at the table in her back kitchen—one way she has maintained her power down through the years. A whistle sails through the golden gap between her front teeth as she laughs; she pats down the fringe of her dress over her great dignified bosom and prepares to testify.

Listen up, now; she ain't going to tell you twice.

———

"I am talking to you 'bout Africatown, now, children, on the outskirts of Mobile, Alabama. About Africatown, out past the old Gulf & Central freightyard, on a little spit of land they call Magazine Point, where they used to keep the city's munitions in slavery times—until one time they exploded. About Africatown, where us descendants of the slave ship *Clotilde* reside. The *Clotilde,* the last slave ship to ever land in American waters. About Africatown, where us writ the American Book of Exodus, black ink on the red shores of this Gulf Coast.

"I am talking about Africatown, children, on summer mornings so hot the bullfrogs are sleeping late, way down in the wet leaves, and the catfish slinking way down deep, in the cool river mud. Africatown, with the morning glories trellising wild, and the blackberry vines creeping up the back alleys behind the shotgun houses, and the fig bushes spicy in bloom. Talking 'bout Bay Bridge Road in the red dawn light, where our people are tending their kitchen gardens of speckled butter beans and corn, collard greens and gumbo. That was Ossie Keeby's garden, long time gone. Uncle Cudjo Lewis's garden. And my mama's garden, with the Cherokee roses my daddy planted for her there." Mama Lulu juts out her jaw. "Hear me, and don't you never forget!"

"Mama Lulu, she is clear as a bell!" exclaims one of her grandnieces, in the living room behind the screen door. They speak of her now, of their love for her, in her presence, as if she will live forever, so you might just as well go ahead and say it anyhow.

"We are all Africans here," says Mama Lulu. "Ossie Keeby. Cudjo Lewis. Kazooma Leviston. Josephine Lee. Saw Johnson. Jabez the Doctor. Ossie Allen. And Uncle Charley—everyone knew *him* so long he didn't need a last name. All full-blood Africans, and property owners, and raised up thirty-six children among them right here, all healthy, and I'm the last one of that generation left alive—a full-blooded African!

"My daddy was Polee Allen," says Mama Lulu. "And here's how he told me us Africans came here. It all began way back in 1858 before the Civil War, when Tim Meaher, who was from Maine, owned a shipyard in the port of Mobile. They say he bet some friends big money he could build a slave ship so fast it could outrun the Navy, slave-running being illegal by then, though it was still slave time. That was Mr. Tim Meaher: he wagered a hundred thousand dollars that he could deliver a shipload of African slaves ahead of the federal cutters."

"It was only ten thousand dollars, Mama Lulu," someone says inside the screen door.

"*Only?* If you-all don't shut up in there, you ain't worth ten cents!

"So this Mr. Tim Meaher outfitted his fast schooner *Clotilde,* and dispatched her to Wydah on the West African coast under a Mobile captain, Captain William Foster was his name.

"Them old full-blood Africans, they didn't like to talk about Africa. My daddy said it broke his heart. But later on, before they died, when they saw they wouldn't never go back in this life, they loosened up some. According to what they told us descendants, there had been over a hundred of them in all, young men and women, that Captain Foster bought from the king of Dahomey at Wydah. They were all captured in slave raids when they were nineteen or twenty years of age.

"The most of us came from a tribe called Tarkars. We lived near the Kebo River—that's where the name Keebie comes from. We were farmers and fishermen—peaceable folks. Our land was rich and fruitful, with all kinds of vegetables in abundance. Corn, cotton, tobacco, and gumbo. Our pineapples grew without culture, the size of an old sugar loaf, and finely flavored. We had spices, pepper, and cinnamon, and honey, too. And all our industry was exerted to improve the blessings of nature, children. And everyone, even the women and children, were engaged in it. From our earliest years we worked side by side with our parents, for everyone had to contribute something to the common stock. We were unacquainted with idleness, children—you hear that? And we didn't live in fear of this sin or that want. Because when a body has things to do each morning, there's no time to worry 'bout what could have been or once was or might could be. The Tarkars believed in one Creator of all things, and that He lived in the sun and was girt round with a great belt. And that He never ate nor drank, but smoked a pipe, which was our own people's favorite luxury. The Creator governed all events—births, deaths, captivity, harvest, or famine. And when the sun crossed the line on the first morning of the first day of their year, all the people raised their rattles and shouted thanks to the skies and held up hands for blessing. Our people's tombs were a kind of small and solitary thatched house, where we attended those that passed, guarded them from bad spirits, pouring a little pure water on their graves to give them something to drink. Water, children, good pure water, mixing with our tears of loss. But as for eternity, I do not remember my daddy ever using that word. We live on in our children, and the good we do here on earth, amen."

"Amen!" from inside the screen door.

"They said the men had more than one wife in Africa, and that was true before the Africans came over here, but still and all it was a woman's world. Do you hear that?" Mama Lulu raises her voice, and her carved walking stick, and shakes it at anybody handy. "The woman was the boss! The woman head the family. And that's the way it should be!"

This is all Mama Lulu has to say on that subject.

"Go ahead and tell it, Mama Lulu!" shout her daughters inside the screen door.

"Those were trying times, children. Slavers and traders coming to the African coast, paying European goods to the chiefs for cargoes of slaves. Drums of war sounding, one people set against another to obtain prisoners and booty. Evil times, children, hard times.

"Now, our people's tillage was worked on a large plain or common, some hours' walk from the dwellings. All the neighbors went there in a body for self-defense. When our people went out to till the land, they not only went in one body, but carried their arms for fear of surprise—bows and arrows, javelins, and shields that covered a man from head to foot. They were all taught the use of weapons; even our women were warriors, and marched out to fight alongside the men. For our whole people was a kind of militia. Dangerous times, children. Every leaf and twig, every whispering breeze, conveyed a foe. And every foe a death.

Our villages had walls, with sharpened sticks all around, tipped with poison, to keep invaders out. But alas, one time when all our people was asleep, the rogues got over the walls and in a moment seized Tarkars from their beds. And without giving them time to cry out or make resistance, they stopped their mouths, tied their hands behind their backs, and run off with them to the nearest woods. They was carried on the left of the rising sun, through all different countries, through the big forests of Africa, till they arrived at the sea coast, where the slave ship *Clotilde* was riding high at anchor, waiting for its cargo.

"They were brought before the king of Dahomey there, children. They say he weighed five hundred pounds. He sat upon a throne made of skulls, set up on a pedestal of human bones, in a ceremonial square filled with poison snakes. They had to fall down on their knees in front of him, or he would kill them right there with his bare hands. And he had them thrown naked into a big pen, thousands of them crowded there together, all sunk down in dejection and sorrow, thinking they had fallen into a world of evil spirits and would all be killed.

"Captain Foster was not a bad man," says Mama Lulu. "I remember my daddy saying that. The Meahers were paying his wages. And as for the Meahers, like those Africans always said, if you can't say something nice about someone, don't say nothing! So they just didn't talk about Meaher. But with Captain Foster it was different. He came to visit us here in Africa-town later on, long after the Civil War, when I was a child. He said he was sorry for what had happened. Said if he'd known what a hornet's nest looked like, he never would have walked into one, because that's just what it was in Wydah back then.

And Foster told my daddy in his own words what happened when he went up before that ebony king of Dahomey.

"He said that when they anchored offshore, the sea was rolling at a fearful height, and they couldn't land their boats. So the king sent out his long boats, manned by twenty strong men, which darted through the waves like fish. On land they put Foster into a hammock with a shade canopy and carried him up into the city, which was several miles from shore. And when he got there, they put him up in the traders' shed, which was just a big roof to keep out the sun, where the slave traders would lay with any woman they chose. He had everything he wanted there—fresh fruits and meats, pastries and cool drinks, and children to fan him.

"Well, the next morning, they took him around Wydah to see the king, with his fifty priests and officials to transact his business. And the king of Dahomey asked Captain Foster how much he would pay. And Foster said he had nine thousand dollars in gold and a cargo of aguardente rum, and he would pay one hundred dollars a head. The king laughed and had his priests surround Captain Foster. And all of them had pythons wrapped round their necks and draped over their arms. The king detained Foster for eight days, till Foster thought he was taken prisoner for sure. But he said his eight days wasn't wasted in Wydah. No, children, not wasted, because all that time he was storing up knowledge of the many sufferings it takes to make this world go around."

"Amen, Mama Lulu!" from inside the screen door.

"Until finally Foster agreed to pay one hundred twenty-five dollars," says Mama Lulu. "They took him down to their warehouse there, let him pick out the ones he wanted. My daddy remembered that. He said Captain Foster just let somebody else pick 'em out for him. He couldn't look them Africans in the eye! As for them Africans, they had never seen a white man before. To them, white was the color meant death. They thought he was some kind of demon. The king's slave drivers offered to brand them for Foster right there. But Captain Foster he shrank back in horror from that, and just said if they would get them out to his ship, he would pay them the gold and throw his cargo casks overboard, for he had got what he'd come for, and he'd seen all his eyes could take seeing.

"They took all them Africans Foster had purchased and they dragged them like meat down to the coast in chains. Sent them out twenty, thirty at a time in the boats, which would return with the caskets of rum. They was just getting the last but one bunch of captives on board the *Clotilde* when the crew spied a pirate ship coming to intercept them. It was a Portuguese man-of-war. And the crew was so frightened for their lives they wanted to abandon ship and swim to shore, every man for himself. But Foster told them he'd double their wages, whatever Mr. Meaher had agreed to pay them back in Mobile, if they'd only hoist the sails and outrun that man-of-war.

"They turned tail and got out of there, as though they were fleeing Satan himself! But there were still some of those Tarkars left on shore that never made it on board the *Clotilde*. One of them was 'Zuma Leviston's brother, and when she saw that ship weigh anchor without him, she fainted dead away on the deck of the *Clotilde*. She never saw her dear brother again on this side of life, children, because he was in the last line to get on the boats, and the last line didn't go. And so one child stayed in Africa and died a slave, and the other child came to America and died a free woman."

"That's how it was!" says a grandniece, but lets Mama Lulu continue.

"They said old Captain Foster didn't make them suffer on the ocean passage. He removed their chains and let them up on deck for fresh air. But when they tried to stand up on that roiling sea—oh, my Lord! They didn't know where they were. In Wydah, they thought they'd be killed for sure, and that was bad enough. But now they didn't know what to think. Who were these strange animals with the red faces and lank hair? Where were they taking them? What for?

"Then Saw Johnson said to all the Tarkars in their own tongue that it sure looked to him like, whoever they were, they'd more'n likely taken the Africans along for food, and they could all expect to get eaten. But Jabez the Doctor disagreed and said they were probably evil spirits taking them to the end of the earth, to throw them over, though he couldn't say why. But they all agreed on one thing: don't tell them your real name. It was their only chance. Whatever happens, children, keep your real name to yourself.

"Well, it was long weeks of not knowing. They knew what real fear was then, hunger, despair. But at least they had each other. That's what kept them alive. Until finally the *Clotilde* reached Mobile Bay in July 1859.

"They sent word to Mr. Meaher, 'The niggers are here!' It was a Sunday they tried to run that slave ship in, because the Naval officers would be in church. So the *Clotilde* could give the federal cutters the slip easy enough.

"Old Meaher had them wait for nightfall. His plan was to tow that ship up the river to a point near enough to his land he could unload and send those Africans on to market without anyone being the wiser. But the river was full of shoals, and the *Clotilde* struck a sandbar. They had to land those Africans any which way, in darkness and confusion. Some of them got carted off to the Selma market. But the Tarkars remembered how it went at the other end getting on board that ship, and this time they had the sense to get back there together in the last line. And Lord have mercy, in all that sound and fury, the last line didn't go.

"And when the sun rose next morning, there they were, hiding in the canebrakes of Magazine Point, just as naked as jaybirds.

"Well, for eleven nights and days they stayed there hiding. Didn't know where they was. Didn't know which way to turn. Didn't know if they was still on earth or not. Didn't know they was still alive or not. Then a circus happened to pass by, on its way north from Mobile to Birmingham. And lo and behold, miracle of miracles, that circus had a elephant. An African elephant, children! Big, slow-walking elephant jes' like the ones they knew at home.

"When the Africans heard that sweet elephant trumpet, Lord, it was music to their ears. They thought they was delivered back to Africa, safe and sound. Then they all came out of the canebrakes together. They lay down there by the side of the road and cried tears of joy to the good sweet earth. And on that very spot where their tears fell, children, why, Africatown was born."

A grandniece now brings Mama Lulu her glass of sweet iced tea. But it's too sweet for her, or not sweet enough. She takes one gulp, growls, and sends it back. She is not Mama Lulu for nothing.

"Us Africans settled down on this here place Magazine Point," she continues. "Meaher never claimed 'em. When the

Navy found the remains of the *Clotilde* and learned what happened, they charged Mr. Tim Meaher with slave-running, but they couldn't make it stick for lack of evidence. He was acquitted. No one knows if he ever collected his bet. Our people were too busy cutting down trees to plant corn and sweet potatoes to pay him much mind. War Between the States passed Africatown by. Us Africans didn't need the Emancipation Proclamation—already emancipated, in our exile and travail.

"Then one day after the Civil War, Uncle Cudjo Lewis was out in the woods cutting trees before planting when Mr. Tim Meaher came by on horseback. And he told Uncle Cudjo they were *his* trees, growing on *his* land, and that Uncle Cudjo shouldn't cut 'em down.

"Well, Uncle Cudjo knew just who he was dealing with, and he said to Meaher, 'Why don't you give us Africans some land? You got plenty, more than you ever need—and you *did* steal us from our homeland.'

"Mr. Meaher, he grinned and said, 'I don't own y'all. I ain't responsible for you, and I don't owe you nothin'. If you want land, you going to have to go ahead and buy it from me.'

"So they did," says Mama Lulu. "The men of Africatown went into the sawmills down by the river at a dollar and a half a week. They went down to the docks of Mobile, screwing those bales of cotton, loading them hundredweight bags of rice and sugar down in the sweltering holds where the sun never shines and it's hot as the fires of hell. They went to work the railroads, lining track, laying rails. And they went out to sea in ships in the Central American trade, 'long the coast of this big green continent. The women of Africatown took in wash, scrubbed floors, starched shirts. You'd see 'em in the streets of the city, carrying their bundles and baskets on their heads like they did in Africa, strong and proud, walking fast, working hard. And the children learned to cook. Lord have mercy if we didn't pull our share!

"My daddy worked at the mill from six in the morning till four in the afternoon. I'd bring him his dinner at noon. He'd always slip a few nails or something into the lunchpail I was carrying because the Africans were building their church back then. We had become baptized for Christians here. I laughed and told my daddy, 'Here you are a Christian building a church, and the first thing you do is go and steal nails!'

"Well, he picked me up with his one big strong hand, set me right on his shoulder, and said, 'We don't own anything here on earth, Mama Lulu, it all belongs to God.' Because they called me Mama Lulu from the day I was born, though no one could ever tell me why.

"Before my daddy and the other Africans built their church, they would go to someone's house to pray and sing. Wednesday, Friday, and Saturday evenings, us Africans all got together to pray and sing, and then on Sundays all day, with time out for dinner, and on into the evening. You never heard such praying and singing as there was in Africatown. The Lord wants to hears his children sing—that's why He gave us the gift of music!

"When my daddy'd come home from the mill after work, then all the men and children would tend the fields together. Everyone had their vegetable patch and their fruit trees, kept chickens, pigs, and milk cows. Banana trees grew everywhere round here back then. The finest satsuma oranges. But you never saw one of those old Africans eat a banana or an orange. That was only for the children. I think it made them homesick. And way down yonder by a place we called Rabbit Warren Tree, they had a big rabbit warren for the whole town. Maybe it isn't there anymore. They been building this place up so fast these days. And you could catch all the fish, crabs, and shrimps you wanted in the river.

"Then long 'bout evening, my mama would say to me, 'Mama Lulu, go tell your daddy his supper's ready.' So I'd run like a galloping pony out to find him in the fields, but he'd say, 'Mama Lulu, go tell your mama I can eat by lamplight, but I can't do the planting by lamplight.' He'd stay out in the fields till way past dark, and I'd stay right there with him till we come home to Mama's supper.

"Everyone in Mobile knew the Africans back then, and most of 'em knew the story of how we got here, due to the evil foolishness caused by Mr. Meaher. We owned our own land, we grew everything here and sold our produce in town. My daddy sold dairy, too. He'd put that old horse in front of the wagon, and we'd climb right up and ride into town together. When the motor car came in, we bought one after a while. My brother was around twenty then, and he was supposed to drive it into town with the produce. But once on his way back he nearly got lynched 'cause the white police didn't think a black man should drive. So my daddy sold the truck, and they went back to horsedrawn wagon. Maybe Bay Bridge Road wasn't nothing but a red-dirt track in those days, but it was still Alabama, children."

"Yeah-you-right, Mama Lulu!" from inside the screen door.

"The Africans have always been hardworking, God-fearing people," says Mama Lulu. "And I want to testify that no one ever missed a meal in Africatown. If you didn't have enough, why, your neighbors give you some of theirs. Come summer, when we held our Africatown church picnics, all the folks in Mobile would turn out for that—black, white, or indifferent. The men would be over here at our house the afternoon before, slaughtering hogs just right, nothing go to waste, and out there barbecuing those ribs all the night before, and the eating would go on all that next day till way past sunfall."

"What-all did you-all make?" a sensible great grandniece asks Mama Lulu from inside the screen door.

And Mama Lulu digresses to a menu of earthly pleasures long as your arm, for the ages to enjoy: "We made cole slaw salad, and potato salad with parsley and mayonnaise, and speckled butter beans in a casserole with smoked ham. We cooked collard greens with bacon so long that nobody could remember they had ever been plants. We made those greens hot with pepper sauce from our own cayenne peppers. And we creamed onions. Then we made cornbread and johnny-cakes—fist biscuits, we called them—and buttermilk biscuits with buttermilk I squeezed with these very hands! And we made green-corn tamales; they had to be boiled in milk for several hours. I would make a hundred of those tamales the morning of the picnic. And we'd take what was left over of that tamale mixture and make green tamale pie. And we roasted ears of fresh picked corn dropped in melted butter and salt. And we made watermelon rind pickles and green tomato pickles to go with the barbecue. And ten thousand hush puppies—that's right! And fried sweet potatoes. And a big bowl of fig compote from our fig trees. Then we deviled a thousand eggs, pickled a thousand beets, but there still wasn't enough. So we angeled cakes, spooned breads, and we made strawberry-rhubarb pies and pecan and hickory-nut pies, banana-cream and peanut-butter pies, and chiffon and meringue pies. Shortcakes stuffed with fruits. Coconut tarts. And my mama made what she used to call her Nutmeg One Bowl Cake. And we washed it all down with pitchers of peppermint tea, kept cold down in Spanish River on the day of the picnic. You learned to cook everything in those days, we didn't have no mica-waves!"

"Was that all, Mama Lulu?"

"Noo, Lord, no," says Mama Lulu. "But if you-all'd quit interrupting, I could finish. We used to smoke mullet. Deep-fry bream. Make crawfish fritters, served with boiled rice, grits, and corn pudding. And hot pickled okra. And gumbo—the real, old-time gumbo. Oh, how my daddy loved my gumbo! If he was alive today, he'd still want some of his Mama Lulu's gumbo. And a big fruit salad, with plenty of watermelon and muskmelon in it. And we made strawberries in cane-sugar sauce. How the boys would die for that one! You could have them eating right out of your hand. People everywhere in Mobile knew: if you came to the Africatown picnic, you got fed!

"The Africans off the *Clotilde* grew to love this land. For heaven sure had kept this little spot of earth blessed, to show how all things were created first. They would never speak to me in African—I don't know a single word of African to this day. I heard how my daddy talked. They'd speak in the African tongue when they didn't want us children to understand. But they insisted all us children learn English, go to school, get an education, improve ourselves. And Africatown started up the first school for black children in Alabama. 'Cause if we don't do it, no one's going to do it for us, children.

"Them Africans knew that none would ever see Africa again in this life. So they built a cemetery on the other side of

Arsenal Road, where the wild daylilies grow, to find their final rest. But before they passed, those Africans taught us to never give up hope. No matter how dark things may get, there's always a way to the promised land. You just keep on moving on, moving up.

"And before they passed, those old Africans taught us to forgive. For if the Good Lord forgives us, why can't we forgive each other? We learned it from the Scriptures, children: 'He who cannot stem his anger's tide, doth a wild horse without a bridle ride.'

"And before they passed, they taught us the gift of kin. Taught us we were all one family of Africans here. And when I was a little-bitty girl on my mama's knee, I remember her telling me, 'This lady is your auntie, that man is your uncle.' All the kids in Africatown were our brothers and sisters and cousins. Because we knew that they were all the same as us, and that we were all different from everyone else.

"But there's only one Mama Lulu—don't you ever forget her! I am Mama Lulu of Africatown, USA, and all the children crave my hugs. All the beautiful little children come to visit me. And I love having them, and I love feeding 'em up on home cooking. But you know, I wonder what it is—I never found a single one ever stay and wash the dishes!"

The Healer: Chronicle of a Lost Expedition

AN ACCOUNT, *given by Esteban de Veras, servant of Álvar Núñez Cabeza de Vaca, and survivor of the lost expedition of Governor Pánfilo de Narváez. Being in the province of New Spain, where the government of their most sacred Majesties was then staying, this man made his testament on the 12th of May, the year of our Lord one thousand five hundred and thirty-seven, before me, Juan Mendez, scrivener and notary public.*

A cocksure and treacherous Moor—Estevanico, as they call him—given to too much talking, babbling, a drunkard, fornicator, and a great liar. Found by Captain Alcazar wandering with Álvar Núñez Cabeza de Vaca on the deserts of Sinaloa, adorned by rich turquoise beads and feathers, carrying a green parrot on his shoulder, and accompanied by a seraglio of seven hundred Indian maidens. The clauses of said testament run literally as follows:

RELACIÓN

I am that blackamoor Estevanico; some know me as the Lusty Arab, native of Azamoor on the coast of Morocco, who accompanied the expedition of Governor Pánfilo de Narváez to Florida in the year 1528. We emerged nine years later on the coast of Tejas. This expedition, my lords, did not go as the Christians planned.

As manservant to my master, Captain Álvar Núñez Cabeza de Vaca, provost marshal of the expedition, I witnessed and survived the shipwrecks and misfortunes, the follies and calamities without end, nine years of futile wanderings, and the true miracles accomplished by Cabeza de Vaca, from the River of Palms in Florida to the painted deserts of New Spain. I was present also when the Christians arrested my master on the deserts of Sinaloa, and enslaved thousands of natives following him through the desert there. I also was beaten, put into chains, and marched to Tenochtitlán. But while my master was shipped back to Spain for trial, I was transferred in servitude here to the Franciscan friars, who converse with the beasts of the field. I know well the many charges and accusations made against Don Álvar Núñez Cabeza de Vaca. He is called a magician, a sorcerer, even a false messiah.

They are none near true. Who knows the master better than his servant? Not his wife. In truth I was more than Don Álvar's wife during our years of wandering the coast of the South Seas, for I bathed and fed him, watched over him when he slept, protected him from a thousand dangers, held his hand through a thousand calamities. I tell you this: he is a healer, nothing more and nothing less. He possesses the skills and powers to make the sick well again. He is a physician without exams and degrees. He does not require the surgeon's knife or the wizard's potions, for Don Álvar cures the soul and lets the body follow. Other than that he is no more than a dunce, like every other man. When he set off for this New World, as they call it, he did not know where he was going, and when he got there, he did not know where he was. All that the Christians on our expedition discovered was that the world does not provide maps for fools. All that Álvar Núñez Cabeza de Vaca ever conquered was his own fears. But when the power of healing came into my master's hands, you could hear the earth sing!

Yes, it is true: I have seen Don Álvar make the dead get up and walk. It is a fact that he has done so. Yet he heals entirely through his faith. Faith—faith alone, and nothing more than faith. Is he to be condemned by the Church for having such strength of faith as to create miracles?

As I am already doomed to guide the Franciscan friars through the land called by the natives Yee-ha, I do not think I shall ever return alive again. I know I shall never again see my dear master, if he is yet alive. So I think I should now do well to say somewhat of the events that occurred to Álvar Núñez Cabeza de Vaca, treasurer and provost marshal of the expedition of Governor Pánfilo de Narváez, during the nine years that we were left on the coast of the New World.

———

It was in June of 1527 that Governor Pánfilo left the port of Sanlúcar de Barrameda, authorized by the crowned heads of Spain to conquer and govern the provinces we would encounter from the Florida Cape to New Spain. The excellent map we took along told us that the land of the Mejicanos was north of Florida. No doubt this was one thing that proved our undoing.

Our expedition consisted of five ships and six hundred men, also officers, and several friars dressed like blackbirds. We carried no women with us, for we were not intending to stay, but only to plunder what the Christian Lord might place in our path. We took few provisions, fewer tools, and no herds, for Governor Pánfilo said, "I am no poor peasant, risking my life in order to plant crops. I am going to find treasure."

This treasure is exactly what the poor nobles of Spain want to obtain. More than all the lands and realms of earth together, it is gold and treasure they covet, for they believe that with it they can enter Heaven. So the boats were filled with men who did not want to die without treasure, but would risk their lives to find riches. Some call such men brave adventurers, some call them reckless dreamers.

As for me, to go or not to go across the oceans, I had but little choice. My master, Captain Álvar Núñez Cabeza de Vaca, was the son of the crusader Francisco de Vera and grandson of Pedro de Vera, who conquered the Canaries. Álvar Núñez, too, followed the soldier's profession. All he knew was dirk and dagger, the sword and the horse-mounted lance. He was a native of Jerez de la Frontera, where his mother, Doña Teresa, resided. He had fought bravely and with distinction at Ravenna, helping the Christians to trounce the Arabs. I myself was taken captive there fighting for the Infidels, as the Christians call us, and was commended to my master in servitude, where I was made to renounce the way of Allah and accept Christianity against my will. I testify that up till his coming to the New World, arms were Álvar Núñez's only profession, while mine was as his slave, to do his bidding and to make him laugh, to outwit him, entertain him, and keep him cheerful in whatever way possible, as his fortunes varied.

Yet when my captain said he would go with Governor Pánfilo, I own, I was glad of it. I saw with my own eyes how the Christians burned heretics in the streets of Spain. I watched them tear men apart limb from limb, burn them alive, suffer them upon the rack, the mace—the most excruciating forms of torture. Daughters of whores, what experts at infliction of pain! And all for the thing they called the Faith, may it groan once loud and die. In the New World I, too, thought somehow to gain the smallest part of treasure; a single gold rattle would have satisfied me. For I wished to pay my ransom, purchase my freedom, and be done with these Christians. I desired only to return to my native country, Morocco, safely away from the Faith. So I hoped.

Together with my master, I had seen Admiral Cristóbal Colón return from the Indies without treasure but with native slaves. I was as curious about them as my master. We stood at the port of Cádiz, admiring their feathers and plumes, their turquoises, their headdresses, their golden nose rings, their gourds and rattles, body paints, and the bright, loud birds they carried on their shoulders. It is a curious fact Don Álvar Núñez often mentioned, that in all our nine years lost in the wilderness we never encountered any natives like the ones Admiral Colón carried back to Spain. The women he had with him were of an unsurpassed beauty, with copper-colored skin and thick black hair like the hair of horses, hanging down like a mare's tail. Not at all savage, they laughed freely and bestowed their favors with the utmost innocence. It was said that these Indian women were witches, for men in their presence often began to drool and foam at the mouth. Yes, I too was glad of sailing for the so-called Indies, but my only motive was to escape all labor and observe these western lands, the source of all these treasures.

My wife, a blind seamstress from Hornachos, came to bid me farewell. On that quay we parted forever. She did not shed a tear, but all present distinctly heard her say to the other women gathered there that their husbands were as good as dead and their sons as good as lost, and that all that was left to them was to look toward whom they might marry next, for that was what she intended to do. Pointing her finger straight at my heart she warned me not to plunge inland into the dark places, for anyone who did so would never come out alive; it would take miracles for anyone to escape, but she believed few would do so. She said those who perished would be the fortunate ones. I gave her a ducat and left the pier. I don't believe in such womanish prophecy, but luck is something entirely different.

Hearing the blind woman's words, our Governor Pánfilo called her forward and demanded to know how she obtained these notions. My wife said that all is written on high, for those with sight to see. At this Governor Pánfilo, who had lost his left eye in battle against Cortés in New Spain, spat in disgust at the insult and turned away. Yet it all happened just as she foretold. Don Álvar Núñez would speak of my wife's prophecies many times during our distress.

—

Our passage to Santo Domingo took three months. There we lost 140 men, who deserted, and one ship, broken upon the rocks. Then we separated, two ships sailing to Santiago de Cuba, and two ships to the port of Trinidad, buying provisions, arms, and horses. In Trinidad the rains started falling, the sea rose high, and the south winds whipped so violently that during the night all the houses tumbled down and the church collapsed. Those who like myself had gone ashore to receive the provisions were forced to lock arms, walking six or seven abreast to keep from being blown over. We tried to make it back to our ships through the forest, but the trees crashed down at our feet. The cows flying through the air struck us in the face and the hurtling pigs boxed our ears. Never had we experienced such a mighty storm. The natives of that place called the tempest *hoorikan*, maybe a demon's name, for she chased us like a vixen. Finally our weak line was split asunder. I was hoisted into the air like a speck of dust, whirled up into the dark chaos, counting myself already among the dead. When I related all this afterward to Don Álvar, who was back on the ship, he scratched his beard thoughtfully and said, "Brave Estevanico, I am of the opinion that we are not in the world anymore."

I awoke next morning as if from one dream to another, for the island was completely changed. Not a leaf, not a limb, nor a tree remained standing. Not an animal stirred, nor a blade of grass. The land was bereft, desolate and ruined. Finding other survivors, we struck along the shore for the harbor. The storm spent, the clouds had completely vanished from the sky and the sea was as smooth and calm as vitreous.

We could not find the ships, only their buoys floating on the serene waters. Wreckage was strewn everywhere, the provisions lost, the horses upended, the bodies of the sailors disfigured from beating against the rocks. Crossing the marshes we saw the most fearsome sight. One of our ships had taken wing and was lodged in the high notch of a tall tree left standing alone by the tempest, with the masts splayed overboard, dead men and horses dangling down like bagatelles from a necklace. Sixty persons this storm made to disappear, and twenty horses died.

When Governor Pánfilo arrived from Cuba, where he had made safe harbor during the tempest, he surveyed the damage and ordered us to embark with him. But the survivors were so unnerved they refused to go aboard again until the governor consented to our spending the winter in Havana.

In late February, Governor Pánfilo arrived in Cuba with an old brig he had purchased and a pilot named Miruelo, who said he knew the cape of Florida like the back of his hand, and a good harbor there from previous journeys. Governor Pánfilo called upon my master, the provost marshal, for his opinion.

Don Álvar said to me, "Shrewd Estevanico, do you trust this pilot Miruelo?"

"He is a drunk and a liar, Master. I will also point out that his right hand is missing and replaced with a hook, perhaps for some old crime, so that when he speaks of knowing Florida like the back of his hand . . . But otherwise he seems no worse than any other Christian."

"Impudent scoundrel! Take that!" He boxed me a blow with his open hand, as was his wont when irritated by my jibes. Then he said, "You are right, we must not put our fate in this pilot's hands."

He went before the governor and told him that the man was not to be trusted. Whereupon the governor laughed and did exactly as this Miruelo counseled.

Next day the expedition set sail with four hundred men and eighty horses, in four ships and the governor's brig. The heralded pilot Miruelo promptly ran us aground in the shoals called Canerreo, where we lay stranded for fifteen days off the western coast of Cuba. We would be stranded there still if a huge storm had not come out of the south and lifted us off. The winds blew so stoutly that we could not cross the straits, and we decided to head for safety to Cape St. Anton. We got within twelve leagues and were pointed toward the harbor, when a contrary tempest came out of the north and practically finished us off, driving us hard all the way to Florida.

We sighted land on Holy Thursday, and came to anchor in the mouth of a great bay. The pilot Miruelo said he knew this bay very well, and that the Indians there were exceedingly friendly. However, as soon as he went ashore, they fell upon him and put an arrow through his neck. With his last breath, he declared this was not the bay he thought it was, though it looked much the same. Several men took fright at Miruelo's death and refused to go forward, realizing we had little idea of our location or route.

The following day, Good Friday on the Christian calendar, the governor put all the men into the ships' little boats and ordered them to shore. We found the houses and habitations of the Indians deserted, for they had fled in the night in their *canoas,* the small boats made from hollowed logs that they use in these lands. Each of their dwellings, which they called *buhios,* was big enough to accommodate three hundred small people, or about one hundred middle-sized people. However, the native Timucuas, for so they are called, are extremely large people, nine to thirteen feet tall. How many of these Timucuas the *buhios* held I do not know. When the Christians ransacked the village, among the shell piles and fishnets was discovered a single rattle made of gold.

Upon learning this, Governor Pánfilo called for his armor, mounted his horse, raised the flags, bid the friars erect the Cross, exhibited his legal documents and took possession of the entire country in the name of His Majesty King Ferdinand. He said the Lord Our God, who had created Heaven and Earth, men and women, and all their descendants, had made us fortunate indeed to be sharing the glory of Colón and Cortés, and that he was sure the source of this gold was nearby.

"Master," I said to Don Álvar, "do Governor Pánfilo's words mean the Christians believe these Timucuas are humans?"

"I would judge it so, yes, thoughtful Estevanico," he said. "Our Governor Pánfilo is not a man to waste words."

"Good, because I need to mate with one of these lithe native minxes soon, and I like to know into what sort of material I am thrusting my business—animal, mineral, or vegetable."

"Ha-ha, you joker Estevanico! Vegetables! What a suggestion! Ha! But you would do well not to thrust your filthy business in my face, rake," he said, still laughing. "If I catch you at it, I'll thrash you soundly."

"I know you will, Master. And if you say you will thrash me, then you will. So that is why I will confine my activities to the darkest part of night, when you are sound asleep, dreaming of your wife's virtue at home in your absence. The silence of my thrusting will make an absence of your thrashing."

The Indians of the village returned next day. Governor Pánfilo summoned them. They were burnished to a red color, very tall, and the men better endowed than any on earth, for they went about in the costumes they were born in, and knew not the meaning of Christian shame. These natives shave their heads, leaving only a knot at the top, which they gather together with brightly colored strings and feathers. The Christians thought it a savage fashion to shave the head, as they stood there miserably scratching the insects in their own filthy locks.

Their bodies the Indians tattoo and paint in wondrous designs of red, black, white, and green, some very festive, others frightening. I saw one with a certain crosshatching filled with circles and crosses, three circles with a line drawn through it. They drew the same crosshatch in the sand with a stick and made a game of it.

Because we had no interpreters, the Christians spoke to the Timucuas in the language of Castile. They made no reply. Then the governor grew vexed, and he spoke again to them, only this time much louder. He said they would be very sorry if they didn't show him where the gold and treasures came from immediately. When they still remained silent, Governor Pánfilo drew his sword and sliced the nose off the *cacique*, or head man, and tossed it to his greyhound León, which he was training to hunt natives at that time. Then he informed them he was searching for a city of the size and wealth of Tenochtitlán under Moctezuma, or maybe a little bigger. He commanded them to say where it was. Whether they knew this Tenochtitlán or no, their many signs and gestures left little doubt that the city Narváez sought was far away, in a hostile land, and that they wished us to go there, the faster the better.

At this the governor shook the golden rattle we had discovered in that place. The natives responded in kind, shaking rattles at the Christians. The governor shook his rattle again. This time the natives shook their bows and spears. Neither one understood the other. At length the governor lost patience. He showed them an ear of golden corn, and bid the Indians tell him where the Christians might find metals of that same color.

Seeing the corn, the agitated Indians pointed inland and shouted, "Apalachee!" Only then was Governor Pánfilo satisfied that they had divulged the location of Cibola, the city of gold, which he was sure must be found nearby. Believing this to be the knowledge he desired, the governor proposed abandoning our ships in the lagoons, as he knew Cortés had burned his ships behind him, in order to prevent the retreat of his men at Veracruz.

Well I remember how my master Don Álvar, as provost marshal, doubted this policy. He asked me, "Black Estevanico, you are uncouth and African, more like these savage Indians than the rest of us, perhaps you understand their grunts and cries. What do you make of this place Apalachee?"

"It is true I have seen more of the world than you, Master, and have learned several tongues," I answered. "I do not command this native dialect, but I deduce from the expression in these sordid native faces that this place Apalachee is not the city of gold, but only a cornfield at a great distance, where their fiercest enemies dwell. They would be pleased if the Christians should go there to kill their enemies and take their corn, for it would save them having to do it themselves. If on the contrary, their enemies should kill the Christians, that too would not go amiss."

"They are setting us a trap, then, clever Estevanico!"

"Yes, a trap, as man's own pride is his trap, and his ignorance the pinion of his chains, good Master."

"Can you learn to speak with them?" he asked.

"Yes, but it will take several days or weeks."

"We can't hold the governor's horse that long," he said.

"More's the pity. 'Tis the overeager warrior that runs into his own lance."

Then Don Álvar made his sentiments known to the governor, saying that it seemed to him that under no circumstances should we forsake the ships before they rested in a known and secure harbor; that we did not, after all, even know our location; that having no skill in the native language, we could not anticipate satisfactory communication with the Indians; that we lacked provisions for a march inland we knew not whence; that we had better re-embark and locate a better landing, since all we saw here was poor sand and scrub pine, naught else; and that as provost marshal he required, in His Majesty's interest, that the governor not destroy the ships, and certify that he had commanded such, under the hand of the notary.

The governor fumed and smoke came out of his ears. "What are you, a lawyer?" he asked Don Álvar. "Better to remain a cowhead, as your name implies!"

Governor Pánfilo brushed all arguments aside with blistering contempt, and bade the notary certify instead that he was leaving the new settlement of La Cruz to go in search of this Apalachee, where he was certain of discovering treasure. Thereupon he ordered the men to muster and said that anyone who so opposed and feared to march inland could go with the ships north to Pánuco and meet him there, and ordered Álvar Núñez to take charge of the ships. Two hundred men immediately returned to the ships, but Don Álvar refused, deeming it better to be charged with cowheadedness than cowardice.

That same evening the governor ordered two pounds of biscuits and half a pound of bacon rationed to each man who was going with him. Upon hearing this, the rest of the men returned to the ships, leaving the governor alone with the clerics and officers. Fearing abandonment, the governor relented, and revictualized to three pounds of biscuits and three-quarters of bacon. Speaking on behalf of the men, Captain Andrés Dorantes demanded three pounds of bacon and three of biscuits each, as they did not know where they were going, so how could they know how long it would take to get there? To which Governor Pánfilo, his good eye bulging out of his head in fury, offered one pound of bacon, two and a half of biscuits, and one hard-boiled egg.

At length the men returned, and we prepared to take up our march northward into the interior. The governor ordered the ships to sail north to Pánuco, to await him there. In the event they reached the port before us, they were to search one year before giving us up for lost. Inasmuch as the port actually lay far to the south, we never saw the ships again. But the Christians did not find that out till later.

—

For fifteen days we marched through an amazing extent of uncultivated lands, covered thick with forests and vast lakes and marshes of stagnated fresh waters. There were many large pine trees, and the country abounded with many kinds of timber—pine, cedar, palm, laurel, chestnut, and cypress. There was little recognizable to the Christians as nourishing. In all this time we encountered not a single person, village, or house.

"Not a good sign, my Lord," I said of the barrenness, as we paused to rest.

"Does it get this hot in Africa, ever-dry Estevanico?" Don Álvar asked.

"Hotter yet. It is not the heat here, but the terrible humidity."

"What is this humidity, some sort of Moorish charm?"

"It is the moisture in the air, my lord, which makes the heat seem doubly oppressive."

"Really? But perhaps you can tell me how one keeps comfortable in such circumstances?"

"You must take a very young girl into the cool bushes, and remain there until long after dark."

"You are indeed a single-minded race," he replied. "But seeing as how that is quite impossible here, have you any other advice?"

"You might begin by removing your iron armor, Master."

"Jackass! How dare you speak thus?" He cuffed me. "What would happen if we were attacked?"

"Why, Master, use good sense: lacking heavy armor you could flee all the faster."

"Flee?" Don Álvar said, as if he had never heard of it. "Really, what a dog you are, Estevanico! Such a one for amusement, eh? Very well, then." He chuckled. "I shall disarm. You may carry my armor."

"Just as I thought, Master. My idea becomes your profit, and your profit becomes my loss. You are just too clever for me."

He grinned. "With this policy Spain will rule the world!"

"And the entire world will hate Spain for it."

"Quit braying now, jackass, and help me off with this chain mail."

We marched and marched, and men began to drop from fevers. The other officers would not let the men shed their armor as Captain Cabeza de Vaca had done; they suffered greatly from the heat, and from sores where the armor rubbed their skin raw. Those on horseback were little better off, for the country was low and watery, thick with shrubs, thorn-bushes, and fallen trees, and infested with snakes. It would have been equally fast for the horses to mount the backs of the Christians.

We came to a wide, deep, swift river, and one of the mounted men, Juan Velázquez, a native of Cuellar, impatiently tried to ride across. The swift current swept him away, and though he tried to grab his reins, he was drowned, along with the horse. His death distressed the Christians, for up till now they had not lost a mounted knight, only common soldiers. To cheer them up, I prepared a fire and roasted the drowned horse stuffed with herbs, pine nuts, and berries. It was so delicious that the meal made them soon forget all about losing the *hidalgo* Velázquez.

The following day we reached the province of Apalachee, unsuspected by its inhabitants. The Christians gave thanks to God to be near their destination and prayed for deliverance from their hardships. The smooth meadows of Apalachee abounded with corn, melons, and beans, and the forests teemed with game. We saw three kinds of deer, rabbits and jackrabbits, bears and lions, and other wild animals, including one which carries its young in a pouch on its belly until they are big enough to find food for themselves. If someone approaches this animal while foraging, it lays down as if dead, a smart ruse I learned to employ during encounters with hostile Indians, but it is not edible, for the back haunches contain sacks of acid which taint the meat, making it acrid to the taste. The birds we saw in abundance included geese, ducks, ibises, herons, partridges, falcons, vultures, eagles, owls, and numerous other fowls. But since the Christians did not know what any of them were, they fell instead upon the Indians' stores of corn.

Apalachee was far less than Governor Pánfilo had hoped, a drab and wretched settlement of thatched huts across a slow river of no great account. All the men were glum, the women were ugly, and the children sullen and lethargic. Governor Pánfilo had the cacique and the cacique's mother brought to him to learn where the source of all the treasure was. Before he even spoke to the chief, he fed the mother to his greyhound León, but as this did not quench his cruelty, he ordered the lancers to run through ten or twelve male children. The friars obliged by pronouncing the little heathens saved even as they commended their souls to heaven. Then they were given a Christian burial.

The chief immediately ordered an attack. All the Indians we had seen so far in Florida were archers. They looked big and naked, and from a distance like giants. Their bows were as thick as an arm, six or seven feet long, accurate at two hundred paces. Armor was no use against arrows in this skirmish. There were men who swore they had seen two red oaks, each the thickness of a man's calf, pierced from side to side by arrows, which is no wonder when you consider the power and skill with which the Indians deliver the arrows. An hidalgo named Avelleneda died when an arrow passed completely through his neck and stuck into a tree. But at length the Indians fled into the forest.

Governor Pánfilo gave the order to search them out and destroy them when found, but Don Álvar petitioned him to send a party to search for the sea instead, that we might find our bearings. The governor said to stop speaking of the sea, as it was remote.

We stayed twenty-five days in Apalachee, making reconnaissances in a country sparsely populated and hard to get through because of swamps, lakes, and woods. The Indians captured there were interrogated separately, but again the lack of interpreters gained us no information of particular interest.

"You won't get very far if you can't converse with these natives, Master," I said again to Don Álvar. "All we will get is deeper into danger."

"You may be right, loquacious Estevanico," he agreed. "Tell me, do you think these Indians here speak the same language as those Timucuas?"

"In truth, I do not know, my lord, but I am willing to try to find out."

"Are you? How will you do that?"

"I will use my brain, my imagination, and my good looks, in reverse order."

"How so? Explain yourself, you rascal!"

"It is quite simple," I told him. "If you will allow me to take a wife among the native women, she will surely teach me every bit of the local tongue down to the niceties in just one week's time."

"Oh, so that's your game!"

"Master, we need to communicate with these natives. You have admitted it yourself."

"You know that as a Christian gentleman, I cannot sanction such fornication," he said, then winked. "But I suppose I could turn a blind eye."

"Yes, Master, be a good Christian gentleman. While I mount one of their mares, you turn the other cheek and see if anyone's coming."

When the chief and his people returned to their village, I was already able to communicate with them when they gathered before the Spaniards. The cacique desired to know who and what the Christians were, from whence they came, and why they were persecuting his people, even pursuing them into the forest.

I said to him, "You want to know why they persecute you and for what purpose they do it?"

"They do it because they are cruel and bad," he replied.

"I will tell you why they do it. It is because the Christians have a God whom they love very much, who is called Lord Our God, and I will show him to you."

They had given me to show him a small basket woven of palm partly full of gold. I said, "Here is the one they call Lord Our God, whom they serve and adore. To obtain this they make you suffer, persecute you, have killed your parents, brothers, children, and deprived you of your homes. For this Lord Our God they will pursue you even into the swamps and kill you, as they have done before in lands like my own in Africa across the sea. Therefore it would be best to give them this Lord Our God so they will go away."

The chief understood, but replied, "We have not seen this Lord Our God. We have none of Him. How can we give what we do not have? Let us dance and entertain the Christians so that they shall not do us any harm. We shall sing for them and smoke the pipe until they become sleepy, for that is our custom."

"It will do no good."

"Too bad," said the chief. "By the way, what kind of animal are these Christians? We see that some of them have four furry legs, but only two thin arms. We observe that some of them have two heads, although only one head like human beings. It puzzles us. Did they come out of the sky?"

"You don't understand, Grandfather," I told him. "You are seeing two animals. The warrior is one, and he is a man. The other animal has four legs and a big head. It is called a horse. The man rides on the horse, you see?"

The cacique only looked more confused.

"Look, the horse has four legs, big head, no arms. The Christians have two legs, two arms, and a head like a human. That is how to tell them apart."

"Ahh, two animals," the chief repeated with evident relief. "We thought one animal. We thought this animal wants to kill us and eat us. Everybody got scared and ran away."

"What do you drink here, chief? Do you make any fermented beverages—drink, run around, get wild?"

"You are a Christian, too?"

"No, I do not worship this Lord Our God. I worship another Lord. Big man called Allah, lives in sky."

"Ah, yes, the sun," he said. "We worship sun, too. We don't worship Lord Our God. Don't worship any metals. We worship big woman, makes crops and babies. Why are you here with these Christians?"

"I am a slave to one of them."

"The one with one eye and red hair? The demon with red hair on face? The one who fed my mother to dog?"

"No, a different one. The one called Head of a Cow."

"And he too would persecute us for this metal?"

"They are all the same."

"And do these animals called horses also persecute us for Lord Our God, too?"

"No. The Christians tell the horses what to do. They are dumb beasts like us."

"Ahhh." He was silent a moment. "Look, I know all you have said, but we are not hiding this Lord Our God from the Christians, for even if we should hide it in our intestines they would get it out of us with their long daggers. Tell them we have none of it. Tell them to go away."

"Chief, they will not believe you. They will become angry. Then they will torture you, baptize you, and kill you in a most gruesome manner."

"In that case we will go hide in the forest again until they are all dead."

"Good idea," I told him. "I will tell them you will dance and sing now, as is your custom. After that you are on your own."

When the natives came forward to dance and sing, they seemed so young, so strong, and so full of energy that Governor Pánfilo demanded to know how they maintained themselves so. I related this question to the cacique, who replied that they bathed throughout the year in a certain warm spring, the waters of which kept all his people vigorous and youthful.

I said to the governor, "There is a certain fountain where the native youth are wont to bathe—"

"What?" he cut in. "Did you say fountain of youth? Hmm. I have dreamt of such a place, and heard of such a thing in certain books of prophecy. Find out where it is. Be quick about it!"

I translated his order. The cacique replied, "Now they want to go swimming?" He pointed inland and said, "It is far. About five days' march, maybe a little less, maybe a little more."

Governor Pánfilo immediately mounted his steed and mustered the men, proclaiming that to discover this marvel would prove even more valuable than seven cities of gold, for in those magical waters youth might return to the aged, new strength to the weak, and new life to the dying. He told them he would lead them on a march inland. The cavalry immediately deserted.

I remember well how Álvar Núñez warned the governor against this rash pursuit of dreams and chimera, which had already caused much hardship and suffering, and that surely the time had now come to exercise caution. He said the Christians had no proof of the existence of this fountain of youth, only the testimony of a heathen. In addition, the year would soon be up, when the ships were to give up the search. The men were all suffering, to one degree or another, fevers, starvation, bleeding wounds, and despair, and it was time to seek the sea, but to march again to the interior was to court utter ruin.

Governor Pánfilo reared his Andalusian charger back on its hind legs and shouted, "The sea? The sea? Always the sea with you, eh, Álvar Núñez?" Then he galloped off toward the northwest interior, in the direction the cacique had indicated.

———

Our journey was extremely arduous, for as I have said the Christians were sick with fevers. I had to abandon the armor and carry Don Álvar most of the way, as he was often too weak to ride. The governor also grew sick, so he had a sling erected, which several of his servants hoisted among them. Those who were not delirious already, the insects drove mad with their stinging and biting and sucking of blood. There is no torment in the world, I think, that can equal those mosquitoes.

After countless days, we did finally reach the spring the natives had spoken of. It was a brilliant blue water, as clear as any on earth, completely sweet and refreshing to drink, but guarded by a mean and ugly dragon about thirty feet long, with a large and dangerous tail, far greater in strength and terror than the crocodiles of the Nile. This monster's tail alone was five or six feet long, which it flourished in the air furiously, lashing the water into foam. The rattling water in its throat, which it forced out in froth and foam, was louder than the bellowing of the angriest lion, and made the earth to tremble and quake. This dragon possessed the strength to vomit on the Christians at twenty paces, a terrible thing to witness, as its spittle burned the skin of whomever it touched.

Without more ado the governor then urged Álvar Núñez to go locate the sea. I went forth with him the following day, with five on horseback and thirty afoot, all volunteers.

"And in which direction do you recommend we travel, Estevanico?" my master spoke down from the saddle.

"West toward the sunset," I told him without hesitation, "until the hour of vespers. My new wife informs me there is an inlet of the sea there abounding in oysters."

"Oysters?" He seemed confused. "Oysters *bueno o malo?*"

"*Hombre!* Try to remember. Two shells. Pry them apart. Delicate, slimy things to eat, like a female between the legs. Good down your gullet with a bottle of red wine."

Álvar Núñez shook his head mournfully. "Have you absolutely no shame, rogue?" he exclaimed.

"No more nor less than the last time you asked. However, I do have more hunger, so let us proceed west in all haste, my lord."

He laughed and coughed violently, then said, "Oh yes, the great appetites of the lusty Arab! Very well, we shall go west. But tell me one thing—"

"Anything. I will answer in perfect truth or falsehood, according to my master's whim, so long as we leave presently."

"Why do you sin so greatly? Do you blackamoors have no resistance to temptation? Or do you not know the difference between right and wrong?"

"Sin is something that must be learned. It is like a taste acquired only after many years of earnest practice, much like the Faith."

"What? You impertinent liar! How dare you compare sin and faith!"

"For example, Master, what is the sin of making love to a willing young beauty compared to the sin of feeding the cacique's mother to a dog?"

"You no good rascal, you." He confessed in good humor, "I agree that that was a disgrace upon the name of Christians. Even the friars would admit it was a shameful and outrageous sin. Governor de Narváez lost respect in the eyes of the men."

"Yes, but not the dogs. It's only dogs Pánfilo de Narváez wants the respect of."

"I will propose we write a letter to the king about that incident," declared Don Álvar.

But I don't think he ever did. After all, how would he send it? We lost touch with Europe for so many years.

We traveled till the hour of vespers and reached the small inlet the woman had mentioned. It was shallow, with a mud bottom. The brackish water inclined us to believe that it communicated with the sea. The tide was withdrawn, revealing, to the joy of the hungry men, vast beds of oysters there for the prizing, plump and salty to the taste. Don Álvar led the charge, cavorting in the muddy flats like a happy fish, giving thanks to God for having brought us here, and shouting, "By the dozens! By the dozens! We shall eat them by the dozens!"

Half the night we were there eating our fill. Then I tucked my weary master into a sandy nest, where he fell asleep merrily yawning and belching, farting and scratching his insect bites.

The next morning the provost marshal dispatched several parties to explore the coast, who came back the night of the second day to report that these bays and inlets were so enormous and cut so far inland that finding the open sea would be a major undertaking, as it was yet a long way off. With this limited intelligence we returned to the Christians' camp on the river the Indians called Suwannee, across from Apalachee. May none have the misfortune to follow in our tracks.

We found the governor and many of the others sick. In desperation they had accepted the rotten meat of a vulture from the Indians, and unable to wait, consumed it raw. Oh, those Spaniards! You could not leave them alone for a single second.

As soon as they were all sick unto death and prone on the ground, the Indians attacked and hacked them to pieces. Wounded and delirious, most of them lay rolling on the ground, bleeding from their many wounds and loathsomely beshitting themselves and their clothing. The stench was so awful you couldn't get close enough to stuff a rag up a dying knight's ass.

Don Álvar reported on our trip to the governor, who was suffering badly from this shitting disease, as some began to call it; he was in exquisite agony. The braggart de Narváez had eaten the biggest portion of the rotten meat. A less noble man than Álvar Núñez Cabeza de Vaca could have taken pleasure in how the governor paid for all his evil cruelty, rolling on the ground and moaning to God to let him die.

Governor Pánfilo was now all for striking out toward the place our reconnaissance party had just visited, but we did not have horses enough to carry the sick, who kept getting worse every minute with this shitting disease. Their bowels ran like rivers. If only we knew of a corksmith handy. Nonetheless, we undertook the journey as best we could. Before setting out, the provost marshal reminded the men that our most reliable help was the Lord Our God. He never wavered in this conviction.

The shitting disease carried many away on the path toward the sea. By the time we arrived at our previous campsite, it was painfully clear to all that we were unable to go farther. The men could not move, and those able to stand duty were very few. The rest lay helpless as newborn babes in a strange and remote land, destitute of means either to remain or to get out, their bowels gushing streams of vile filth, their heads ablaze with fever, blood flowing from their wounds, their eyes glazed from the heat.

Then, as if matters were not bad enough already, the cavalry decided to desert, judging that their chances were better on horseback without having to assist the prostrate governor and his prostrate infantry. De Narváez called the cavalry officers into his presence and capitulated completely, begging their advice, one man at a time, and promising to do whatever they told him in order to escape this dismal country.

We didn't need a prophet to know we had to reach the sea and escape by water. To stay where we were was certain death. But how could we get away without boats? The officers concluded the only way was to undertake the formidable project of constructing vessels. This seemed a near impossibility, given the fact that no one knew the first thing about boat-building, and there were no axes, saws, iron, forge, oakum or pitch. But Don Álvar gave this advice to the younger officers: "Let us get to work, and trust in His will."

The next day one of our infantrymen, who had once been a blacksmith in the Old World, came forward and said he could make wooden pipes and a deerskin bellows. Don Álvar issued an order in the name of the governor that the men turn in all their equipment—stirrups, spurs, crossbows, body armor—to make nails, axes, saws and the other tools we needed. The hidalgos decided to kill a horse every three days to distribute among the workers and the sick.

The work proceeded rapidly. It was a sight to see the Christians making nails and saws out of their arms, for where did not the Christians conquer with the sword? After two months, four barges were ready. We made pitch from certain pine resins. From horse tails and manes we braided rigging. From our shirts we made sails. We flayed the horses' legs, tanned the skin, and made leather waterbottles. When the men and supplies were loaded, the barges remained hardly half a foot above water, and were packed so tight that no one could move.

"Master," I pleaded, "this will not succeed. Look here, the barges will capsize."

"Be calm, faithless Estevanico," he said. "The Lord will deliver us."

"You are mad. We will sink. Those who can swim will live. The rest will be drowned."

"Sink or swim," repeated Don Álvar. "Perhaps we will find that is the rule of life in this New World which no one can avoid. Such is the harsh power of necessity that we should hazard the sea, none of us knowing the first thing about navigation."

"Nor how to swim," I mumbled. Neither Don Álvar nor I could manage a single stroke.

We ate the last horse and pushed off, satisfied in but one regard, to see Florida at our hindmost quarter. But the waves soon broke over our heads. One of the barges, under command of Captain Tellez, had hardly gotten clear of shore when it capsized. All forty-seven men aboard, none of them swimmers, sank like stones and were lost. Then we sailed seven days among waist-deep sounds, always hugging the shoreline. We had no idea if we were close to the main, or when, at this snail's pace, we should reach the open sea.

Hunger and thirst grew daily more intense. We reached a strait leading out to the sea, but only recognized it as such when the barge under Captain Penalosa was sucked through by currents and winds and disappeared toward the horizon. It was never seen again. Another forty-seven men were lost. All that were left now were ninety-four men in the two barges, one under Governor de Narváez, the other under Cabeza de Vaca.

For thirty days we crept on like this, the two barges moving listlessly along the coastline, dragged by winds and currents. No one aboard had the slightest intention of propelling the barges forward, or setting a course. Governor Pánfilo's skin had all sloughed off from too much sun, and he lay draped over the tiller like a living skeleton, pointing his bony finger and giving delirious orders that no one bothered to obey. We drifted sometimes alongside the governor's barge, sometimes within sight of it, but often without any sight of it whatever for hours and days. Thirst was killing us. Once five men sprang to the side before they could be stopped and drank the salt water. They died in great agony.

The waves overwhelmed our barges many times each day. None aboard doubted that his death would come any minute. Álvar Núñez said then, "I would welcome death rather than see so many around me in such condition."

"Really?" I said, "Is that so? Then allow me to run you through with your sword this very instant. Allow me this one last act of loyalty before you die."

That changed his mind. I should say that of all the men left on our barge, only Don Álvar made any attempt to keep the Faith. He did not doubt for a minute that the Lord would ultimately deliver us. Even when the men started to eat the dead, he was serene in his belief. They did not so much eat them as cut them open to drink their blood, for no one had the stomach for consuming the corpses raw, and there was no way to cook the flesh on board the barge.

"May God have mercy on their souls," said Don Álvar.

"Yes, and may God bless their meal. Do you think the zombie Narváez is gone for good? We haven't seen his barge in four or five days. Maybe it has capsized and he has drowned."

"Let us hope so, friend Estevanico," he began, but realizing what he had said, he grew sullen. Just then we entered a slow eddying current. It spun us round and round, and the water became brown. We had reached the vast mouth of a big muddy river, where we found we could take fresh water from the sea, the river emptying into it in such volume. As it would be dark soon, we tried to head for shore to gather firewood, but all our efforts to breast that determined current pouring from the river resulted only in our getting carried farther out. The north wind rose from shore to drive us the rest of the way to the high seas. For two days we toiled to gain the shore against bitter winds, as it was the month of December. Seventeen men were washed overboard and drowned.

Then the seas calmed suddenly, and whose barge should appear, less than twenty elbow lengths away? It was our leader, Governor Pánfilo de Narváez. We saw him still slumped over the tiller in pitiful condition. He was a living corpse, surrounded by other corpses. You could see his bones sticking through his skin. *Zopilotes*—the birds of death—were already picking at his eyeballs, and his ears swarmed with buzzing flies. The men still alive in his barge were lying prostrate, begging for someone to finish them off. In that terrible hour, I saw grown men wailing for their mothers like helpless infants.

When we saw how it was with the governor, I said to Don Álvar, "Let us keep going, and let death take the governor as it sees fit."

"A Christian cannot leave another in such dire straits," he said.

"Then a Christian is a fool, Master, for the Grim Reaper is swinging his blade as we speak. I'll wager the gold rattle against my freedom that he'll be dead by the hour of vespers."

"I forbid you to speak that way, ever, you clown! Though I admit his case looks hard." But he took compassion, and shouted to the governor that we would come to his assistance. At first we knew not if the governor understood. His ghastly head listed slowly in our direction, his slack jaw flapped open, and a dry, whiny, high-pitched voice, which sounded like death itself, asked my master what he thought we should do.

Don Álvar gasped, but loyally replied, "We'll throw you a rope, Señor Governor! We shall lash our barges together. We must avoid abandoning each other. Let us share a common fate."

The governor, as if startled, began a wheezy laugh like dice rattling around in his rib cage, and he replied, "Oh, no, I'm not falling for that old trick, you dunce! Lash our barges together indeed!"

I said in a low voice, "He is cracked, sir, as I warned you. Let us get away from here."

But no, Don Álvar would not hear of it. He shouted across that he awaited the governor's orders.

"We shall make for shore in our two separate vessels," the governor said. "And you, Álvar Núñez Cabeza de Vaca?"

"Yes, Señor Governor?"

Governor Pánfilo, shaking from head to foot, coughed his words out as if with his last breath. "I want your four strongest men on my barge! Now, fool!"

The Christian forebearance shown by the provost marshal under such circumstances was remarkable. Don Álvar did not begrudge him the four men who could still stand duty. We only had five. "Do you wish to go first and have us follow?" he asked.

"No more tricks, dunce! No more tricks!" the governor shot back sharply. "Do as you wish. I don't give a damn. Every man must save himself. *Hasta la vista.*"

And so saying, having taken our four strongest men, he pulled away in his barge. We never saw him again. As my master is fond of saying in other circumstances, "Thanks be to God."

We knew we would have to row if we were to ever reach shore, so Álvar Núñez and I, with the one sound man left and the navigator, all put our arms to the oars by turns. It grew bitterly cold that night. Our one sound man collapsed and died during his second turn. While the navigator took the tiller, Álvar Núñez and I huddled together on the deck, but neither of us was able to sleep.

"The navigator will also die during the night," I said. "I'll wager you that gold rattle he will be gone before dawn. Then it will be just us two, alone at last." I planted my lips on his.

Don Álvar pushed me away in disgust, crying, "You rogue, to make your evil merriment at a time like this! I forbid it!"

But the navigator did not die during the night; a different fate was already awaiting him. As it got light, we saw we had drifted to the shore. Before we could do anything, a wave picked up the barge and tossed us like a horseshoe out of the water onto some rocky beach, the navigator striking his head and dying instantly, poor man, just as the sun rose over the sea.

Of our expedition, only the Provost Marshal Captain Álvar Núñez Cabeza de Vaca and myself now survived. Out of six hundred, we two were left. We crawled up the shore till just out of reach of the tide, exhausted but thankful to be alive, and naked as newborn jaybirds in the nest. There we fell into a sleep so deep it felt like death itself, and when we awakened some time later, the barge was still there half immersed in the sand, the vultures had picked clean the carcass of the navigator, and we were surrounded by two hundred natives armed with bows and arrows, and wearing drawn faces.

"They must be the cannon balls Admiral Colón described," Don Álvar said, rubbing the sleep from his eyes.

"Cannon balls?"

"Oh, cannibals!" He turned on me. "No time for your surly jokes, slave Estevanico. Find out who they are, and if they intend to sacrifice us to their heathen idols."

I turned and spoke to them in the tongue I had learned in Florida, which they seemed to comprehend; perhaps these native tongues are all dialects of the same language.

"They say they are called the Tejanos," I told my master. "They call the land here Yee-ha!"

As soon as I repeated that word by which they call their native land, all the Indians stamped their feet and shouted, "Yee-ha!"

"They wish to know who we are," I continued.

"Tell them we are Christians," said Don Álvar.

"I have done so. They reply they have never heard of Christians."

"Then tell them we are lost, that we have lost everything, even our clothes."

"Master, have mercy on a poor fool like me, but they can see that for themselves. They can see we have lost everything. Their eyes inform them better than words that we are two lost souls."

"I do not know what else to say, fellow survivor Estevanico." Don Álvar was downhearted. "If they wish to sacrifice us to their idols, there is nothing we can do to stop them. It is all in the hands of the Lord."

"Very well for you," I told him. "But what shall your Lord do for me? If we are both to die at the hands of these wild savages, I doubt I will accompany you on your journey to Heaven to join the angels."

Then my poor master wrung his hands. "I am sore with sorrow at having brought you into this, trusted servant and old comrade. If we are to die together in this moment, I regret that I cannot make it up to you in some way."

"Make it up to me? Oh, that's all right, my poor good-hearted señor," I comforted him. "I can serve the devil as well as the Christian. What with my luck, the devil will be a Christian. But you could do one thing to make amends, easy as can be. To tell you the truth, I never planned to return to Europe anyway. Whether to die there or here does not especially pre-occupy me. For Esteban de Veras, even if it ends now in death, this expedition has probably turned out for the best. What I want, *mi jefe,* is my freedom. I fancy dying a free man. I don't fancy to enter the afterlife as a slave."

Then Álvar Núñez Cabeza de Vaca said these words, to my exact recollection: "I grant your boon. You are henceforth free, Esteban de Veras. I only ask that you not leave me alone, that you will stand by my side as a free man, a friend, and brother."

"Where else would I go, good dunce? And what would I do without you to hector?"

Don Álvar said, "If we live to see another day, we will rise up naked in the morning before the eyes of the Lord and go about all day under His watch. From now on, we will only go where the Lord takes us."

"Is your God testing us or punishing us? At least let me know that much."

"Truly, I wish I knew, blaspheming Estevanico. All I know is that we are alone in this New World. We must begin life over again here. We must be born again. We shall most likely have to forget everything we ever learned in Europe."

At this I could not help rocking with mirth. "What? All those years of crusading and ravishing virgins—all for nothing? All that sacking of cities, carrying the standard for the Faith and Ferdinand and Philip? All the gore and the trumpets in vain? I cannot believe it. All we learned of life in Europe about using lance and dirk to rule over people by force now useless? What a sad day, indeed!"

Then my captain Álvar Núñez Cabeza de Vaca said, "I was a professional soldier for Ferdinand, and good at it. I liked my calling. If I had not marched for the Faith, perhaps it would have been for another standard or kingdom. Now there is nothing. No kingdoms, no saddles nor horses, no dirks nor daggers, no enemies. I am as shorn of my privileges as I am bereft of my garments. And you, knave, who know only how to laugh and gamble and to make sport with low women, are you not oppressed here?"

"Not yet."

He grinned through his tears. "No, you have the skills that will lead us through. Perhaps all a man needs in this New World are those things we first learned as babes in our mother's arms. Perhaps only those lessons will be useful to us now."

And so saying, Don Álvar sat down and cried like a baby, bawling and bawling, shedding copious tears. Yet I do not think he cried for himself alone. He was grieving for the six hundred men who had died due to Governor Pánfilo de Narváez's malfeasances, greed, anger, deception, stubbornness, ignorance and conniving ways.

Naturally, to see my former master thus broken down in grief and tribulations saddened me immensely, but what really struck my heart was the thought that we had miraculously survived our voyage on the barge only to be washed up at the feet of these supposed man-eaters. They were still surrounding us and listening to our talk, their faces long and unfriendly. Then I, too, broke down in a flood of tears to relieve my sorrows. I sobbed and sobbed. It was a duet of tears. The cruel north wind commenced to complete our chorus, and our wailing and lamenting only grew fiercer.

Then the Indians, sitting in the sands all around us, understood our plight and burst into tears of woe, too. They joined us in our grief, sometimes outdoing us in its expression. They tore at their hair and beat their heads with their fists. It was amazing to see these so-called savages, who would have us for dinner according to their custom, howling like wounded dogs. They felt our pain more acutely than ourselves.

When all our tears were shed, the cannibals then brought us to their village. We awaited the hour they should make us their victims, but instead of slaughtering us for sacrifice, the Indians brought us to the houses of their sick and urged Don Álvar to heal them.

"Estevanico, *qué pasa?*" he asked. "Do you have any idea why they think I can do something for these sick people? It's nothing you told them, is it?"

"No, no, a thousand times no. Me? Tell them what? Well, *tú sabes,* I might have mentioned something about it; I really can't remember. But look at the way they are all jumping around. They think you have some talents, your honor. They say they have some of their people in the hole with their back to the wall, and they want you to turn them around."

"But I can do nothing for them," Don Álvar said. "I'm no doctor. And as for miracles, my own conscience is stricken with guilt at my many sins. I have not the power nor the right to make miracles or cure anyone. Should I now add to my sins by playing the false healer?"

"What have you got to lose?" I suggested. "Maybe you don't have to worry about them eating you; there's hardly a mouthful of meat left on you. A thin broth of skin and bones is all they could make of you. But what about me? Why, there's still plenty of good dark meat left on me. Why don't you see what you can do for those poor folks under their rugs?"

Still, Don Álvar would have no part of it, until at length the Indians got very angry, beat us with their clubs, and drove us from their village, naked and starving.

—

Then began our wanderings. For almost three years we went from one tribe of natives to another. In all this time, traveling among all these Indians we saw a sparse, infertile land with few trees growing, and no crops planted among any of them. Everywhere we went Don Álvar was asked to heal the sick, the wounded, the suffering. They said their gods had told them a white healer would come to them. But since he always refused, we were both soon reduced to slavery in order to eat. We had to grub roots in the water or underground in the canebrakes. Our fingers got so raw from this work that if a straw touched them they would bleed. The broken canes often slashed our flesh. We had to work amid the natives without benefit of clothes. Sometimes we were handed over from one tribe to the next, like items of trade. Other times we were put in wooden cages, poked, abused, beaten, and sodomized, then chased away, until some other men happened upon us.

During all this time, I kept reminding Álvar Núñez that even should he try to heal the sick and fail, we still might find ourselves better received by the natives than by simply rejecting their pleas outright. "After all," I said to him, "if they are willing to place their faith in you, how is it that you aren't willing to place faith in yourself? You have said many times that we are only agents of Lord Our God. Let Him decide."

But Don Álvar was only slowly won over. It seemed long ages and whole lifetimes that we rambled and roamed, and always among these starving, inarticulate peoples, all mired in hostilities and vengefulness. It was as though they had only discovered the joys of warfare and murder on the previous day. They could not stop killing each other long enough to put something in their mouths to eat. Warriors with arms and legs cut off in battle, we saw by the hundreds. The wounded begged Cabeza de Vaca to put their branches back on before they bled to death. Most days the sick and the dying lined up to see him.

Under these circumstances, life became too hard to bear for Don Álvar. Week by week he became a changed man. He was no longer the Spanish hidalgo, the Christian gentleman, with his Arab horse, his Arab manservant, and his chaste wife. But who or what had he become? The Indians called him Mr. Nobody and gouged his fingernails for refusing to help them.

In order to escape, we contrived to move among more northern tribes, who lived in the forest. There was more to eat in the forest, and more to trade. We became traders of a kind, going from one tribe to another. Our principal wares were seashells and conchs used for cutting, sea beads, and mesquite beans, which the Indians value very highly, using them for medicine and in a ritual beverage in their dances and festivities. As merchants we were neutrals, and could cross from one tribe to another, safe from the constant warfare.

We returned to the coast, and continued as traveling merchants between the coast and the inland. The heavy loads we carried on our backs caused the cords to cut our arms. Yet this occupation well suited us. We could travel wheresoever we liked to find food with no obligation to work, as we were not slaves. Our reputation spread; everywhere we went the Indians treated us honorably because they liked to barter for our commodities. Still, many were the daily privations, the hardships, many storms and frosts. In the winter we nearly froze to death; in summer we were constantly tortured by the mosquitoes. They poisoned, inflamed, and exasperated us so that our bodies looked as though we had an incurable sickness that would deliver us to death's door. We wandered this coastal region nearly six years, alone among the Indians and, like them, naked.

Each year in the autumn, some tribes went to a certain place on the banks of a great winding river to eat the nuts of the tree called *pee-kan*. These nuts have a soft shell, and gathered from the ground furnish the sole subsistence of the people for two months of the year—though not every year, because the trees only bear every other year. The nut is rich and sweet, the trees massive and numberless. Many other animals that love to grow fat upon these fine nuts also came into the orchards.

In the course of the gathering season, the Indians worked a great distance upriver, and we with them, though always we camped by ourselves at a distance. It was while here gathering *pee-kan* nuts that an Indian told me that other Christians were alive among them, so Álvar Núñez begged that he take us to their abodes.

As we approached, Captain Andrés Dorantes, a young hidalgo from our expedition, came out to see who it could be. When he saw Cabeza de Vaca he was terrified, for he had long considered us dead, and all the Indians had confirmed our demise.

We assured him otherwise, though perhaps we looked more dead than alive. At length Dorantes calmed down and wept with relief, for he had believed all this time, as he told us, that he had abandoned his superior officer the provost marshal to his death when first the barges separated, and was sure, on seeing us, that Don Álvar had returned from the other side of death for revenge.

For Don Álvar this was a day of great joy. He gave many thanks to the Lord for preserving us through such adversities, so that we might again meet together. Dorantes knew of still another Spaniard, Castillo, held by a neighboring people. They were called the Mariames and had a bad reputation. Although Dorantes and the Indians he was with—the Yguaces—warned us of the danger, Don Álvar decided to go there immediately to rescue this Castillo.

On the way to their camp we heard from Dorantes of the fate of the men with him on the third barge. Adrift on the open sea, one by one they had begun to die of cold and hunger. Captain Pantoja, in charge of the barge, used them so severely that at last they could no longer endure his high-handedness. The camp master Juan Sotomayor got into a fight with him, and clubbed Pantoja in the head; he died instantly. Their number went on diminishing. The living dried the flesh of those who died. So Esquivel fed on the corpse of Pantoja, and Sotomayor fed on Esquivel. When Sotomayor died, only Castillo and Dorantes were left. According to Dorantes, Castillo began to feed on the dried flesh of Sotomayor. But later on Castillo said it was Dorantes who ate Sotomayor. We never learned who was telling the truth.

At long last their barge drifted into shore, where the Indians found them, along with the gnawed bones of their companions. They took Dorantes with them, but Castillo refused to come. Dorantes said he had pleaded with Castillo to seek the way to Pánuco together, but that Castillo had said he'd had more than enough of looking for this or that place by now, so he asked the Mariames to receive him as a slave. Dorantes fled on foot, and roamed widely from this time, almost like ourselves. He returned at the time of the nut harvest to see if Castillo was still alive and try to get him to come away with him, for among the Mariames he lived every moment in dread of being killed.

When we reached the village of the Mariames, we could see that things were not well with poor Castillo. A woman had dreamed the night before that her son would kill the Christian, and the next morning the dutiful son went to work torturing him to death. For the Mariames, as Dorantes told us, are always obedient to their dreams, carrying out whatever atrocities come to them in their sleep, this being their form of superstition. Thus enthralled to their custom, they destroyed even their male children on account of their dreams. With his thumbs tied together and suspended upside down, Castillo said that only yesterday he had seen parents burying alive their boys of eight and nine years old because their dreams had told them to murder their children. Rarely, he said, do they let a girl child live.

While we were lowering Castillo to the ground, a mother, herself crippled horribly, cast her baby daughter on a mound of earth and walked away. The village dogs immediately devoured the infant. No one lifted a hand to save her. Naked and without a sword, Don Álvar watched this with terrible suffering on his countenance. With me as interpreter, he demanded to know of this witch, who would destroy her own children without qualms, why she would do so.

The mother replied, "We Mariames must cast our daughters away at birth. All other nations are our enemies, and they all hate us. If our daughters grew up to marry them, our enemies would multiply until they overcame and enslaved us. We annihilate our daughters rather than risk the making of a single new enemy."

When I told her answer to Álvar Núñez, he grew crimson with rage. "But why don't you just marry them to your own kind?" he sputtered.

The woman said calmly, "That would be a disgusting and shameful thing. The Mariames purchase wives from among our enemies, leaving fewer young women among them to give birth."

Thus the Mariames' slaughter of their own children took place in absolute obedience to the twisted mathematics of their nightmares.

"Dear former master," I said to Don Álvar, "let us not stay here among the Mariames, but make haste away. I doubt I could sleep a single wink among a people so savage."

"It is truly more a curse than a disease, this epidemic of murdering their own children," he said, "but we must bring Castillo away with us."

"*Mira*, Don Álvar," I said to him. "You have heard Captain Dorantes say that Castillo wouldn't leave with him. He is a volunteer among the Mariames. And you are no longer provost marshal of anything. What if one of these Mariames dreams of us?"

However, the very evening of our arrival some of the Indians came to Álvar Núñez and fell on their knees, begging him to cure them of terrible headaches.

At first Don Álvar waxed wroth at me. "Is it your wagging tongue again, Señor Gossip Estevanico?"

"I might have dropped a word; I really can't remember. It was so hectic here today, what with Castillo getting tortured while the dogs were eating that baby girl. Is it any wonder the conversation slipped from my memory?"

"You must tell them in all frankness, honesty, and sincerity that there is nothing I can do for them. Tell them to go away."

He folded his arms.

"You don't have to cure them," I suggested. "Maybe you could just cheer them up."

"That is your part to play, fool," he replied.

"Very well, then," I said. "But prepare yourself for some bad medicine."

When I told the Mariames what Don Álvar had said, they got wild and fierce with anger, blaming me as the messenger of wickedness. They took us all captive, tied us to a stake, and vowed they would let us starve to death there, withholding food until Don Álvar complied with their wishes.

That did it. After two days in the burning sun without food or water, Don Álvar said, "It is time to do as they bid, thirsty Estevanico."

"You have no choice. Act the part of the healer to the Mariames or we are all done for."

"You know that I would rather die than pass myself off as something I am not, claiming powers that I do not possess, which is a crime before God."

"I know that, Don Álvar. Yet you don't want to arrive in heaven with the deaths of Dorantes, Castillo, and innocent Estevanico so freshly recorded in your account, do you?"

Then Don Álvar began to cry like a baby again. "But what if I fail, Estevanico?"

I said to him, "Don't fret your brain about such matters. Failure was the stuff of the Old World. Here it is no crime to fail. The only crime here is not to try. The sun rises from a different angle in this land. The drum beats a new rhythm. You must lift your old carcass up, go out there, and try. Give it all the faith you have. I know that you can do it."

"I can't do it," he babbled through tears. "I can't, I can't, I can't!"

"Yes, you can," I told him. "These Indians believe you can. The Christians believe you can. You can do whatever you want if only you keep the Faith and try hard. You can perform miracles, Don Álvar. Now go do it, for God's sake, and save our lives!"

Dorantes and Castillo picked up the call and cried out, "Do it! Do it! Save our lives!"

So finally, much against his own will, did Álvar Núñez Cabeza de Vaca undertake to cure the Mariames of their terrible headaches. First he found out what their own method of cure was, which was not working. They told him that first they gave the medicine man all they had, and the medicine man used a sharp pointed stick to make a hole in the sick man's head, then blew on the sick man's body, the breath supposedly casting the infirmity toward the hole made in the skull, until finally he sucked the sickness out and cauterized the wound. They insisted Álvar Núñez use the same treatment to cure them.

"You are not going to suck their heads as they request, are you?" I asked.

"Can you think of another way, resourceful Estevanico?"

We agreed on a different method, which we made up then and there. It was for Don Álvar to bless the sick where they lay in front of us, to breathe upon them, to recite a Pater Noster and an Ave Maria, and to finish by removing the loincloths they wore to cover their genital parts and to wrap the cloths around their heads, praying earnestly to God all the while for their recovery, and concluding with Álvar Núñez, Dorantes, and Castillo, as well as myself, giving the sign of the Cross.

The first patients he tried it on, as soon as we had made the sign of the Cross, instantly got up completely well and said that all pain had vanished.

"You see?" I rejoiced to tell the new surgeon after the operation. "And you said it wouldn't work!"

Don Álvar was so stupefied and exhausted that he temporarily lost the power of speech. We stood guard by him as he slept on the ground. One of the Indians he cured had previously killed all his children after a bad dream, but as soon as his health was restored he set out directly to spread the news of the Healer. In the next days one after another of the Mariames were relieved of their illnesses and maladies in the same manner by Don Álvar, so that by the time the Indians left for the place where many tribes went to eat the prickly pears at that time of the year, the Mariames were so well recovered that not a single one dreamed of annihilating his sons or daughters. So happy had they become at the miraculous cure that they danced and sang in festivity for three days and nights. In appreciation they presented us with food and skins, offered us their own wives, and gave other tokens of their gratitude, which Álvar Núñez did not accept. The Indians wanted us to stay among them, and promised to feed us only venison and blackberries and to always treat us kindly. But how could you trust the Mariames? One headache and it would be all over for us.

So as soon as possible we commended ourselves to God and made a break for it. We ran in haste as far from the Mariames as we could. We thought we were fleeing toward the coast but came to the mountains instead. Night overtook us, and we thought we should freeze, but found a burning bush, by the warmth of which Don Álvar, Castillo, Dorantes, and I passed that cold night.

We did not know that the burning bush was a kind of signal for the Indians who lived in the mountains to gather. But next morning a crowd of Indians came, bringing sick persons, some with severed limbs.

"Please, please!" I had to tell them. "It is too early for patients. The doctor is asleep. He cannot cure anyone till after breakfast. By the by, have you brought anything for breakfast?"

All they had were prickly pears, so that was what we were paid in. Don Álvar would perform the cure, and I would tell them, "That will be fifty-five prickly pears." Don Andrés Dorantes was put in charge of collecting the fees from the Indians after treatment, and Castillo, who was still recuperating from his savaging at the hands of the Mariames, helped keep the waiting people in line. Don Álvar performed the cure from dawn until late.

The ritual we created for the curing was perhaps useless. Don Álvar did not require such hocus-pocus. When he prayed the power came into his hands like lightning bolts.

Then he bestowed health so bountiful that every patient got up the following morning as sound and strong as if he had never had an illness. Truly, the doctor was as astonished as his patients. At times he would become silent, deeply lost in a trance, his eyes lifted to heaven, staying that way for hours, as if listening for an answer. At last he would say, "I have always trusted to His providence and that He would lead me out of captivity."

"So be it," I replied. "We are no longer captives here. We are not prisoners or slaves. We can go where we like."

"Then let us make our way to a Christian country," Don Álvar said.

"Good doctor, have not we had enough of Christian countries?"

But who was I to say no to Álvar Núñez Cabeza de Vaca, the Healer, as the Indians called him? I said nothing more, as I did not wish to disrupt his faith, by which he could heal the sick at such a fast rate. In any case, I did not believe we would ever find our way to a Christian country again. For my part, I believed we would end our days on earth traveling on this parched coast.

Every year at a certain month in the summer, the Indians gathered to eat the prickly pears. Among the tribes were Cultacuches, Malicones, Coayos, Susolas, Atayos, and others. The Indians all through this region talked only of the wonders the Healer wrought, and individuals sought us from every direction in hopes of obtaining Don Álvar's blessings. We turned away no one. Why should we? The Healer's powers seemed to become stronger with more use. Soon we were doing thirty or thirty-five cures a day, and taking in more prickly pears than we ourselves could possibly eat.

Dorantes, whom I began to call the Ledger, calculated that it took no more than eight handfuls of prickly pears a day to satisfy one of us, but we soon accumulated them by the thousands. Every time the Healer cured another group, they gave us all their prickly pears in tribute, until we struck on a plan to start giving away the surplus. Don Álvar would say to the Ledger, Dorantes, "Give those starving old people a thousand prickly pears."

And it would be done. Consequently, hunger was soon vanishing from the land. This only made the Indians love the Healer all the more. They came in a great multitude to show their gratitude. I brought their cacique before the holy man and interpreted their talk.

"The chief wishes to know if the Healer has come from Heaven. He asks if you are a child of the sun."

"Say I am a humble Christian, a child of God like any other."

I told this to the chief. He also asked Don Álvar if hunger was gone for all time, or only until the next bad harvest.

The Healer smiled and said, "In the New World, the Lord has provided plenty of food for all. Tell him the strong and the wicked have too much, the meek and poor too little. But if all would follow our Lord and become Christians, I would teach them Christian sharing."

When I related this to the chief, he grew indignant and replied hotly, "You must be God of Fools, old man. Look at this, our land. It is a barren desert. It is burnt and dry. Nothing good to eat grows here. It has not rained in twenty-three years. Only a few beans, maybe a squash. Do not preach to us about sharing. Only bring us rain. Can your God make the clouds open? If so, we will gladly become Christians."

When he heard this, Don Álvar puffed his chest out like a partridge, as he was wont to do at times when his pride was pricked. But at length, considering the matter, he sagged and said only, "Tell them I cannot make it rain. This is clearly beyond my powers."

Don Álvar often sailed backward into his greatest miracles. It once more fell to me, the sinner, to minister to Don Álvar, the holy man. "How do you know you can't bring rain if you don't try? Remember how you said you could not heal anyone? Now look how much better things go for us. Maybe you can make it rain if you just stop thinking no all the time!"

But Don Álvar was not convinced.

I told the cacique the Healer was not pleased, and desired them all to go back to their villages and homes for now so that he could rest and pray.

But the same cacique returned the next day, his face disfigured with fear. He begged the Healer not to be angry with them or kill any more of his people.

"What? Kill his people? Estevanico, ask him who is killing Indians. Tell them I had no hand in this misfortune."

But they would not be persuaded. The chief said that many Indians had fallen ill on their way home, and the next day eight died. He ascribed their deaths to the Healer's displeasure. It seems that this chief had misunderstood Don Álvar's talk. Nevertheless, I had to inform the Healer that the natives blamed the recent deaths on his anger. When he found this out, he blamed me, and gave me a sound slapping, not to mention pummeling, a punishment I had not experienced for ages.

"Ow! Ow!" I complained as loud as I could. "Leave off, my dear physician. For what malady is this a cure?"

"It is you who must leave off, knave!" Don Álvar was shaking with rage. "You, not even a Christian. Leave off your licentiousness once and for all!" (For he knew I kept several women nearby, as a sport and a pastime when I was not being called upon to interpret with the Indians, get directions, arrange dispersions of prickly pears, and resolve a score of other wearisome problems.) He said, "These natives are not dying because of my anger. They are falling because of your bad translations!"

Then I leapt to it and informed all the Indians that neither the Healer nor Lord Our God was angry with them, and they need not fear falling ill or dying on that account. I said that something had gone wrong because the Healer was trying so hard to make it rain, that we would investigate the cause, and that if they brought those who had fallen to the presence of the Healer, he would see about restoring them immediately and without charge.

Luckily the clouds were then covering the sky, and the day darkening with the threat of rain. The Indians accepted our corrective policy.

———

Among those patients to whom Álvar Núñez showed his healing skills was a young boy already past death's door. This child's parents had brought him across the desert to find the Healer, but the infant had stopped breathing on the way. The father and mother scooped out a shallow grave in the sand and covered their son's body with rocks, supposing that it would soon be the prey of vultures and jackals. Then they walked on together until they came to where we were.

When he heard what had happened, Don Álvar got down on his knees and prayed. We canceled all other appointments for the day. After several hours bent forward on his knees, he was not praying; he had fallen asleep. I nudged him with my foot. He lifted his head in a fog and said immediately to the parents, "*No es muerte.* He is not dead."

Don Álvar spoke these words, which had come to him as a result of a dream, with such certainty that the parents turned in their tracks and without a word trotted off through the mesquites and tumbling weeds, back miles and miles to the rock cairn, where they had buried their child. They removed the rocks from the tiny body and listened at the infant's sandy mouth. There was indeed a shallow breath; the boy was alive.

Throughout the land the effect was profound wonder and fear. People talked of nothing else, and wherever the fame of the Healer reached, they set out to find us so we would cure them or bless their children. For eight months, reckoned by moons, people came seeking us from many parts, and telling us we were truly children of the sun—the Indian way of saying holy men. Up till this time, only Álvar Núñez was practicing cures, but what with the crush of people now coming to us, the Ledger and Castillo soon took up the profession as well. They took over the daily blessing of the crowds so that Don Álvar could deal with the hard cases. I did not take part. One of us needed to keep his feet on the ground.

Then some Indians came, begging the Healer to rid them of someone they called "Mr. Bad Thing." An aged cacique with a wrinkled forehead said this Mr. Bad Thing was a little man who wandered through the region causing havoc. He was all burned up, had a pointed beard, horns, and a forked tail like a certain type of lizard. The chief said a blazing brand would shine at the door when this Mr. Bad Thing rushed in and seized whom he chose, gashing him with a sharp flint, then reaching his hands inside the gashes, pulling out the person's entrails, cutting a section two palms' length, broiling it on the embers, and tossing it down his throat while still blazing from the flames.

Álvar Núñez listened with alarm, then said to me, "Sharp Estevanico, does not this sound like someone we know?"

"Yes, indeed, it sounds like a Christian surgeon," I ventured, still sore from my last beating. Don Álvar Núñez could still appreciate a joke now and then.

This Mr. Bad Thing, the Indians continued, would merely touch his victim on the shoulder and thus sever a limb with the delicacy of a butcher. They told how Mr. Bad Thing would swoop into a village at night, causing their lodges to fly straight up into the air, then come suddenly crashing down to earth, mangling the inhabitants. Next morning they found villagers in the trees, pierced through from head to foot by branches. They paraded the wounded and mutilated in front of us to show they were not making up this tale.

The Healer said, "It appears to be the Evil One himself."

"The horns and beard would lead to that conclusion, not to mention the blazing brand and the forked tail."

"If I had known it would come to this, I would never have taken up this business of cures."

"It is still questionable whether you took it up or it took you up."

"Old friend Estevanico." Don Álvar's voice sank. "I suppose I am or have become a sort of healer, as they call me, and these methods have given good results, but this does not mean I am prepared to confront Lucifer."

"You always said God had a plan for you, Holy One. You just never knew it was this."

"True. And you think that now I know God's plan?"

"So it sounds to the ears of Esteban de Veras."

"But why me, estimable Estevanico? Is there no way back?"

"Back? Back where? What could you mean? If this is the Lord's plan for you, you must go through with it."

"Through with it." The Healer sighed in disbelief. "And there is nothing else to do?"

"Nothing else you can do."

"We shall certainly not survive this time," he said in sorrow.

"Be brave! Screw up your courage! Don't let Mr. Bad Thing get you down. And remember, I will be right behind if you need me, so don't worry. It will be the Ledger and Castillo, then ten or twenty thousand Indians, and then I'll be right behind them."

"You are my great comfort."

Then we went forth together to the place where the Indians said Mr. Bad Thing lived. It was a big crevice underground in the desert, guarded by owls and gila monsters.

"I am certain Mr. Bad Thing lives here," Cabeza de Vaca said. "Cannot you smell it?"

"I surely can! Someone has been cooking beans in four directions." For the stench was magnificently unbearable. Even the ground was extremely hot, trembling as if about to explode.

The Healer fell to his knees and began to pray, but perhaps some part of the prayer went amiss, or this Mr. Bad Thing deflected it, for suddenly, as if in a dream, we were bodily transported away from that place in the desert to some other place. It was the only time his powers went awry. We had to walk back eight days' journey in the desert to where Mr. Bad Thing resided.

It was not easy to beard that Mr. Bad Thing. After the false start, the Healer required great energy and total concentration. In truth, I doubted him capable of winning this battle. I remarked what changes this expedition to the New World had wrought upon my former master. He had become an old man now, with a long white beard that hung down to the ground, and skin like elephant's hide from years in the sun. In the old days I would have suited him up in his armor for battle and he would have ridden out to meet Mr. Bad Thing on his charger, with his heavy lance in front and his plumes flying behind, his family mace hanging from the saddle, to crush Mr. Bad Thing's head. But now he remained perfectly naked, calm, and frail as a cane reed, as he was during all his cures and blessings, for Don Álvar was never one for shaking. He never liked to wear clothes when he was practicing medicine. But who does? In the period of our wanderings, we shed our skin twice a year, like snakes. I also never wore clothing, but had obtained a buck deer's head, which I wore for the pleasure of acquiring antlers. The Indians would not let the Healer begin to pray against Mr. Bad Thing until they had painted a large insignia on his back, a superstition for obtaining good luck. It was the same crosshatch we had seen so long ago on the coast of Florida.

The Healer lay flat on the ground and prayed fervently. He prayed through a day and a night, and the day that followed. He prayed up and he prayed down. He prayed backward and he prayed forward. He prayed straight and he prayed bent. Then he commanded in the name of God almighty that Mr. Bad Thing stay under the ground from thenceforward.

I expected to see *el diablo* hurtle forth from the ground. For who was Álvar Núñez Cabeza de Vaca to make the devil remain in hell? Instead, froth and bubbling liquid fire began to issue from the holes. The earth turned red-hot as a cinder under our feet. Plumes of black smoke billowed into the air, and then masses of maggots issued forth from the crevice; millipedes of a tremendous size crawled out; angry hornets swarmed from the openings; armies of red ants marched; battalions of scorpions, all rattling their stingers, and another kind of lizard we did not know—with a great long tongue, a lizard that could run on two legs like a man. The sky grew black as night. Everywhere was smoke, when suddenly bats bolted from underground. They flew out by the millions, in a great screeching swarm. The sky was entirely blotted out. Later only a few snakes slithered forth, coiling together in hideous fury, but not so many in number.

The test of faith was over in a matter of hours. A final and tremendous belch shook the earth, then all fell silent, and the scorched ruins steamed. The dead hosts of all the creatures piled up in mountains.

I had covered my head with my arms to avoid the flying creatures, but now peeped out. "Psst, Master?" I spoke in a hush. "Psst, psst!"

"Over here," came a low voice nearby.

"Still alive?"

"Yes, boundless thanks to God," said Don Álvar.

I found him and helped him to his feet. "I think your cure has taken effect."

His eyes were glazed, circled by dark rings of fatigue from all his efforts. "It did?"

"Shall I inform the Indians they need fear this Mr. Bad Thing no longer?"

"They don't?" he seemed dazed.

"Congratulations and blessings, Don Álvar. It seems you have beat the devil in his own lair."

"Thank you," he said weakly. "Thank you so much."

—

If he was popular before, there was no reckoning it now. Tens of thousands of Indians started for our presence all at once to thank the Healer for banishing this Mr. Bad Thing—whom we had never laid eyes on. The Healer spoke to them as one, all gathered there, to convert them to the Faith. He raised his arms up to Heaven, and taught them, "In Heaven is a man we call God. If you would only believe in God and become Christians, you need never fear Mr. Bad Thing again, nor would he dare come and inflict wounds upon you."

The Indians all raised their arms. But the caciques said they already knew about this God, only that he lived in the earth, not in Heaven, and furthermore was a woman, not a man.

The Holy Man threw up his hands again; so did all the Indians. So it was that although the Indians in our retinue did not yet know much of the Christian faith, yet they believed whatever Don Álvar told them, for they now considered themselves his children. He had them muster each morning before us and lift their arms together toward Heaven. They repeated this ritual at sunset.

The country virtually emptied to meet us. We got no rest at all after this. People from everywhere hysterically crowded upon us, everyone competing to touch the Healer first. We were nearly killed in the crush. Whereas sometimes prior to this we had not eaten, but always slept, now we always ate but could not sleep a wink. After all our travails, battles, run-ins with death, the many pangs of hunger we had suffered together, and our years of wandering the coast of the South Sea, we would in the end, it seemed, be killed by adoration, the victims of our own success. Though they pursued just to touch us in innocent affection, it cost us many hours going through them.

Involved in the constant pushing, tugging and grabbing, Don Álvar appeared to be wearing away like the sole of a boot from too much use. Trying to get away from this throng, we plunged inland again, as we had done before, always with the same disastrous consequences, and this time it was no different. We got lost till we came to a town called Soyopa, where rain was falling so heavily that we could not cross the swollen river and had to wait fifteen days.

In Soyopa, Castillo happened to see an Indian wearing around his neck a little sword belt buckle with horseshoe nails stitched to it. He took the Indian to Don Álvar, who bade me ask the Indian where he had obtained the amulet. The Indian said the charm had come to him from Heaven. When we inquired who had brought it, he said that some bearded white men had come to that river with horses, lances, and swords. They had lanced some natives and taken many away in chains.

Hearing this, the Healer grew so excited I thought his head would burst. "Be quick, speedy Estevanico, and find out what has become of these bearded men."

"I will do so for your sake, but speaking quite frankly, I would just as soon not know."

"Ask casually," he warned, "so as not to arouse their suspicion."

"All right," I said. "And shall I inquire, too, how many children have been slaughtered and how many young girls raped?"

"Why would we wish to know that?"

"Why, because then we would know better if these bearded men were Christians."

The holy man was not too weak to administer a swift kick to my buttocks.

"They have gone to the sea," said the Indian. "They got into the water, and we saw them moving on top of the water into the sunset. We hope they won't come back." He wished to know if the Healer could make the bearded men fall into the sun.

I was certain we were on the trail of Christians. But upon hearing this news, the Healer fell to his knees and gave many thanks to the Lord Our God, so glad was he, having almost despaired of finding Christians again.

We turned direction again, following the base of the mountains toward the sea. But soon we were hastening through a vast territory abruptly vacated. The country and villages were burned with fire. Not a lodge was left, nor a field of new green maize, nor a hut, nor a garden of spreading squash and climbing beans. Our hearts grew heavy as we looked over this fertile, beautiful land, now abandoned and ravaged, and saw the thin, weak people, confounded and hiding in fright. They were reduced to eating roots and bark, too alarmed to stay anywhere very long, preferring death to a repetition of their recent horror. All the people said the bearded men had attacked without warning, razing towns and fields, and carrying off half the men, and all the women and children. Those who had escaped were wandering about as fugitives. The horsemen had marched many Indians away in chains.

As we traveled farther, the initial joy of Don Álvar turned to trepidation. We could see the Christians' tracks and found the remains of their camps. Everywhere they had been, the villages were wasted and without inhabitants. The hand of hunger was upon the survivors. One morning our Indian heralds returned, saying they had spied on the Christians from behind trees and seen them marching away columns of Indians in chains in the dead of night.

The barren ruins of the country and the intelligence we received terrified our Indian escorts, many of whom fled to hide. We tried to reduce their fright by assuring them of the Healer's protection. We followed along a great river for sixteen days. When we saw from stakes in the ground that we were drawing near to men with horses, Don Álvar and Dorantes gave thanks to God for bringing us out of our wretched exile. But when Don Álvar insisted we quicken our pace, Castillo became very angry and said he would go his own way from now on. He departed, heading to the west. His final words to Don Álvar, as I recall them, were "Tell them I died on that barge long ago. Tell them I died in their hell, and was reborn here in Paradise! Farewell, good Doctor, and may fortune smile upon you." We never saw him again.

Within days we came upon four Christians with their horses. We three, the sole survivors of the Narváez expedition, approached their camp, hailing the Christians from a distance in the Castilian tongue. Even at a great distance they were struck dumb at the sight of Don Álvar, a shrunken, naked figure like a newborn bird, bald on top but hairy as a gopher under the chin, and in the company of so many Indians. It was curious the way the Healer had grown old, far more so than Dorantes or myself. He had lost a full two hands' length, and his beard had turned completely white. From so many years as a Christian knight, his legs had long since bowed. But the habits of the horseman were useless in this New World, where everyone went only on foot. We had walked thousands of leagues, then thousands more. It was not a physical feat, but one of pure spirit. Now Don Álvar seemed to totter forward across the plains on bandy legs, with his elbows sticking out, almost as if he still wore body armor and carried a rusty lance.

Still, his single-minded spiritual devotion showed in his face. He had sprouted a supremely serene countenance, with a tranquil, unhurried expression. He had the curious habit of keeping his eyes closed much of the time, so that it was hard to know if he was praying or sleeping—an old man's trick, and his very favorite. The changes medical practice had wrought upon Don Álvar made his aged face look sage far beyond the forty-five or forty-six years he had. He was more serious than he had once been; he was gentler, too. The gentleness he showed to the Indians was nothing short of astounding to the Christians.

None of the Christians replied to our greetings. For a long time they simply sat dumbfounded in their saddles, staring at us in disbelief. The one in command, whom we later found out was Captain Diego Alcazar, looked from Don Álvar to the Indians following him and licked his chops. Then all started to talk at once.

"I'm completely undone," said Alcazar. "We've been out here for weeks unable to catch any Indians. The men are tired and hungry. Now this old dwarf comes along with all the Indians you could want, and he looks like he knows where there are more."

"Shall we torture him to find out?" said another of the Christian officers.

"Wait, we must be careful," said a third. "He could be the homunculus we have heard about in tales."

"Greetings! Greetings!" shouted Don Álvar like a long lost brother. "You do not know how long we have been praying to let us meet."

"Careful," I said to him. "It may not be us they care about meeting. Look at the way that one with the yellow hair"—this was Alcazar—"is eyeing those Indians."

"We know him," said one of the Indian caciques. "He is a weak and vicious man."

"They would not harm Indians under my protection," said the Healer.

"He does not know me very well," said Alcazar.

"He is a weak and vicious man," said the cacique again.

"Here is the plan," said Alcazar. "Let us make slaves of the Indians in their train. Take these three prisoner also. Force them to lead us to other Indians."

"But who are they? That is what we still don't know," said another Christian officer.

"We are also confused," said a cacique. "Which are the Christians here? Is it the Healer or these others, the bad ones on horses? They both claim to be Christians. But how can that be so?"

"You are my prisoner," Alcazar spoke to Don Álvar.

"Foul plot! Can this be true? You cannot conquer through violence, only through gentleness," the holy man answered.

"There is a crafty scheme afoot," I told him.

"We are bound by custom to turn the Healer over to other Indians," said the cacique. "We do not intend to leave you in the charge of these marauding Christians. We would die if we returned to our homes without fulfilling this sacred obligation."

"Interpreter," said Alcazar to me, "tell the savages that this old man is a member of my race who has been long lost, and that we are the lords of the land, who must be obeyed and served."

"Tell them yourself."

"It is indeed curious, but I once resembled that one, tall and blond in the saddle," said Don Álvar.

"Shall I kill the rebellious blackamoor?" said one of the Christian officers.

"By all means," said Alcazar.

"I rode tall in the saddle, just like that *teniente!*" gasped Don Álvar.

"These Christians lie," said the cacique, "for the Healer came from the sunrise, and they came from the sunset."

Another cacique said, "The Healer heals the sick, while these others kill the sound."

"We are naked and barefoot," the Healer proclaimed.

"We are clothed, horsed, and lanced," spat one of the Christians.

"I will never believe you are of the same people," said a cacique.

"Let's kill some of these Indians before they kill us," said Captain Alcazar. "That will teach the rest to be good Christians."

"He is a bad and capricious man," said an Indian. "His evil comes from his weakness."

"I am shocked," said the Healer.

"We are shocked also," chorused the caciques.

Don Álvar said, "I fought for Felipe of Aragon. I was an *hidalgo*, tall and blond in the saddle. Ten years ago you could not have told me from this Christian knight."

"You are all my prisoners!" said Alcazar.

"You were like him?" said the Indians.

"Those days are long gone," I said. "New days are beginning. Let us wake up from this dream, with as much of nothing as we desire to keep. Mark well that Christian's face, Master, for once you were a Spanish gentleman like him. Once you were a man who had the power without; now you are the man who has the power within. There is the one you were, Don Álvar Núñez Cabeza de Vaca, but only here the one you are now!"

"The man I was and the man I am," said the Healer in a faint whisper.

At this point they put us all under arrest and marched us through forests and wastes so that we could not communicate with the natives.

———

I, Esteban de Veras, affirm that this document, contained in sheets, is my testament, for I have dictated it and caused it to be written down, and have signed it with my name.

Made in the city of New Spain, twelfth of May, in the year of our Redeemer, one thousand five hundred and thirty-seven.

White Cranes

You might as well call me Bubba—everybody else does. I've been Bubba since the day my parents first set eyes on me in the Houston hospital, and I'll most likely remain Bubba till they lay me in my grave. All my life, it's been Bubba-this and Bubba-that. First it was the Bubba bike. Then the Bubba mitt. Later on the Bubbamobile. Hard to tell what started it all. Bubbas are all males born below the Mason and Dixon line. The nickname is as southern as fried chicken. Some say it's baby talk, from trying to say "baby" or "brother" and coming out "Bubba" instead. Some say it's a certain contented or sleepy look in a boy child's face, or even how much he weighs at birth. I weighed more than twelve pounds, which immediately qualifies you for Bubbahood, plus a probable spot on the future football roster of one of our fine temples of miseducation, otherwise known as public high schools. I was also born with a complete caul, which is the membrane that protects a fetus's head inside the mother's womb, that maybe only one in a million babies still has intact after birth. In the South the old-time conjure women who used to deliver babies at home said a child born with a complete caul had some special gift or destiny and was touched by God, though the only talent I ever displayed was for running off at the mouth, and running behind the times.

—

My real name is actually Charles Cincinnatus Coxmoor, Jr., but who the hell's got time for all that? Things are slow enough down here in Port Aransas, Texas. Bubba Coxmoor will do just fine. I'm forty-five years of age and a Vietnam veteran, with a college degree in wildlife biology I got with my G.I. benefits from the University of Texas. When I finished my studies in Austin ten years back, there weren't many jobs out there, since the Reaganauts were busy making the environment safe for corporate polluters. But my wife, Katie Alice, and I were lucky enough to buy an old eighty-five-foot wood-hulled, open-sided party boat that takes tourists out to see the whooping cranes in the Aransas National Wildlife Refuge, which is located behind Matagorda Island on the Intracoastal Waterway. Katie Alice quit her job as a ranger at the refuge, and for the last ten years we've been operating the boat together out of Port Aransas.

I had a rough time growing up and assuming responsibility. I was only a college freshman when I got busted for smoking pot at a Saturday night dance. Actually, smoking it *and* distributing it. They were hard on underage felons in Texas in those days, but since it was my first offense, I was given the choice between enlisting in the Army or going to prison with a criminal record that would follow me all my days.

I got shipped to Vietnam in 1968, where I stepped on a mine near Pleiku during the Tet offensive and lost my left leg. They sent me home with an honorable discharge and eventually fixed me up with a space-age prosthetic that left me only semi-gimpy. After I got back from Nam, I wasted many a year trying to recapture my lost youth. I'm one impulsive son of a bitch, like the time I rammed a fireplace poker through the TV set because they were showing a program on Vietnam veterans I didn't happen to agree with. I have also been known to be reckless and undependable, like the time I lost my job at the Houston shipyards because I went turkey hunting on opening day, got loaded on Jack Daniel's, fell out of a tree stand and broke both elbows. I still smoke pot, wear a beard and my hair in a ponytail, listen to the same Janis Joplin records I acquired when I was seventeen, and still choke up when I hear "Me and Bobbie McGee." Though I'm too familiar with my own patented brand of Bubba bullshit by now to think I'm some kind of rebel. I see what happened to a lot of Vietnam vets, ones who made it back and ones who made it partway back, and I thank my lucky stars I met Katie Alice, who was the one who pushed me to go back and finish my education and to buy the boat in the first place. Without her to keep me running on the rails, I'd be lost. We've got a little girl, Sara (Sally), who is eleven years old and talks and looks like a female Bubba wind-up doll: chunky body, round face, straight brown hair. The two of them and the boat are the best things that could have ever happened to a world-class underachiever like myself.

I'm not a religious person, but I try to do God's work, and we try to give the folks who go out on the boat their money's worth. You talk about a preacher's flock; well, those whooping cranes have become a kind of ministry for me. The Church of the Immaculate Bubba. I feel like a zealot who takes Muslims on the pilgrimage to Mecca, hoping a little bit of Mecca will rub off on him.

It's something about those cranes. Katie Alice and I have both learned a lot about them over the years. There's less than one hundred of these huge waders left alive in the world. Their numbers have been dwindling down all through the last couple of centuries due to a variety of factors, all having to do with humans. In Colonial times, there were still great flocks of cranes on the Gulf Coast, around the Florida peninsula, and supposedly right on up the East Coast as far as the Outer Banks of North Carolina. Back then they hunted cranes for food and feathers. Audubon shot a bunch of 'em with one blast of his goose gun.

Then the coastline got settled. As the pioneers hit the road west, the marshes where the cranes nested were gradually drained for agriculture during the nineteenth century. Without anyone realizing it, whooping cranes started fading away. Flocks got rarer, sightings got fewer. Last seen in Illinois in 1891. Last found nesting in Iowa in 1895. It was already almost too late in the 1930s, when some ornithologists from the Audubon Society realized there was only this one flock of birds left—fifteen birds in all at that time. Fifteen whooping cranes come to the end of the line, nothing standing between them and extinction. By chance this little speck of Texas Gulf Coast on the Blackjack Peninsula was the winter habitat of the last flock of whooping cranes left alive on earth.

It was President Franklin Delano Roosevelt who created Aransas as a refuge for the cranes. After the Second World War, the federal government launched a big campaign to save the whoopers. Magazine articles and television programs were made about them, and the whooping cranes soon became the first and most famous of all endangered species. Schoolkids used to follow their migration between Aransas and northern Canada twenty-five hundred miles away, where our flock has its breeding grounds. Hunters were alerted everywhere not to shoot them, and none have been shot since the early 1950s. In fact, since they were protected, the whoopers have been increasing in number, though very slowly. No one really knows enough about their biology to know when and if they might form a second flock.

People come to us from all over the U.S. and Canada to see the whooping cranes. A lot of folks make the trip special. The whoopers are about the biggest tourist attraction we got on the Texas Gulf. We're one of only three boats licensed by the Fish and Wildlife Service to take people into Aransas. Every year we take more than twenty thousand visitors, lots of groups from foreign countries, especially from Japan and Asia, where cranes are symbols of long life and marital fidelity. I'm Captain Bubba up in the wheelhouse, and Katie Alice gives them an orientation lecture about the birds and the area till we get out in the Intracoastal. Most of the time we skirt the coast near shore till we locate a pair of cranes, then cut the engines, drop anchor between the channel and the shore, and let the folks watch the whoopers through their binoculars.

We have the most well-behaved passengers anyone could ask for. Never had to throw off a drunk, like on fishing boats. I like to go down to the deck and answer people's questions. I get so tickled watching them watch whooping cranes. Little kids and old grandmothers. Never a boring moment. When they see a whooping crane for the first time, they just light up. It's like seeing a legend in their own time.

The whooping crane has got to be about the most graceful and elegant bird you can think of, a real aristocrat of nature. What we usually observe from the boat is cranes stalking the shoreline in pairs or family threesomes. They are deft predators. Their stature is nothing short of kingly. They stand about five feet, tallest of all North American bird species. Beautiful lithe, white necks, stilt legs varnished black. Their white plumes have a kind of satin shine to them. When they sight prey in the water, they stand over it perfectly silent, moving about one millimeter per second, till they get down to where they can strike. And then—splash!—in less than a second they've speared it, brought it out of the water, and are tossing it down their gullet. They'll hunt for fifteen or twenty minutes, then stand still as stone, creamy white like a Greek statue in marble against the flat greens of the salt marshes and the blue lagoons.

Like Robert Johnson sang, the whoopers have "Elgin movements from the head down to the toes." Every step they take is like they're following a grand duke around. The mates don't stray far from each other's side, so that most often all their elegant stepping is usually done in deuces.

Our boat is too big for the cranes to recognize it as something dangerous in nature, so they don't pay it no mind, and we can move in as close as twenty-five or thirty yards. As long as no one makes noise or waves their arms, the birds will go on about their business as if we weren't there. But if any kind of crane-recognizable intruder comes into view, that male crane will snap his head erect like a samurai warrior, take one fierce look around, glaring down his javelin beak from behind an iridescent deep-purple-colored patch over the forehead, then emit that big blast from his vocal chords that gives the whooping crane its name. There's nothing you'll hear in nature to match it. Katie Alice, who has actually worked around cranes longer than me and knows them as good as anybody, says that sometimes they whoop to ward off intruders, while other times it's more like a warning call to alert other cranes to danger. I've tried to describe that whoop a hundred times. Best thing I can come up with is that it's like a wilder version of a high-school marching band trumpet, if that makes any sense. Anyway, that potent whoop can easily be heard more than a mile away on a still day.

Every hour or two we move the boat along when the whoopers take off. They will start announcing their flight intentions with an unfurling and flapping of their immense wings. The bird's neck lances forward, legs thrust straight back, and the white wings with jet-black tips spread out over seven feet. It requires a lot of energy to get these big babies airborne. We'll see them flap in slow motion only a few feet over the water. Suspended in air, they seem to have all the time in the world. When they flock up they'll fly in these perfectly synchronized formations. Lots of times our passengers will burst into applause, like it's the final number in a stage show. Maybe for one little instant, they see how the world looked before the first Bubba had rototilled the Garden of Eden.

Like I said, the whoopers are creatures evolved in slow motion. Every move they make is slower than molasses, and their lifestyle is just about as slow as their movements. For a bird, whooping cranes take a long time to mature—three to five years. We often see all the young 'uns together. Driven away by their long-suffering parents, they form their own youth gang. They will associate with each other for several years—typical teenage pissants—till the young cranes start to court, settle on a mate, and separate into pairs. They don't rush into mating like humans do, overheated by the passion of the moment. An available young female crane will try out one young male for a while, hang out with him, go fishing every day with him; then, when he's likely all goony in the gonads to finalize the deal, she'll drive him away and try another one.

The females aren't coldhearted or calculating, only extremely particular. Their migrations are so long and dangerous, and their parenting is so extended, that selection of a mate is the keystone of the species' survival. Once cranes find a mate, they stay together for life, which some biologists who have studied them think could be as long as fifty years, barring accidents and predation. We always take our boat tours to see a newly mated pair if we can locate one, because crane romance is a sight to see. The young lovers splash around the shallows together, preening, displaying, and performing their mating dances. The male crane bows his head, slowly lifts his wings, then leaps straight into the air three or four feet, tossing his head back till his bill points up to the sky, like a combination of Baryshnikov and Moses Malone. The female responds by spreading her wings and gliding around her mate in a spectacular water ballet. Then she springs straight up, too, and they both start leaping up and down together like they're on pogo sticks.

Once they do finally hook up and form pairs, the cranes fall into a regular migratory rhythm, which also determines our season on the boat. In late January, they start their breeding cycle with their amazing mating dances. A lot of birders and other folks will come down to Aransas toward the tail end of winter, which is mild down here anyway, just to see the cranes dance. Then on a certain day in spring, the whoopers start to flock up together. They circle around the refuge gathering the tribe for a couple or three days. I say they're polishing up their formation flying before commencing their migration. Katie Alice says they're all hyped up because they're going home to their nesting grounds in northern Canada, where the cranes lay their eggs—only one or two at most—and birth their young. We won't see them again till they arrive back in the autumn. That's another real exciting time to visit the refuge, when the cranes first arrive at Aransas with their new fledglings.

We usually haul the boat out in the off-season, scrape and paint the bottom, and attend to routine maintenance. There's always work to do when you own a boat, and I need to keep busy to stay out of trouble. Since I don't have time to do much hunting or fishing during the tour season, I make time to do some summer fishing in the Gulf. Every autumn before the cranes come, Kate Alice will get all nervous, God bless her, in case something might happen to one or more of the cranes on migration. It's about a twenty-five-hundred-mile trip for them. The autumn migration south is even more dangerous than the spring trip north. Any new parent can imagine what it'd be like to take a four-month-old on a twenty-five-hundred-mile trip. They travel south in family groups, slowly imprinting the route on their young, but anything and everything can happen: a hurricane or tornado, an early snowstorm, a stupid kid with a .22 rifle, eating something poisonous, a pack of wild dogs, or crashing into high-tension wires. After ten years, we pretty much know the long-established pairs of cranes on sight. If one doesn't make it back to Aransas in the fall, we'll know within a few days exactly which one. We breathe a deep sigh of relief when they finally start landing at Aransas. We take volunteer spotters from the Texas Audubon Society out on the first days of the tour season, who tally the whoopers to see if all are present and accounted for, and to start keeping stat sheets on the young cranes.

We have been at this long enough to know within a few days of accuracy when the Aransas flock will take off on the spring migration, which marks the end of our tour season, and we publish the date April 15 in the brochure about our boat we send out to travel agents and put in the motels. So at first we were stumped when we got a call from a Washington, D.C., travel agent, who said a Vietnamese government delegation visiting the United States wanted to charter the boat beginning April 16 to see the famous whooping cranes at Aransas. They were offering to pay what we would have charged for a full boatload of tourists for each of three consecutive days to have exclusive use of the boat, which we call *Cutter's Way* after an old movie about a Vietnam vet and gimpy-legged kid that I like.

Katie Alice told the woman over the phone we'd be glad to accommodate the delegation, but that if they wanted to catch the whoopers they should try to push up their schedule, since the birds were unlikely to remain at Aransas that late in the season. The travel agent didn't think there was any wiggle room in the delegation's schedule, but said she would relay our doubts to her clients and get back with us. However, the next thing we knew, a check arrived in the mail from the travel agency, covering the costs of a three-day private charter for April 16, 17, and 18. I was seeing a new outboard for my fishing boat in the immediate future.

"Should I call back and cancel?" Katie Alice said.

"Heck, no," I told her. "That money'll come in handy in the off-season."

"Can I go, too?" said our little girl Sally.

———

We didn't know what to expect, but we didn't have any trouble depositing the check. The weather turned fine at the end of March, and we had a run of great days for crane watching. The sun warmed up the bays and ponds at the edge of the salt marshes, and the new fish hatch provided an abundant source of food for the birds to store up fat before their long journey north. At the same time, the warm weather keyed up the male cranes, and they were doing more than a Texas two-step to seduce those lady cranes. They were prancing and dancing, their best show in years, and we had a lot of satisfied pilgrims.

About the end of the first week of April, right on schedule, the cranes started to flock up. The last days of the season are always some of the best at Aransas, because as the flock start to gather you can see their excitement about the coming trip. They'll be out there practicing their collective takeoffs and landings like the Air National Guard. They'll circle overhead

and whoop in harmony and do all kinds of strange and interesting things. There was one pair with their yearling, for
example, that seemed to fail to pay heed to the flock as it
came overhead. Well, that whole flock of cranes put down not
far from the family and started whooping at them, chewing
them out for not behaving more sociable, I guess.

April 15 came. We didn't hear anything from the travel
agency up north, so we figured the delegation was on. We
thought there was still a slight chance there might be a few
straggler birds in the area, but there wasn't much we could do
but give it our best shot. The night before, we decided to let
Sally come along with us; she's a big enough girl now to help
out with the passengers and in the snack bar, and it was her
spring vacation. Besides, she was twisting with curiosity to see
the Vietnamese.

We assumed we were going out on three consecutive day
trips, but when we came down to the dock in the morning, the
Vietnamese delegation was already waiting there with their
gym bags and little rice cookers, several large bags of rice and
such, as if they were heading up the Mekong River.

"Well, this is all highly irregular," I said out loud to Katie
Alice.

"Shhh, you'll offend them, Bubba," she said.

"They probably don't speak no English, Katie Alice."

"What are they doing, Daddy?" my daughter wanted to
know.

There must have been about thirty members of the delegation, but they sure didn't look to me like government officials.
They were dressed like any other Oriental tourists, in cheap
Chinese sportsclothes and sneakers, but maybe they'd
stopped at a Wal-mart before they came to us. They were all

lined up in three rows of ten in the parking lot off the side of the dock doing some kind of slow exercises in unison. There was an old yellow man leading them at the front with his eyes closed, who moved just as smooth as malted milk. He looked about seventy, I'd guess, with one of those real calm Oriental faces and a steel-gray crewcut. He wasn't dressed like the others, but had on a pair of baggy gray pants and a military-style gray jacket, though without insignia.

We went aboard to get the boat ready, and after they finished their routine the delegation scrambled across the little boarding steps, all smiles and clicking cameras and happy chatter.

"I am Dr. Duc To, head of delegation," said the old gent with a formal bow.

"Glad to know you. Welcome aboard. Did you say Doctor Doctor?" I couldn't hope to get his name right.

He handed me his business card, which straightened me out. It said: "Dr. Duc To, M.D., Ministry of Public Health and Welfare, Department of Ancestral Relations." I passed it on to Katie Alice.

"I'm Captain Bubba Coxmoor." I extended my hand to shake, but when he reached out and just lightly grazed my fingertips with the outskirts of his thumb and index finger, I felt such a strong buzz, like an electric current, passing through me that I nearly got thrown against the wheelhouse wall.

"Okay. This is my wife, Katie Alice. She operates the boat with me."

"Morning!" She did her best squink. Squinking is something southern women do. It's a combination of making a high-pitched squeaking sound and winking with both eyes at the same time. It's how you know a southern woman is trying to be friendly, like their mamas teach them.

"And this is our daughter, Sara Coxmoor."

The old gent bowed again. "How do you do, litter gel?"

"Hey," said Sally, momentarily stunned into shyness, but watching him like a hawk.

The delegation's translator, Miss Phuong, introduced herself next. Like the leader, she hadn't adopted the discount store uniform either. She was a handsome middle-aged woman with skin the color of amber and tiny, birdlike bones. She piled her black hair elaborately high on her head, covering it with a patterned silk scarf, and wore a long tight skirt down to her ankles. Her big dark glasses gave her a definite air of mystery, like she was someone with a lifetime of sorrows she didn't want the world to see in her face. She spoke English with a French accent, and when she leaned over to shake hands I noticed she was wearing perfume; it reminded me of the scent the bargirls used to wear in Saigon, but maybe that's the only flavor they have in Vietnam.

I said to the translator, "Before we get started, maybe you could explain to your delegation that the cranes start their migration north this time of year. We know the main flock left Aransas a few days back. We'll try our hardest to find some whoopers, but we can't guarantee you'll see any. It's just that they may have all left already. We sure don't want y'all to go away unhappy in case we can't find any. We tried to inform your travel agent about this."

Miss Phuong didn't bother to relate what I said to Dr. Duc To, who stood with his feet apart and his arms folded on his chest, nodding approval as she said, "Dr. Duc To asks you not to worry on behalf of delegation. You appear to be a man who eats and sleeps well, like zee happy spirit. We are certain you will help us fulfill delegation plan, Capitaine Coxmoor."

"Ya'll can call me Bubba. Everybody else does."

Miss Phuong looked at me a little strangely—probably never heard the name Bubba before. While she was talking the old gent started rummaging in his rucksack and brought out a map, which he unfolded for me to look at. It was a highly detailed topographical map, not only of the Aransas refuge but of all the surrounding territory in Aransas, Calhoun, and Refugio counties. Every point, I mean every single bay, was labeled in Vietnamese. There was even a red line marking a route. I could not imagine where he could have obtained such a thing, but I reckoned it wouldn't be polite to ask.

"Dr. Duc To ask to conduct delegation here." Miss Phuong traced the red dotted line with her long painted fingernail.

"That's fine," I told her. "Like we say in America, the customer is always right."

This Miss Phuong did translate, and Dr. Duc To actually laughed and said, "Very sensible, cunstumer right! Okay, now we go."

I could see from the look on Katie Alice's face that she was just as impressed and puzzled as me by Dr. D., Miss Phuong, and especially the map. It was all as queer as a three-dollar bill.

Sally had wiggled in between us, not one to be left out of anything, and she was checking out the map, too. "Hey, you mean they already know where to go?"

"Honey," said Katie Alice, "will you go up to the bow, please, and throw off the mooring line when we tell you?"

"But, Mama, where in hell—I mean, where in tarnation did they get that map from?"

"Go up to the bow *now*, please."

—

Before leaving the dock, a bunch of the women came up to Katie Alice on deck and asked if they could hang this piece of embroidered silk they had from the center pole in the passenger's cabin, which is really nothing more than the center deck with a roof made by the wheelhouse, plus a canvas extension and roll-down clear plastic awnings for the sides in case of rain. They had brought with them this small octagonal symbol of some kind. Katie Alice squinked 'em and made friendly signs, but told them they'd have to ask Captain Bubba. Actually she just wanted me to see the thing.

The women had no objection, so she brought it up to the wheelhouse. It was an octagonal shape, about six inches on a side. Inside the octagon was an eye, and inside the eye a red heart.

"What do you make of that, Bubba?" she shouted over the engine, which is an old 225-horsepower diesel and makes more than its share of noise.

"You know I ain't for sure. Maybe it's to keep hippies away!"

"Well, you were over there; ever seen anything like it?"

"If I did I was running too fast to recall. Probably just some kind of good luck charm to keep away the evil eye."

"Well, I'm going to nail it up in the passenger cabin. But don't you go playing cards with them, Bubba, 'cause if this thing works, they'll take all your money!"

———

Cutter's Way left the dock at Port Aransas a little after 9:30 A.M. We headed out through Aransas Pass, then our usual way up the Intracoastal Waterway past Fulton and Lamar to Blackjack Point, where the fifty-four-thousand-acre refuge starts. There's plenty of deep water out there, and like always, I steered the boat right beside the channel in order to avoid all the tankers, barges, derricks, and such servicing the oil industry that make the Intracoastal like a foamy interstate highway. God forbid there should ever be a major oil spill there because it'd just wipe out the cranes with one swipe.

Katie Alice and Sally stayed down on the deck with the delegation. From up in the wheelhouse, I could see that they had all moved to the bow and were crowded around Dr. Duc To, who had the only set of binoculars—banged-up military binoculars, probably around since the Vietnam War. Later on we found out he'd been a medical doctor and a colonel in the NVA. Even chatting and relaxed with his people out there, you could kind of tell he was held in awe. They hung back a little bit, as if intimidated by him, and formed a semicircle around him like disciples to catch his words. They let him do the talking and reacted with the same expressions whenever he delivered a comment. He was watching the oil service craft. Once he must have said something funny, because they practically fell over laughing at what he told them, though usually they just nodded in silent agreement.

The ride up to the Point only takes about forty-five minutes. It was a spectacular morning out on the water, and I decided right then and there that even if they didn't get to see any whooping cranes, I'd take 'em around and give them a gold-card tour of the whole Aransas area. Hell, we got everything from dolphins to Texas barbecue and mariachi bands.

We were coming up to Blackjack Point when Katie Alice climbed up into the wheelhouse again with Miss Phuong.

"Should we go up into St. Charles Bay?" We usually start by splitting off the Intracoastal and going up into St. Charles Bay, which is protected by the peninsula, so the shoreline is prime hunting habitat for the whoopers.

Katie Alice conferred with Miss Phuong, who didn't seem to hesitate to call the shots on her own.

"They say they don't want to lose time, especially if there are probably no cranes up there anyway. Why don't you stay on the outer shore, Bubba, and we'll work the bays one by one!"

"Sounds good to me!"

If you go up the outer shore there's a series of shallow bays that stretches all the way up the peninsula for a good twenty miles. At low tide the whoopers will come out to the exposed mudflats to hunt for crabs. The outside route was also along the red route on their map. Like I said, the customer is always right, especially if he agrees with you.

Then commenced an exhaustive and fruitless search. We went from one little crease in the coastline to the next all morning and well into the afternoon, but all we saw were some herons and egrets, which I thought about trying to pass off as whooping cranes, only they don't whoop. I stopped several times to talk over the loudspeaker with fishing-boat captains I know, but none of them had seen a whooper all day. We finally dropped anchor in a cove of Ayres Bay to let the delegation eat their lunch. Katie Alice and Sally opened up the snack bar, but they could have saved themselves the trouble. The delegation members rummaged in their gym bags and pocketbooks, and much to our surprise, brought out McDonald's bags. Then they sat down in place on the deck, crossed their legs, and ate cold french fries with ketchup—probably left over from a stop at the fast-food parlor en route to Port Aransas. They'd even brought their own tea in thermoses. Katie Alice fixed the three of us some hot dogs and Cokes, and after lunch we took off again.

For the better part of the afternoon we worked our way north, still hugging the shore, up San Antonio Bay and around False Live Oak Point. From there it's only another five miles to the northern border of the Aransas Refuge. We were skunked; the cranes had flown. We had been heading north by northeast, then northwest around the point, but long about 4 P.M., I knew we would have to turn back if we were going to make Port Aransas before dark.

I throttled the engine down to a gurgle and asked Katie Alice over the loudspeaker to come up to the wheelhouse. I was hoping for a word with her myself, but the clattering of high heels on the metal stairs told me Miss Phuong was on her way up, too. Even Sally came up, holding on to Miss Phuong's hand like she was her newfound friend.

"Miss Phuong's going to teach me to talk in Vietnamese, Daddy!" she cried. "She's already taught me how to say 'white crane.' It goes Hi ... um ... um ... pow ... ah ..."

"*Pai hao liang,*" said Miss Phuong with a slow, repeat-after-me lilt. As she put her arm around Sara for encouragement, my intuition told me she was a woman who had never had children, or maybe had lost them in the war.

"*Pie how long!*" Sally pronounced it perfectly.

"That's great, sugar," I told her. "Because if you want to talk Vietnamese, Miss Phuong is sure the best one to teach you."

"So what do you say, Bubba?" asked Katie Alice.

"We better call it a day if we're gonna get these nice folks back at a reasonable hour."

"Honey, I don't think they're really intending to go back to port, from the fact of their having brought all their gear and food and stuff. Miss Phuong," she turned to the translator, "could you, like, please explain to Dr. Duc To that we charter the boat by the day, and we have to turn back to port now, and we can go out again tomorrow morning?"

Dr. Duc To was up on the bow, with his hands behind his back, gazing out over the water in a serenity no one would dare disturb. I guess the Vietnamese don't believe in hands-on management.

"Capitaine Coxmoor, our highest venerable Ong Duc To say on behalf of delegation he would like to express warm thousandfold thanks. You and lovely wife try so very hard to locate zee cranes."

I said, "Well, we appreciate it, Miss Phuong, and we're glad to have your delegation aboard, too. I can't think of a nicer bunch of folks we've had out, isn't that right, Katie Alice?"

"You right about that, Bubba!" She squinked Miss Phuong. "And you could tell Dr. Duc To that we'll try just as hard tomorrow, and we'll go up the back way in St. Charles Bay, where there may be some straggler cranes."

"Unfortunately, delegation cannot lose time returning," Miss Phuong continued pleasantly but firmly. "Delegation must move forward to fulfill collective goal. Have we not paid for ze s'ree days boat?"

"Yes, but see, we don't have sleeping accommodations for the delegation on board. No place to sleep. No food."

Miss Phuong continued in the same determined way. "Delegation requires no such assistance, but wish only to continue on red route to zee twenty-eight degrees, twenty minutes north latitude, until we reach estuary of Army Corps of Engineers freshwater feeder number three fifty-two."

"What the heck are you talking about, Miss Phuong?"

"That must be one of those irrigation channels they dredged in Refugio County," said Katie Alice.

"I've never even been up there. They dredged those things back in the fifties. How could they know about that? I'll tell you one thing, these Vietnamese are either major drug runners or the most determined damn bunch of bird-watchers I've ever seen the likes of. I sure don't want to offend them, but I'm inclined to turn back anyway. I just don't know which way to turn on this thing, Katie Alice. I feel like Bill Clinton with a foreign policy crisis on his hands. Why don't you play first lady and decide for ole Bubba?"

Katie Alice didn't have a doubt in her head. "They *did* charter the boat for three days, Bubba. They probably thought they could go like they wanted. I mean, who knows if there's even such a word as 'day trip' in Vietnamese?"

"Maybe if we took 'em all out to eat Tex-Mex tonight?" I was grasping at straws.

"Well, I'm with Mama. We should keep going like Miss Phuong says," piped up Sally. "We've slept on the boat lots of times, and anyway I want to see where that map leads. I'll bet Dr. Duc To knows where he's going."

"Dr. Duc To ain't the captain of this boat, little girl," I remonstrated, but when you start arguing with your kids, you know you're licked. Anyway, it was thirty-two against one.

"Okay." I gave up. "We'll keep going. But, Miss Phuong, I want you to make one thing crystal clear to Dr. Duc To and your entire delegation, if you would, please."

"Yes, please, Capitaine Coxmoor?"

"We cannot run this boat at night in the shallow water. That is out of bounds. We haven't got the lights, and it's against Coast Guard regulations. If we run aground on the bottom up here, some people could get hurt and I could lose my captain's license. Besides, it'd cost a fortune to get someone out here if we needed to get towed off a bar. If I take the boat up to where y'all want, I'm dropping anchor and waiting out in deeper water overnight. Can you relay that to the head of your delegation for me, please?"

That's when we found out about him. Miss Phuong said Dr. Duc To was eighty-five years old, so she didn't want to keep pestering him about the details of our cruise. She had worked with him for twenty-five years, since the end of the war, during which he had been the responsible military official for civilian health in the entire "liberated zone," as she called it. For twenty years since "liberation," he had been a leader in the reconstruction of public health. "We understand you do very best to help us fulfill delegation plan. Safe operation of boat eez your duty, Capitaine Coxmoor. In this we do not interfere. Do you wish to follow map?"

"No thanks, not necessary. I got my own charts, and anyway, I couldn't read yours in Vietnamese if my life depended on it. I'll just follow the shoreline, same as we've been doing. But since y'all seem to know the place better than us natives, you can stay up here with me if you want."

"Yesss!" Sally lifted her left arm in a fist of victory. "Daddy, does this mean we've been hijacked?"

———

We chugged along the coast for another hour, then put in for the shoreline as the sun was starting to set. We'd edged around the hump of the refuge, so that the sun was going down over our shoulder, so to speak, back over the wetlands. The flat sawgrasses were all lit up orange like a million sparklers, and the sun was a geometrically perfect red ball. It was one hell of a Texas Gulf Coast sunset, only without whooping cranes.

The Vietnamese shifted toward it like a mass of multicolored gelatine oozing over to the stern. Then they put their palms together and shut their eyes in a kind of Buddhist-looking gesture. I'll say one thing for them as tourists, which I've noticed in other Asians we've had on the boat, though maybe to a lesser degree: they did everything together except go to the bathroom, but nobody had to tell them what to do. They were organized without anyone organizing them. Like they all thought the same thing at the same time, and *enjoyed* doing the same thing at the same time. During the war, we were told it was because they were brainwashed or because they were an inferior race, but I've met enough Orientals to know now that's total bullshit. I believe it's that they take a certain amount of pleasure in doing things the united way, is all, like a baseball team or a herd of longhorns.

Just watching the delegation gave me a touch of the blues because it put me in mind of the Vietnam War, and I hadn't thought about the war in some time. I'm not a man to hold a grudge against the Vietnamese. The war's been over more than twenty years. You got to try to put the past behind you and move on in this life: that's the Bubba way. Any memory will fade with time, whether your tragedy came on the battle-field or in the bedroom. But that evening I did recall how during the war it always felt like it was every man for himself over there. Enlisted men against officers, officers against the brass, blacks against whites, pot-smokers against straights. We weren't only fighting the VC and the North, we were fighting each other—fighting ourselves.

There was only another hour max of daylight left, but my navigational charts showed the Army Corps's irrigation canal, and I found it, no problem. The military used to use Matagorda Island as a bombing range, but agreed to stop when the feds protected the whooping cranes. The Corps of Engineers had plenty of dredging and filling projects to keep them happy back when Matagorda was a target range, but afterward they had to use up their excess institutional testosterone creating bulkheads and irrigation canals nobody ever used because the soil is so sandy in this part of Texas that nobody has tried to pasture cattle on it for a hundred years, let alone farm crops. The mouth of the canal had been bulkheaded with concrete work and is about thirty feet across, entering the bay from scrub country decorated only by a few floating buzzards.

"Here you are," I said. Miss Phuong and Sally had stayed up in the wheelhouse with me.

"Eez freshwater feeder number three fifty-two?" asked Miss Phuong.

I handed her my binocs. The Corps had left a little plaque affixed to their concrete work. There was no current to speak of in the canal but what the Gulf gave it, and they'd dredged the bottom good, so we could sit twenty feet off it.

Miss Phuong just flashed the fieldglasses up to her face for an instant, like she didn't know how to use them, then said, "Now we eat and rest till morning. On behalf of delegation, I wish to reassure you, Capitaine Coxmoor. We do not want to cause you or lovely family anxiety. Dr. Duc To ask you to put yourselves in heez hands, like any patient in hands of doctor. Vietnam people say, as morning mist rises to reveal river, all will become clear. Now Miss Phuong will go down to help wiz zee meal."

I noticed my daughter didn't say a word, and led Miss Phuong down the steps like her seeing-eye dog.

The women set up their little charcoal braziers on the open deck. They'd brought their own charcoal in a big burlap feed-bag, and pieces were handed around. By nightfall *Cutter's Way* looked and smelled like a Vietnamese junk full of boat people. They boiled rice in their woks, and each delegate contributed a piece of the remains of a Big Mac, which they chopped up and stir-fried, so that everyone had a bowl of rice and meat. They sent us bowls, too—even chopsticks to eat it with, though the eating implement of choice for me is a plastic spoon from the 7-Eleven. Then they brought out their tea kettles, boiled water, and stretched out on the deck in the heat of the evening, drinking hot tea and smoking cigarettes. My daughter took it upon herself to go around out there and tell each and every little group that smoking was bad for their health. I could see them nodding politely in agreement, even the ones who were smoking. As it grew darker, the women's faces glowed red and orange in the light of the charcoal cinders. The drifting smoke kept the mosquitoes off. The delicate voices of the men ran uphill and down like some pale melody.

We decided to bed down on the floor in the passenger's cabin. Katie Alice spread the storm blankets we always carry, and the three of us lay down together, with Sally in the middle.

"Can't I sleep with Miss Phuong—please, Mama?"

"Try to get some rest, sugar," said Katie Alice. "You'll see Miss Phuong in the morning."

"But Mama!"

"Hush up, now, Sara," said Katie Alice. "Did you hear what your mama told you?"

"Daddy, you're not scared, are you?"

"I reckon not. Nothing to be scared of, spending the night on our own boat. Why, are you?"

Our Sara isn't one to admit she's scared of anything. She was silent for a long moment, then said simply, "I'm not if you're not. Oh, man, but I like Miss Phuong. Wish I had her as my teacher."

"Well, that's all right, darling," said Katie Alice, "because these are good people. They're just different from us, is all, so sometimes it's hard to understand each other."

"But Bubba was over there. He understands them, don't you, Bubba?"

It was the first time she had ever referred to me as "Bubba." I wished I could have told her yes; I had to tell her something. I said, "Well, that war was a long time ago. Your daddy was just a common grunt soldier over there. They didn't tell us fighting men much about it. It was a bad war. We shouldn't have been over there in the first place. But once we went, we should have gone in there with our six-guns blazing and got it over with fast. Only thing I understood in Vietnam was to keep my butt down and try to shoot them before they shot us. But I didn't, so it don't matter nohow."

Then the predictable questions started. What was it all about? What's a communist? Is Miss Phuong a communist? Did I ever kill anybody? This jabbering, which Sally inherited from me, can go on all night once she gets started unless you put your foot down over her mouth and hold it closed. I warned her, "If you don't hush up right now and go to sleep, I'm going to take some stringent measures."

Suddenly Katie Alice jackknifed up straight. "Shhh— Bubba, what's that? Y'all hear that? Listen!"

At first all I heard was nothing, just the water lapping against the side of the boat. It was a still night, without much breeze. Then from a long way off the whoop of a crane drifted across the marshes and out over the water. It was unmistakably a whooper, but it didn't sound like any other whooping crane I've ever heard. It wasn't that brassy trumpet, but more soulful, like a sweet and low saxophone from one of those old-time New Orleans jazz bands. The notes hung in the heavy air for a long time, then sort of evaporated like sky writing.

"It's a ghost," said Katie Alice. "Oh, my Lord, it's a ghost whooping crane."

—

I woke up before dawn feeling moist and unwashed, to say the least. My stump throbbed, as it will do in wet weather. A heavy, drippy fog had moved in during the night—not cold, just that thick Gulf Coast humidity blanket that makes you feel like a fungus eager to multiply. As it got light, all you could see past the rail was a gray blot, which kind of matched my mood. Puffs of mist drifted over the delegates, who were already awake and performing their morning exercises together. I stood for a while with a blanket over my head, drank a Coca Cola, and watched them. They were so silent, so slow. Their bodies sliced through the air almost without friction. Not one of them made a sound. Their hands and arms described slow circles. Big circles with their arms, little circles with their hands. Circles to the north, circles to the south—graceful circles in all directions. Sometimes they looked like they were holding on to invisible basketballs. They stepped forward, shifted back, reached high, swung low. They rotated on their heels and waved their arms in front of them, just like the passing clouds. The moves flowed into each other smoothly; you could probably only get that after years of practice. It was more a dance than a martial art. They ended up with their hands crossed in front of them chest high, palms turned inward—the final circle formed between their arms, hands, and chest. They remained in that pose for several minutes. I concluded they were either meditating or sleeping standing up.

I was meditating, too, for what it was worth. *We ain't going nowhere till this stuff lifts; could be here another hour, maybe two. How the hell are we going to accommodate all these people in the bathrooms? I hope the head doesn't back up from all the traffic.*

"Auspicious day!" Dr. Duc To interrupted my reveries, entering the passenger cabin with Miss Phuong.

"Well, I've seen better. Hope y'all got some sleep. I know it couldn't have been too comfortable out in that ground fog."

He shrugged it off. "Vietnam people experience much worse. Here all is harmony."

I didn't know he could speak such good English. I said, "I fought in Vietnam."

"Then you have known more bitter mornings, too, Captain Bubba. May I ask, you lost leg during war of liberation?"

"Uh-huh. Course, we didn't call it that."

"I am medical doctor," he said. "May I ask where you received such wonderful prosthetic leg?"

"Here in the States. It took years till they got it to fit just right, but now it's state of the art. Cost eighteen thousand dollars. Government paid the bill."

"Ahhh, yes. I so wish we could have such prosthetics, but Vietnam is poor country. We have many thousands amputees after war of liberation."

I changed the subject. "I noticed y'all doing your exercises out there." Is it tai chi?"

"Yes," said Dr. Duc To. "Tai chi chuan. It is ancient Chinese way of inner healing."

"And why is it that you Vietnamese practice a Chinese way?"

"Vietnam proverb: Borrow from the tiger, lend to the rooster. But you look cold, Captain Bubba. Need tai chi to warm up inner self. We prepare tea now. You and lovely family will take tea with us, please."

"You mean hot tea?" Which is an abomination to anyone born and bred below the Iced Tea Line. But I found myself saying, "Sure. We're not going anywhere till this mist lifts."

"When zees will be?" asked Miss Phuong.

"Hard to say. It should start to dissipate after the sun comes up."

We rousted ourselves and went out to the deck to have breakfast with the delegation. Each delegate now brought out what had to be the last of his or her provisions: a quarter piece of the Big Mac bun carefully squirreled away for the morning meal. These the women dipped in cooking oil and fried in their woks, then served with soy sauce or sugar. The Vietnamese gobbled them up standing, with steaming cups of hot tea. Miss Phuong and Dr. Duc To personally served Katie Alice and Sally and me.

Before we finished, the sun started to burn through, highlighting a patch of glittering water here, a sunny bar of land there. After about an hour, the last clouds finally lifted in a salty swirl, leaving a soft deckle edge on the sea and shore, and that's when we heard the cranes again. Their whoops widened out from well inland. There was a bunch of them, trumpeting and hollering with that same ghostly vibrato. It was the only time the Vietnamese broke ranks: they rushed over and stood there nailed to the railing, searching the western sky with their naked eyes.

"Cranes!" Sally cried, as she'd heard her mother and me do hundreds of times. "Cranes at eleven o'clock!"

They were flying in tight formation, a grand congregation of them, about forty-five degrees up in the sky. They circled over the flats and headed right for us. As they moved out over the water, we counted 'em. A hundred and fifty-three beautiful white whooping cranes. They came in directly overhead and shook the boat with their powerful squawks. The Vietnamese *ooh*ed and *ahh*ed and pointed and congratulated each other, just like all our other passengers do. But this wasn't like any tour we'd ever made. It was like the cranes knew we were coming. They circled over the boat, then floated back to the shoreline and set down together on the banks of the mouth of the canal, where they stretched up to their full height and flared their wings before tucking into a slow walk, like a bunch of old men with their hands behind their backs, strolling and gossiping along the shore.

I was completely jazzed. Katie Alice was, too, because up in the wheelhouse she leaned over and hugged me and kissed me behind the ear. "Did you see that?" was all she could say, over and over.

We didn't have a clue how Dr. Duc To could have known there'd be cranes in that particular spot, let alone 153 of 'em, which is more than the entire Aransas flock. But he *did* know. That old man knew it right along. Probably had the number written down on his magic map. I was no longer inclined to ponder how such a thing could be. Things are bound to happen to you in this life that don't have an explanation. It might hit you twenty-five years later, or it might always remain a mystery. I'll never know why I survived Vietnam, while guys right ahead of or behind me got killed or maimed worse than me. Seems like we all take part in events written by others, who probably know a lot better than Bubba Coxmoor how it will all turn out. So when Miss Phuong came up to say that the cranes were a sign that the "harmonious orientation" was to head up the canal, I just saluted and said, "Yes, ma'am."

That was a day like no other. The mouth of that freshwater feeder was hardly wide enough to accommodate *Cutter's Way*. We only draw six feet, so I took her slow and steady. But a half-mile or so inland, the waterway widened out about double width and turned into a slow-moving muddy river. The cranes led us on. They would fly upstream round the next bend, then set down till we got them in view again. As we crawled along at a snail's pace, the landscape changed before our eyes. Instead of the prickly-pear Texas scrub country we were used to, green rice paddies stretched out in all directions, broken up by thick green and yellow clumps of bamboo. In the paddies, men and women worked in black pajamas and pointed bamboo hats, like I remembered the peasants from Vietnam. Some were transplanting bundles of rice stalks in the flooded fields, others padding rhythmically behind their water buffaloes. They all turned from their labors to watch us as we passed by.

The sky turned milky with haze. Vietnamese men on loaded black bicycles followed a road along the left bank of the water. Little boys in single file balanced shoulder boards, from which hung beaked baskets. Fishermen's sampans passed us port and starboard. The river ran right up to houses lining the banks, so it looked like whole villages were floating on the water. Farther back, the tops of pagodas peeked out from the green screens of palm and bamboo. At the water's edge, women pounded clothes against the rocks while their kids frisked in the shallows.

Sally came running up to the wheelhouse with Miss Phuong in tow. She was so hyper she'd like to croak right then and there. "Daddy, Mama, you know what? Miss Phuong says we ain't in Texas anymore!"

"We can sure see that!" said Katie Alice. "Everything looks so neat and proper."

"Yes," said Miss Phuong. "Like my village in Vietnam before war of liberation. It is perhaps familiar, Capitaine Coxmoor?"

"Well, in a way it is, and in a way it ain't."

I couldn't find words, but naturally I knew what was missing. It was the din of the choppers and the smell of burning hooches. It was the cries of napalmed peasants, the incoming artillery, the booby traps and automatic fire, the cursing of wounded men, the whole nine yards of nightmare. More than anything, what was missing was the terror of getting yourself killed every damn second, and the almost worse dread of killing anything that moved just to survive. If this was Vietnam, it was a Vietnam I'd never had the chance to see.

Miss Phuong caught my meaning. She said, "Miss Phuong cast eyes down in deep apology, Capitaine Coxmoor. Now you will please allow Miss Phuong to inform you of delegation mandate. You have heard of Caodaist Vietnam religion?"

"Not really."

"Vietnam people believe in repose of ancestors. If ancestors cannot find rest, they may become demons and bring down woe to people. Prosperity of family depends on good-will of zee dead."

"You mean like how we pray to saints?" blurted Sally.

"Yes, perhaps so," said Miss Phuong, caressing Sally's face. She asked, "Miss Phuong, if all these people are like saints, are we in Vietnamese heaven?"

"No, Sarry," she smiled. "But there were many unhappy spirits of those killed during war of liberation. Then we had not time for our rituals honoring dead. Too many dead. Too much killing. Many spirits of our ancestors cannot rest, and wander through zee world till they find place of peace."

Katie Alice looked at me and I at her. We both said at the same time, "Texas?"

Then Katie Alice leaned over and whispered to me, "Bubba, that's what it meant on Dr. Duc To's business card. Remember? 'Department of Ancestor Relations.' "

"What about the cranes?" I asked. "Katie Alice, you don't think those cranes are the ancestors of our flock, do you?"

"They are guardian spirits in Caodaist religion," said Miss Phuong.

"The cranes are our guardian spirits too, Miss Phuong."

Miss Phuong smiled mysteriously. "We know zis. Did you not wonder why we choose you to guide delegation?"

That afternoon we reached a village that started at the riverside and stretched back along a straight canal. The flock of whoopers set down at a solar pond back in among the paddies and waited for us to catch up. Miss Phuong said we would stop here, and showed us the spot on the delegation's magical map. Every hooch in the village was marked with a red dot or square. Starting from down the river were two long, narrow legs of dwellings, so that they all had access to the water, where they kept their sampans. Then the village widened out in east and west wings. At the head of the village was a circle of temples and pagodas, and a large house where the priests lived.

"Do you know what is zee Feng Shui, Capitaine Coxmoor?"

"Can't say that I do."

"Feng Shui is spiritual science of geographic placement. Dr. Duc To practice Feng Shui. He can map zee harmony with elemental forces. You see zis village? It is shaped like white crane on map. Good omen in Feng Shui. It means ancestors' spirits find peace here."

"That'll give Texas something new to brag about," said Katie Alice.

Under a soft sky, the delegation made their way through the village from house to house, carrying their gym bags. The cranes chanted from the paddies like a brass section from an old big band playing some rocking gospel. From every house the ancestors filed out in their black pajamas to welcome their families. There were children and old men with white beards. It was nothing like a Texas family reunion. They greeted their relatives with modest bows, without any outward show of emotion. Sometimes the delegates got down on their knees and kowtowed before them. Then the ancestors joined our procession, and we all walked down along the canal together till we got to the temples.

Dr. Duc To went up to greet the priests, while Miss Phuong stayed in the rear with us. "We will now begin zee ritual for repose of dead," she said.

"Is this something we shouldn't see? I mean, if it's more comfortable for y'all to do this in private, we can go back to the boat and wait."

"Not at all, Capitaine Coxmoor. We are your guests on boat. Here you are our guests. We welcome you and lovely family in warm hospitality."

The ritual was a simple one and only lasted about twenty minutes. They'd come halfway around the world for this unfinished business. There were three altars set up outside one of the temples, each decorated with flying silk banners depicting cranes. In one the cranes formed a diving line down the sky, while a single peasant carried buckets of water on shoulder boards. In another the birds passed high between jagged mountains. In the third was a shadowed valley, a grove of leafy trees, a pagoda on the edge of a cliff, and two cranes.

In front of the altars was a long table. The delegation came forward and kowtowed in front of the altars, then approached the table and started setting out dishes of rice and fruits and other foods they must have carried in their gym bags from the other side of the world. No Big Macs here, I noticed. Their relatives buzzed about them, their voices rising and falling in that singsong way. It seemed to me they were making sure their relatives did right by the ritual. I'll tell you one thing: if I was an unhappy spirit, I'd want the folks to do that ritual just right, too.

At last the table was all set. Miss Phuong leaned over to whisper, "Now delegation will fulfill mandate of heaven. We must make fire to cleanse memory and banish zee evil." In the old tradition they would set fire to rice stalks, she explained, but since the war the ceremony had changed slightly. Now it doesn't matter what they burn, long as it catches fire.

And that's just where the bags from the Golden Arches came in. They put the greasy hamburger wrappings on the altars and set a flame to them with a Bic lighter. A cloud of black smoke raced to the sky and turned gray there as the flames ate up the offerings. Everyone kowtowed in silence. That was about it. Then they retired to the temple courtyard for a feast that lasted the rest of the afternoon.

—

We reached Port Aransas next day, where a charter bus was waiting to pick up the Vietnamese delegation. Dr. Duc To and Miss Phuong, still in her Jackie O sunglasses, said good-bye with Vietnamese bows and American bear hugs. Sally got hugs and kisses. Dr. Duc To offered to take her back to Vietnam for what he called "fundamental education." He said, "American children well fed, strong, and healthy. But don't go to school?"

In the effusion of their leavetaking, they forgot to take their Bac Quay with them, the embroidered symbol hanging from the centerpole in the cabin, though maybe they forgot on purpose. We left it hang; we wholeheartedly believe that eye inside the heart protects us from evil spirits, and believe me when I tell you there are plenty of them still hanging out in Texas.

We hauled the boat out during the summer, and I went off fishing with some shrimping buddies. I didn't say a word to anyone about our mystery tour with the Vietnamese, but after five or six Buds, when they started badmouthing the "gooks" and "slants," which is what we American heroes call the Vietnamese boat people that have settled down here in Texas, I took strenuous issue with them and told them they didn't know what they were talking about. They blame the Vietnamese fishermen for catching all the shrimp, but I told them the shrimp are out there for anyone with the gumption and enterprise to catch them. If those people want to live fifteen on a boat and work seven days a week to earn their living here in America, then God bless 'em.

The summer months drag on down here till hurricane season, and it gets so damn hot. I couldn't wait to get back out on the water, back to the tour boat, and back to the cranes. We always thought there was something holy about the whoopers, and now that we knew it for sure, we waited for the flock to reach Aransas like it was the Second Coming.

The same week the cranes arrived at Aransas in October, a package with Vietnamese stamps came in the mail. It was wrapped in plain brown rice paper and tied on four sides with a red ribbon. It didn't contain a letter, only a color photograph of me with a single whooping crane. In the picture I'm standing face to face with the crane out in a flooded rice paddy, stretched up on my artificial leg and my left arm raised. I look like Dr. Duc To practicing one of his tai chi poses, though I have no recall whatsoever of that photograph having been taken. In the background is a delicious green jungle of bamboo and banana trees.

We know we need to get back there somehow. Katie Alice and I have discussed the possibility of some weekend taking our little fishing boat with its new outboard, paid for with the bonus we took in from the Vietnamese delegation's charter, and heading up that freshwater feeder to see if we can find the Village of the Ancestors. But now that it's the whooping crane season again, we'll be pretty busy till the Aransas flock flies out next spring.

JONATHAN MASLOW is as peripatetic in the
United States as he is abroad. He was recently
a writer in residence at Louisiana Scholars
College, is the editor of the *Cape May Geographic
Society Bulletin,* and is on the faculty of the Governor's
School for the Environment in New Jersey. He
has done documentaries for the BBC and PBS, has
been a Guggenheim Fellow, and has written for
Atlantic Monthly, The New York Times Book Review,
and *The Philadelphia Inquirer.* His most recent book,
Sacred Horses, recounted his exploration of the
Akhal-Teke breed in Turkmenistan, which also
resulted in his documentary *Saddle the Wind.*

ABOUT THE TYPE

The text of this book was set in Janson, a misnamed
typeface designed in about 1690 by Nicholas Kis,
a Hungarian in Amsterdam. In 1919 the matrices became
the property of the Stempel Foundry in Frankfurt. It is
an old-style book face of excellent clarity and sharpness.
Janson serifs are concave and splayed; the contrast
between thick and thin strokes is marked.

HPL
GENRE LIST

Texas Fiction

HOUSTON PUBLIC LIBRARY

R0l030 78358

ISTKW 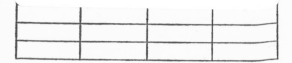 S MASLO

MASLOW, JONATHAN EVAN
    TORRID ZONE : SEVEN
STORIES FROM THE GULF
COAST

S MASLO

ISTKW

HOUSTON PUBLIC LIBRARY
CENTRAL LIBRARY

1,3/__   OCT 96